PRAISE FOR
PERISH
BOOK TWO OF THE JACK HARPER TRILOGY

"In *Perish*, Barlow sings the siren song of anger and revenge, expanding the universe of the terrible, and introducing us to even greater threats as she builds a world of the awful."

—Weston Ochse,
Bram Stoker Award Winning Author of *Bone Chase* and *Burning Sky*

"Cults? Misplaced loyalty? Betrayal? Violence? This book has it all and then some. The rare sequel that evolves and improves upon the first, leaving me eagerly awaiting book three."

—Luke S., NetGalley Reviewer

"As the second book in the series, [*Perish*] picks up where the first book leaves off, and spins a dark and strange series of events that lead Jack Harper down a path of self-discovery. I was surprised at how well the author handled so many heavy and dark topics. From death to abuse to drug addition, this book has a myriad of dysfunction that weaves together the aftermath left by the conclusion of book one perfectly."

—Abigail, BookSirens

"Overall, this is a well written and interesting story that I highly recommend to mature readers that like their stories dark and gritty. It was an excellent reading experience all around."

—Gabriella, GoodReads

"I was once again left looking Harper trilogy. If the third book second did to the first, then this

the Jack ıd, as the r most."

Sarah Buck-Mayr, GoodReads

PERISH

PERISH

BOOK TWO OF THE JACK HARPER TRILOGY

L.C. Barlow

A California Coldblood Book
Rare Bird Books
Los Angeles, Calif.

THIS IS A GENUINE CALIFORNIA COLDBLOOD BOOK

A California Coldblood Book | Rare Bird Books
Los Angeles, Calif.

californiacoldblood.com

Copyright © 2020 by L.C. Barlow
ISBN 978-1644281376

Set in Minion
Cover design by James T. Egan of Bookfly Design LLC
Typesetting by Glenn Sarco2000

Printed in the United States
Distributed by Publishers Group West

Publisher's Cataloging-in-Publication Data

Names: Barlow, L. C., author.
Title: Perish / L. C. Barlow.
Series: The Jack Harper Trilogy
Description: Los Angeles, CA: California Coldblood Books, 2020.
Identifiers: ISBN 978-1644281376
Subjects: LCSH Cults—Fiction. | Magic—Fiction. | Brainwashing—Fiction.
| Paranormal fiction. | Horror fiction. | BISAC FICTION / Occult &
Supernatural | FICTION / Horror
Classification: LCC PS3602.A77561 P47 2020| DDC 813.6—dc23

Dedication

For a little Inn up in Maine, filled with writers every winter. It provides hot tea, finger sandwiches, and cookies at three-thirty in the afternoon sharp. Its warmth calls to one across the snow and occasional blizzards, sometimes traveling down the United States, all the way to Dallas, Texas, and makes a southern woman long for the north.

For Mom, Dad, Sebron, Adam, and family and friends who make life worth living—those who are here and those who are beyond.

Also, and always, for Inga.

CHAPTER 1
ON THE OUTSIDE LOOKING IN

THE FIRE CURLED ITSELF AROUND the house like an affectionate beast. From the beast's back, smoke billowed up, glowing near the top of the flames, before it rushed into the black night. I stood at a distance, watching. The heat pushed at me, even from so far away. Lutin waited on my left.

The grass where he stood greened, the air around him cleared. He wore black sweatpants and a gray sweater that had once been moth-eaten but no longer revealed holes or dust. Through the refreshed cloth, glowing tendrils of orange light, about the width of a sword blade, spread up over his arms, legs, and torso, curving every which way like a vine. Even when he did not move, the interior brightness shifted, as though stoked by his breath, becoming brighter, then softer as the intense light flowed over him in waves.

His face shone pale in the night, except around his eyes and just below his cheeks, where dark lines swept, as though drawn in charcoal. His black hair flowed like wheat in a light breeze. His dark lips tensed, rigid as a statue's. Love and relief emanated from him, reminding me of a warm fire on the first cold day and the smell of petrichor, the catalyst of all change.

His four brothers, whom I had resurrected, looked just like him. Veins of fire also crossed them, and dark lines contoured their skin, but they were not Lutin. No others compared, no matter their ethereality.

This creature had survived ten long years in Cyrus's basement. This creature had provided me the ability to resurrect. This creature had deemed me worthy of preternatural power. I owed everything to him.

Lutin's glance flicked toward me. He smirked, as though he read my mind. We shared his smile, warmth building in me. With him, I was home, and everything would be all right. He was, after all, the creature that returned people to themselves, returned color to the world, returned life.

I blinked.

He vanished.

No puff of smoke, no whoosh of air, no lightning strike, no thunder roar. He simply disappeared. Only a patch of grass remained, a bit greener where his feet had been.

I scanned the forest to my left and the bit of lawn between me and the burning mansion. Nothing. No one. I stood alone. Lutin had said before that he needed to leave me; he would return when I learned to stop biting.

Above the distant roar of the flames, a strange rustling sound rose from my right.

I turned.

Two of the many trees that separated the burning mansion from the converted red barn about a quarter of a mile away shook. I walked toward them, hand on the gun in my jacket pocket, suddenly thankful for the cool night air that managed to reach me despite the blaze.

The sweet, electric air woke me; all the tiny hairs on my skin prickled, and everything flashed vibrantly. I had just seen my "father" killed—not just killed, but torn apart, particle by particle, by Lutin, the mysterious being from another world, the creature I set free. The night air and recent demise of my Machiavellian mentor cleared my mind as I fearlessly moved toward whatever creature lurked in the low grass.

I reached the tree line. In the twilight was the shape of a white-haired man with long legs. He crawled in the dirt. He wore black pants and shoes, but the majority of his shirt, excluding several dark stains on the fabric, flashed as white as his hair. He glowed in the darkness. Thick, dark liquid that smelled like a mixture of copper and sugar coated half his face. The other half was clean, recognizable. I knew him. Julian. How he had survived the whole night, the whole ordeal, remained uncertain, but I was happy he had. Yes, I was very, *very* happy.

"You're the one who hurt the children," I said.

The man stopped, aware of me for the first time. He glanced at me. His face kindled dread, and I reached for my knife, flicked the blade free. A gurgling sound escaped him, and he flung himself down and attempted to crawl away. I stomped one foot firmly on his leg, stopping him, and retrieved my gun. I pointed it at him. In the dark, the black metal reflected the red flames. Julian froze. His elbow wobbled, threatening to collapse; he could barely prop himself up. His whole body shook with exhaustion.

"Why'd you do it?" he asked. He meant, why had I betrayed my father, let loose the creature in his basement, diverted the children they planned to send out into the world to bomb churches and schools, and squashed Cyrus's evolution.

I owed him no answer, and my own aching exhaustion kept me silent.

"Why'd you kill Cyrus? He gave you everything."

Jealousy simmered just beneath the accusation. He lay in the dirt, his ribs heaving, his body shaking. One of Cyrus's loyal devotees, he had determinedly worked his way to the top. Julian would have cleaned the underside of Cyrus's shoes with his tongue if Cyrus had asked. He'd played dead time and time again, convincing children they had killed him, that they were unworthy, unclean, and needed Cyrus to lead them. I pictured him on the gurney, fake blood pouring out of him, as a young boy stood with a scalpel in his hand, shocked. "You are too dark," Cyrus told the boy, pretending the child was responsible for Julian's "death." "It's a good thing I am here to save you from your darkness." The child, probably eight years old, nodded, fully believing those words, and a new follower was created. Cyrus and Julian traumatized children in such a way that they no longer trusted themselves. Instead, they trusted Cyrus.

I moved my pistol slightly, motioning for Julian to rise.

"No more screwing with people's heads," I said. "The cult is dead. So are you."

Julian cocked his head, his chest still heaving. "How *did* you do it? And *why*? We were so close! So close to bringing about Cyrus's transformation! We only needed tonight!"

I remembered what the ferrics told me after I had resurrected them— that the box Cyrus used to gain supposed power was a toy through which the Builder made murderers out of men. It was how Cyrus made followers of children, only one step further up the chain.

"That was a lie," I told him. "The box was never going to give him preternatural power. It was suggesting that only to influence him to murder a large number of individuals. No one was going to evolve. There wasn't going to be a revolution."

"*No*," Julian yelled, his eyes wide. "*That's* the lie! We owned *a box* from the Builder himself. Cyrus perfected a system for growing it—he fed it pieces of Lutin's soul. A ferric's *soul*. We were becoming so powerful. Do you know what you've done? You have destroyed one of the most powerful and protective systems in the world, created by your father."

I blinked and took a deep breath. This man would never understand. "He destroyed the lives of hundreds of people. Of children just like me. *You* helped him." I glared at Julian.

He stared, wide-mouthed, up at me, as though he couldn't believe that his words didn't convince me.

I gestured with the pistol again. *Up*, it said.

The red barn loomed in the distance, the place where they had kept the children. It remained safe from the blaze. When Julian did not rise, I knelt on the grass and leaned toward him. He scrambled backward, as though I might eat him.

"How about," I said kindly, "we stop worrying about all that's just happened and do what needs to be done."

"What's that?"

Fear rolled off his breath.

"I want you to show me what's in the left side of the barn."

"What are you talking about?"

I smiled. "When Cyrus gave me the tour, I didn't get to see the whole place. You think I didn't notice the side door? You're going to open it."

Julian shook his head, his gaze dropping to the grass, as though his mind refused to entertain the idea. I jammed the back of my left heel straight down on his damaged leg. He screamed. "*Okay!*" he shouted. "Okay okay okay!"

He grabbed a low branch from one of the trees and hoisted himself semi-upright. He wobbled dangerously and then stabilized. One step at a time, he limped ten feet in front of me. I followed. In less than ten minutes, we reached the red barn. The lights inside brightened the path near the entryway.

Instead of entering through the front, into the cream-colored, modern lobby, we angled to the left, away from the lights, in the sooty dark. Behind us, the shimmery light from the burning mansion and the smell of smoke in the cold air seemed dreamlike.

Julian glanced back at me once, red light coating the left side of his face, his blue eyes hazy and glazed over. He paused, oddly still, as though he wondered if I were about to shoot him. "You're not going to like what you see."

"We're in a little corner of hell in this world. That's to be expected." I pursed my lips. He stared at me for a few seconds longer and then turned to continue limping forward.

As we rounded the building, Julian said, "Jack," in a voice so low, I almost missed it. "You could lead the cult, you know. With the red box, you could do anything." Julian's words barely pierced the ringing in my ears from the explosive night.

He struggled through the grass, a trail of blood behind his right foot. He didn't yet realize how much Lutin, his brothers, and I had destroyed. Nothing remained. Anywhere. "The red box is gone," I replied matter-of-factly.

He stopped. Behind him, I couldn't see his face or his reaction, but he slumped, wilting, like a flower in a sudden freeze.

"This thing, whatever it is—a cult, a following—is dead. It's gone."

He turned and looked at me with tears in his eyes. That shocked me, and the tip of my pistol dropped a millimeter. I corrected it.

"The Builder help us all," he whispered.

His steps slow, his shoulders drooping, as though expecting death, Julian continued. Along the side of the barn, two doors faced us, a weathered gold padlock securing them together. Julian leaned an arm against one door. From his pocket, he retrieved a set of keys. He ran his fingers through them and located a gold key. He inserted it into the padlock, turned it, and tugged. I stepped back and readied my weapon. An *arca* might be inside, perhaps in the shape of a blue box this time, that would release white smoke and devour our souls.

"Think of you, out in the world," Julian said, his gray-blue eyes lifting to meet mine. "Think of all the people you will kill. All the lives you will ruin. It will be like unleashing chaos in the world. The best place for you, Jack, was here, in the following, with Cyrus. Out there, you'll self-destruct, or you'll kill them all. You were built to."

"Wrong audience," I said, tired of him. Only poison left his lips. "Open the doors."

He merely stood there, blocking my way, my view. Before I could say anything more, he lifted the padlock away and opened the left door, then the right. The black interior obscured everything. I scanned the void wildly, waiting for something to jump out. Julian slid his hand just inside the door.

I cocked my pistol and aimed, certain he found a weapon. Something clicked.

Brilliant light illuminated the room. Releasing a pent-up breath, I loosened my grip on the pistol. I forgot Julian.

A giant mound of toys rose to three times my height. Maybe a hundred teddy bears, twice that many Barbie dolls, yellow plastic trucks, cans of Play-Doh, pink necklaces, ponies, dolls, stuffed animals of every kind, piled like the greatest Christmas gift a child could ask for. Shiny purple, green, and pink bracelets littered the floor.

"What the hell is this?"

Before Julian answered, it came to me. This playroom bounty belonged to the children they had stolen. My back stiffened, and my grip tightened dangerously on the pistol still pointed at him.

I scanned and rescanned the pile of toys before I studied the room surrounding them. To my left, a table supported a pile of papers.

One eye on Julian, I walked forward, into the barn. I stepped over several wooden letter blocks and arrived at the table. Stacks of identical sheets of paper littered its surface. I lifted one from the top. A figure-eight symbol in bright, heavenly blue lay on its side, like a toppled hour-glass. Over the figure eight, two lines came to a point so that the whole thing looked like a triangle or pyramid. The word Infinitum floated within. Below the figure-eight, the print read, "Down on Your Luck? Nowhere to Go? Don't Know What the Point Is Anymore? We Are HERE for You." Below this, in smaller print: "Come join us in Basille, Louisiana."

I turned to Julian and held up the page. "What is this?"

He looked from the sheet of paper to me with no expression. "It's us, Jack."

My eyes flicked back to the page. Cyrus had never mentioned the word Infinitum to me before. Queasy fear of the foreign and unknown washed over me. "Us?"

Julian nodded once. "Those are what we distribute—were what we distributed—to people to get them to join. These movements don't just build themselves."

As I stared at the page in my hand, the reality of Cyrus's death hit me hard. I had assumed that when he died the unrelenting and unwieldy feel of life would disappear. Instead, it worsened. The contours of my ignorance ran deep. "Infinitum," I said, testing the word in my mouth. "Infinitum following. Infinitum cult." I had never seen these words before, but I had never been on the outside. I had only ever been on the inside.

I swallowed, and my throat clicked uncomfortably. Out of the corner of my eye, a flash of movement registered. My head jerked, and I pulled the trigger. Wood fragments exploded out of the wall exactly in the place where Julian had been before he bolted.

I rushed out into the night. As I rounded the corner of the barn, he appeared in the distance, his white hair shining in the moonlight. I crouched low, readied my pistol, and took a steadying breath.

In the distance, a wail rose.

My head swiveled; my jaw dropped. Had I mistaken it? No. A high pitched sound that shifted low and then back, like it was traveling round and round, wailed, unraveling, speeding up and slowing down. Police.

My senses keen, my body reacted before any thought arrived. I stopped bothering with Julian and ran. I leaped to my feet, racing over the grass back toward the burning mansion, straight to the garage.

The sirens pulsed louder; blue and red lights shone in the distance against the tall trees. I jumped into Cyrus's car and jammed the key into the ignition. The Lexus hummed soothingly. I shoved the stick into reverse and slammed out of the drive, the gravel crunching violently under the tires. I sent one more look toward the ever-brighter house engulfed in flames, saw the red and blue police lights cresting the hill, and sped away. I drove the opposite direction of the sirens, keeping my headlights off. My heart pounded violently.

The light of the full moon barely illuminated the road's lines. I drove on the edge of my seat, glancing in the rearview mirror for any sign of the police chasing me. No one and nothing followed. After several minutes, I released a heavy breath and slowed my speed. I turned my headlights on.

Light flooded the road, and something flashed into view. I slammed on the brakes and swerved to the right. A nauseating crunch erupted as the car clipped something. A large gray object flew up and forward.

The Lexus screeched toward the side of the road, the headlights spotlighting a set of trees. The vehicle came to a stop five feet before I would have hit them.

What the hell was that?

I unclipped my seatbelt, opened the door, and stumbled out of the car, not yet processing what happened. Down the road, the object lay in the middle of the pavement—a bicycle covered in reflective tape. The detached rear wheel rested ten feet away. Farther up the road, something—someone—moved. My mind went blank.

Cyrus's burning mansion, barely a mile away, lit the sky pink. Smoke suffused the air, and multiple police sirens moaned. I needed to get out of there. Adrenaline coursed through me and urged me to get back in the car.

But the person moved and… squeaked.

I clenched my teeth. Abandoning Cyrus's car, I walked toward the individual on the road. All the world seemed to crash down when the shape became clearer. A young boy, helmet on, looked dazedly up at me. His left arm contorted, bending at the elbow the opposite direction it should have. His hand rested next to his shoulder. Blood pooled beneath him. His chest and hips twisted so that he faced behind himself.

I suppressed a violent urge to vomit. I knelt down, my knees banging against the asphalt. I did not touch him.

Blood bubbled from his lips as he silently stared at me. His red tongue attempted to push free of the pooling blood, his eyes dim with shock.

How could this have happened?

I thought of the power that Lutin had given me only weeks before. The powerful being Cyrus locked in his basement, siphoning off his abilities for himself, had forced a piece of himself upon me. Buried deep in my breastbone, next to my heart, it fluttered at the sight of the distorted boy. But my new ability didn't grant me the capacity to heal. It gave me the capacity to resurrect.

"I can't help you," I said, panicking. "I can't do anything." My breath shuddered out of me, and my eyes welled up. No, I couldn't help the child… Unless I…

The creatures I had resurrected in the past month—the dog and the girls—always came back to life without scars, without any imperfections. The dog had returned without bullet holes. The girls had returned without poison in their veins. "I can't heal you," I said, more to myself than him, "but…maybe I can help you." I thought of the gun in my pocket. I couldn't heal him; I could only bring him back to life.

Julian's words rebounded in my head. *Think of all the people you will kill, all the lives you will ruin. It will be like unleashing chaos in the world.*

"*Shut up,*" I said out loud.

With no energy, no resolve, I walked off the road so the boy couldn't see me and wiped the tears from my eyes, steadied my trembling hands. I retrieved the gun from my pocket, my heart pounding, tears slipping from my eyes as I emptied the single useless shell from the .38 and filled it with a fresh one. I didn't have many left.

The sirens howled louder, as though they might be a hundred feet away. Cars might appear around the bend at any second. What would I do if they did?

I returned to the boy in the middle of the road.

Pressing the gun against the boy's neck, I looked away and pulled the trigger. The air filled with the sound of a firecracker. I felt the result instantly—a subtraction from the cosmic space, like a star in the night sky extinguishing. Slowly turning back to the child, I beheld his blank, bloody face and couldn't breathe.

I grabbed his twisted body and hauled him from the middle of the road. His dislocated arm and leg dragged on the pavement. Once the body rested safely on the shoulder opposite the Lexus, I returned and carried his bike, placing it close to him. In my shock, the world appeared swimmy, and I waded through it.

I sought the sensation that was like an epiphany, like magic, like hope and goodness rolled into one. Despite the dark night and the deaths that had occurred, despite shooting this boy, I fought for calmness, the sensation of circulation returning. I urged my power to trickle to my fingers, rolling it around my palm. It grew and frothed until I held a tiny, invisible tornado that could rip the world apart. I pushed the cyclone forward, urging my power toward the body on the ground harder than ever before.

The vortex whirled down into the corpse. When I blinked, the boy's body revivified whole and restored. He lay perfectly balanced on the grass, as though sleeping, his chest silently rising and falling. Blood coated his hair, and dark spots bloomed where the road had scraped his skin, but aside from those blemishes he appeared perfect. I dropped a long, weighty breath.

I wanted to curl up in the dirt and leaves and lie there for a long, long time.

He opened his eyes and sat up. I nearly screamed. I jumped to my feet, turned away, and jogged back to the car.

"Hey!" he yelled from behind. "You hit me!"

I dropped into the driver's seat and slammed the door. I reversed back from the tree and pulled onto the road, headlights on, driving carefully out of the city.

For the next five hours, I gripped the steering wheel tight and, at exactly the speed limit, drove 400 miles—far, far away from Cyrus's mansion, Julian, the city, and the boy.

CHAPTER 2
EXPOSED

HEADING NORTH, I DROVE UNTIL dawn approached. At six in the morning, I stopped on the side of an empty road, utterly exhausted but still electric and alive. I craved laudanum or something heavy to put me to sleep but had nothing to calm me. I turned the car off and took a deep breath, closing my eyes. My body shook from adrenaline—from killing my father, resurrecting five of Lutin's brothers, setting Lutin free, letting Julian escape, and from the boy in the street. I felt trapped in the memory of the mangled boy, like a flailing ant caught in honey. After saving so many, I had killed a child just a mile from Cyrus's home. Was this fate?

Over the next five minutes, no cars passed. The road, I hoped, would remain empty. I crawled into the backseat, positioned myself on my side as comfortably as possible, my head against the padded door and my feet curled up. Despite the fact that my body shook from the dregs of adrenaline, I drifted into a dreamless sleep.

When I woke, afternoon sunlight illuminated the inside of the car, impossibly bright, as though the fire that had torn through Cyrus's mansion had followed me, burning the forests I passed.

My muscles twinged, and my clothes reeked of smoke. I stared at the sunny car roof above me. For the first time, the permanence of my situation washed over me. There was no Cyrus to return to, no Infinitum. The ferrics I had resurrected had fled. Lutin was free, and so was I.

As I stared up into the beige roof, it came to me that I had a choice— either ask someone to tell me how to be normal or to make my own norms. It took me less than a second to decide. My life would be what I made of it. I would become what I made of myself. Something like Infinitum, someone like Cyrus, would never have any say over me ever again. Free of the following, I would build my life, one brick at a time. God help anyone who tried to stop me.

Wiggling my fingers and toes, forcing my stiff muscles to move, I sat up with a groan and climbed into the driver's seat. I took a deep breath and tried not to think of the boy on the bike or the sound when the car crushed him.

Think of all the people you will kill, all the lives you will ruin. It will be like unleashing chaos on the world.

I winced. Julian's words echoed in my unconscious. How many years would pass before those echoes died?

I turned the key and the engine smoothly idled, drowning those inchoate mutterings. The bare road stretched before me. On and on it went.

I licked my parched, sooty lips, put the car in drive, and continued for a few more hours. When the gas gauge hovered just above empty, I pulled into a Shell station.

After I paid cash for the gas, only a twenty-dollar bill remained. The pathetic amount of money in my pocket couldn't be ignored. Under Cyrus's care, money had never been a problem. He paid me for the assassinations. When I needed more money, I just asked.

Survival required more energy and thought, now. Instinctively, my mind sought a resource.

In the distance, a man in the parking lot with his back to me talked on his cell. He wore a crisp gray suit. His hair appeared molded in perfect waves. I licked my lips as I stared at him, wondering if I was too exposed to act on what called to me.

I glanced at the front of the convenience store and noticed a boxy gray surveillance camera just above the rusted propane canisters pointed toward the front doors, the opposite direction from the man. My stomach grumbled with hunger, and my mouth went dry.

My glance flicked back to him. What if I killed him?

I thought of the boy on the road and resurrecting him. If I accidentally killed the man, I could always bring him back to life. My safety net was permanent.

After glancing once more at the single surveillance camera, picturing that single twenty in my pocket, tasting the salty nothingness in my mouth, and dreading the hunger-based mind fog that began to descend upon me, I slipped my gloves on. I took a deep breath and crept up behind the man. I gripped the gun in my right pocket by the barrel. He spoke into his cell phone as though danger was the last thing on his mind, but it lurked right at his elbow.

I raised the gun butt and slammed it against the back of his head. He dropped to the ground. I knelt, smelling his expensive cologne and the lingering scent of cigarettes. The gravel and broken glass that glittered on the pavement dug into my knee. I reached into his pocket, found his wallet, and retrieved two hundred dollars and some change. That would hold me for a while. I replaced the wallet in his pocket, checked his pulse, and left. I returned to Cyrus's car.

About to open the door, I glanced at the car parked behind Cyrus's Lexus and was startled. A wide dent stretched above the front right wheel, as though a large pole had scraped against it. The scratched and yellow plastic of the headlights obscured the bulbs. Inside, holes pockmarked the front seat's fabric. On the backseat rested a package of diapers.

I bit my lip and looked at the money in my hand. I thought of all the children Cyrus had stolen, some from poor parents. He never said anyone willingly gave him a child, but I wondered. Had he really stolen them all? I closed my eyes briefly. Children. It seemed I would do anything for them. I approached the beat-up old vehicle and slipped half the stolen cash through the barely open window. It dropped straight down on the driver's seat, looking oddly crisp on the soiled tan fabric.

A police siren rose on the breeze. The hairs on my back prickled. I wadded the rest of the money and shoved it in my pocket. I hopped in my car and continued north. As I drove, the sound of the sirens died. It was just me and the blessed pavement once again.

I stole more money from twelve individuals in the same way as I traveled. By the time I reached my destination—New York City—I'd amassed enough cash for several nights in a hotel plus groceries.

New York City seemed to be center of everything. Every type of person, every type of food, every type of entertainment, every type of experience existed in New York City. A melting pot, it dramatically diverged from anything I had experienced. I determined to let it infuse me, evict the inbreeding of the cult. I wanted to wash away images of young children in hopeless circumstances.

I reached Manhattan midday and found myself stuck in traffic for an hour and a half, surrounded by yellow taxis that appeared to have their own language on the road. They reminded me of my language with the knife. Everyone drove violently. Eventually, I located an empty street, pulled to the side, and parked. People walking by my car laughed. When the purr of the engine stopped, I savored the musical sound of honking horns, people chatting, and the whoosh of a nearby air conditioning unit. Taking a deep breath, I exited the car.

A blend of fresh, oily food and trash perfumed the air. Buildings towered overhead, reflecting the sun. A little girl with two golden braids that flopped against her shoulders passed me, holding her mother's hand, the pair speaking French. Hot dog vendors chatted with customers. A café boasted ristrettos across the street. An ice cream parlor sparkled at my right. Beside the parlor stood a pizza place advertising slices for a dollar in neon pink. A tourist shop beckoned beside it. The road seemed to stretch infinitely before me, the valley between the mountainous buildings clearly laid out. Woozy, overloaded, I backed against a wall to remain on my feet. It was all so colossal, reminding me that I no longer lived in Cyrus's world. Infinitum was gone. This strange, unwieldy world more than replaced it.

The sensation of being swallowed whole overcame me. The city and all its activity doused me with nausea. Cyrus's mansion, which had once seemed so large, was nothing compared to this. My past no longer seemed real. I wondered if anything else existed in comparison to the city, even my ability to resurrect. Perhaps my past had all been a dream, and I was simply a person in need of serious psychiatric rebalancing.

That's when I knew I had landed where I wanted to be, needed to be. New York was a megalith that destroyed the possibility of Infinitum ever existing. The city's vast variety promised to erase the monotony and impossible strangeness of my earlier life. Its very existence suppressed my trauma.

I strolled along those streets that erased me. When I passed a building advertising apartments, I entered. I asked the man standing at the front desk with black hair, large, almond eyes, and dark skin about rent. He stated a one-bedroom apartment was $4,500 a month. I nodded. I noticed an application on the desk and reached for it. He slipped his fingers over the sheet, pressed down, and slid it away from me. Our eyes locked. As though realizing his rudeness, he cleared his throat, cocked an eyebrow, and glanced toward a man wearing a crisp clean suit in the small room behind the desk. The man in the back nodded, and the clerk released the application. I reached for the page, noticing a smear of blood on my left hand. It wasn't mine. I dropped my hand to my side and smiled at the man behind the desk. I scanned the application and tapped the employment question with my right hand. "What if I don't have a job?"

He chuckled like he had predicted such a question. His smile revealed large white teeth. "Then you couldn't make rent."

"I can make rent," I replied. Sure, I could. Couldn't I? I had been capable of everything else in my life. I managed to claw my way out of Cyrus's cult, to destroy him and rescue thousands of individuals across the nation. I succeeded in healing a young boy by killing and resurrecting him. What was rent in the face of that?

"Well…" He half-laughed, half-smirked. "You can always pay in cash up front, with a year's rent as a down payment, which you'll get back when you leave."

"That's $54,000," I replied, astonished. "$108,000 total for that and the year of rent."

He nodded once, his lips twisted and eyebrows raised. "It's Manhattan."

I blinked hard a few times, as though clearing away fog that obscured my vision. My heart leaped and informed me it was tired of leaping. It wanted to lay down on a soft patch of grass somewhere and sleep for a long, long time. I hadn't expected the world beyond Cyrus to be so daunting and unforgiving. I slid the application back toward him as though it were a losing a poker hand. How did anyone survive in this city?

"Thank you," I said.

"Of course." He returned his focus to his computer.

As I left the building, I glanced back at the golden front doors with grim sadness. A woman wearing a white fur coat securing a small dog between her elbow and side opened the door and walked in. Her red shoes clacked on the marble entrance with an ominous sound. I looked away.

I toured the city, taking in all of the sights, keeping an eye out for dark alleys, abandoned buildings, buildings under construction, and parks. My eyes lingered over them like fingertips over black piano keys. I walked beside a large park in the middle of the city, saying hello to strangers sharing the sidewalk. A few people responded to my obvious I-just-arrived friendliness by warning me in passing not to walk alone there if I didn't have to and not to stay after dark.

"I'll keep that in mind," I said to one woman with long gray hair who informed me that in Central Park crime was the norm.

I rested on one of the benches along the gravel walkway and looked up at the trees that blotted out the sun. As a strange sadness flooded me, I shut it down as deeply and quickly as possible. I couldn't bear sorrow on top of everything else. I didn't have access to Cyrus's ever-flowing bank account. Things in this city were far different, down to the atomic level—an unimaginable place. How would I survive? I could kill and resurrect… That was all I knew. I suddenly realized why Infinitum was able to exist. Without a cult, life was hard and random.

I headed back to the car through the deafening blare. I could sleep there while I figured everything out. Exhaustion consumed me. The sun beamed too bright, the pedestrians spoke too loudly. The day, with its noise, activity, and disappointments, took a strange, nightmarish turn. A few hours of sleep couldn't keep up.

A helicopter buzzed overhead, the whirling blades reverberating between the buildings, magnified into machine-gun fire. I winced, willing it to go away. It disappeared from above the street, but its noise continued to boom over the tall buildings.

In the window of one of the souvenir shops, several televisions broadcast an image that cooled my blood. I cocked my head and strode purposefully toward the shop, pushing my way past several individuals, until my nose rested against the glass. My car—Cyrus's car—filled the screen. My heart pounded, and my vision funneled.

The bird's-eye view from some sort of news report then switched to street level. At the bottom of the screen, beneath the scrolling closed captions, crawled the words Cult Leader's Vehicle Found in Manhattan. My jaw dropped as I read the scrolling words. "*Louisiana cult leader Cyrus Harper, who was recently exposed as the mastermind behind a near mass-bombing in the United States, has potentially been located this afternoon at the corner of 31st and 4th. A vehicle was found illegally parked, and upon running its license plates, police discovered they had located the car they have been seeking for the past three days...*"

"Why do all the psychos come here?" a man beside me exclaimed. I jumped. From beneath a thick wave of gray hair, a set of green eyes glittered. Wrinkles lined his face, and his nose protruded like a beak. He wore a camel-colored trench coat and carried a briefcase. His grip on the handle tightened, whitening his knuckles. "Glad they found the fucker, though." A folded magazine rested in the crook of his arm. A familiar image decorated its front—a painting of a woman in a sapphire gown, diamonds ornamenting her neck.

I winced. My mouth dried, and my voice cracked. "You...you know about Cyrus?" My thumping heart threatened to explode, repeating the pattern of the night before. This seemed impossible, and my consciousness threatened to abandon me.

His expression sharpened, as though he thought me insane. "Been all over the news nonstop for three days, now, kid. They're calling him one of the biggest terrorist threats the US has ever seen. They haven't been able to find him. I thought he'd fled to Mexico. For some fucking reason, he came here." He threw a hand up in the air. "I don't know. Never understood this world." He lifted his chin as if saying good-bye. "Stay safe, kid. He could be anywhere." He pushed through several people who had lined up and melted into the crowd.

A shrill female voice beside me chittered. "Hope they catch him and give him the death penalty. I'd gladly fry him myself."

My eyes flicked between the long-haired blonde with bright pink lips and the screen. People all around me knew about Cyrus. Impossible. Infinitum had always been concealed. No matter what I did, no matter where I went, I had been able to complete the most atrocious assignments for my mentor with zero threat of detection. Now, apparently, the whole world knew of him.

An image popped into my mind of the peeling red velvet box that delivered blacker-than-black stones on a small golden shelf that unfolded inside. Beneath that shelf, flames flickered. Cyrus had used that box to identify people who blasphemed. Their names arrived written in gold on the ethereal black stones. If he dropped the stone into the fire, it obliterated an individual. That box, Cyrus told me one cold evening, also ensured our anonymity. It shrouded us from the outside world. With the power Lutin had given me, I resurrected his ferric brethren, and they burned that box. It seemed their action ended all the protection and unearthly concealment.

I was fully in the world now. Dropped and immersed.

I turned from the television, the heat of exposure warming my face. I racked my brain—had I left anything terribly important in the car? My gun, wallet, and money rested in my pockets. The only things remaining in the car were in the trunk—an ice scraper, a blanket, a tire pump.

My heart continued to pound, and my head ached.

Did the police know that Cyrus had lived with children? Did they know Alex's name or mine? Did Alex know that I fled in New York? He must. I had no idea where Cyrus sent him before I destroyed everything, but it wouldn't take him long to find me. All he had to do was turn on a television.

I was smart to have chosen a city with millions of other inhabitants. One in two million is a lot harder to find than one in forty thousand.

Sirens echoed through the street, announcing more police vehicles approached. I jammed my hands in my pockets and lowered my head, resisting the urge to clutch my jacket around myself. Taxis made way for the patrol cars that flashed by. I exhaled completely.

The world without Cyrus was not the same world. The rules were clearly different, and if I didn't figure out how to play according to them, something terrible would happen to me. Even if I figured out how to play by these new rules, something terrible might still happen.

I stopped and asked a young man in a baseball cap, "Do you know where I could use a computer for free?"

He ignored me and continued on his way. I walked along, stopping to ask two other people who also ignored me. At last, a woman with spikey pink hair and a nose piercing shrugged and said, "The library?"

"Where is that?"

She pointed, and I followed the line of her finger to an immense building with two large lion statues on guard atop the front steps. Above the massive archway, the words NEW YORK PUBLIC LIBRARY carved themselves into the structure.

"Thanks," I said, but the woman had already moved on.

I jogged to the building and climbed the stone steps. Inside, a gorgeous, massive entryway greeted me. It smelled aged and sweet. An older woman seated at a desk on the left confirmed that guests could obtain computer access on the fourth floor for thirty minutes. I thanked her for her help and found the stairs. Thirty minutes would be enough.

I arrived at the fourth floor and located an available computer among the rows upon rows of desks. I dove into the dozens of news stories about Cyrus, looking for any mention of my name.

It seemed that the police became aware of Cyrus and his operations when a fire station in Basille, Louisiana, discovered his burning mansion. Reports announced that firefighters had doused the flames, which took approximately ten hours to fully extinguish. When police entered, they found evidence of Cyrus's plans to bomb hundreds of cities across the United States. This, plus other unidentified evidence, informed investigators that they had happened upon just one section of a massive nationwide cult that called itself Infinitum.

None of them mentioned an Alex or Jack Harper. Several articles reported that Cyrus's following had abducted an unknown number of children, but they did not elucidate the extent of those abductions.

I leaned back in my chair and sighed. The police might not be searching for me, had no idea I existed. That was how I wanted it. As for Alex, I would deal with him myself.

I bent forward in the chair, slipped my hands into my hair, and swallowed hard. I had no money, no car, no contacts, and no place to live. I fumbled through my jacket pockets, absentmindedly seeking a cigarette. When I patted my inner pocket, I came upon something unexpected.

A woman's name and number, stamped on a card the color of bone, appeared.

Margaret Wilhelm's card.

She lived all the way down in Louisiana, but still... Perhaps I could call her.

Tapping the card on the table, I stood. I took the stairs down and discovered payphones at the far end. I found a handful of change in a pocket and hoped it was enough. Dialing the number on the card, my heart pounded, and my hands trembled. The phone rang.

After the third tone, someone picked up. "Hello?" a woman said.

A giant space, pure quiet, lingered between us.

"Hello?" she said again. "I can't HEAR yooouuu." The teasing falsetto voice on the other end undoubtedly belonged to Margaret. Her image flashed in my memory—an older woman with bright red hair and a big smile wearing a cloche hat. Her telling me to call her if I needed help.

My heart beat faster and harder, and my mouth went dry. My eyes clenched shut, and I winced in anger.

With a rush of adrenaline, I slammed the phone down in its receiver and sealed my mouth.

I should not have called her. If she helped me, even if she knew someone in New York who could, that would only lead to something terrible happening. Somewhere down the line—in a week, a month, a year—somewhere, Alex would learn about her. Margaret couldn't be involved.

I fetched the lighter from my pocket and set fire to the card then and there. The last remnants charred on the greasy marble counter, marking it with black dust. A tear filled my eye. The card burned, ashes its only remnant. I wiped them away. I walked out into the bleak day.

I would take the difficulty and hardship, and I would make them my own. My specialty was death and resurrection, and I had my gun. That would have to do.

When dinnertime came, I paid a dollar for a slice of pizza and felt as though I had just eaten plastic. It soothed my stomach but not my mind. I grew tense, worried, agitated.

Manhattan boomed, despite the swarm of police, powerfully active, and I wandered through thousands of people. About two in the morning, in the deep dark, the city slowed. I made my way to Central Park, the place everyone warned me not to go.

The moon glowed nearly full through the trees that shimmied back and forth in the wind. I waited in the dark, until what I sought found me. Something sharp poked into my back.

"Turn around," a voice said. My heart rate accelerated. I did as I was told.

A thin man dressed all in black loomed before me. A ski mask covered his face. Staring at him, I thought, *They said I would be robbed, and now I'm being robbed. Like clockwork.* Rules governed this brand-new world, after all.

He twitched with adrenaline or the effects of some drug. The gun wobbled in his hand.

"Give me your fucking *money,*" he half hissed, half shouted, thrusting the gun between my eyes, hard against my forehead, bruising skin against the bone. Blood trickled from the top of my nose. It tickled, and I wiped it away.

"How long have you been robbing people?" I asked.

"Are you crazy, bitch? I said give me your fucking money!"

I shook my head. "No." That was not how things were going to go.

In a quick series of movements, movements I had learned as a child and perfected over a decade, I twisted the gun from the man's hand, nearly breaking his finger in the process, and turned it on him.

He cursed and clutched his fingers. When he saw his own gun pointed at him, he threw his hands up and immediately backed away. "Shit! Shit! Shit! Please don't shoot me!" His voice boomed deep but oddly unsteady.

Moving erratically, he jumped and shivered as oddly as any person high.

I considered shooting him. But the revolver would be loud, and I needed it.

"You shouldn't steal from people," I told him.

He nodded vigorously, backing away from me.

"Promise me you won't steal from anyone ever again, and I won't shoot you."

"I-I promise."

I motioned for him to go, and he did. He bolted, looking back only once. I smirked momentarily and rolled my eyes.

I strolled along Central Park until I spotted a man walking alone. Thinking of the boy on the bike bitterly, I pushed the memory away, and snuck up behind him. I slammed the gun against the back of his head, knocking him out, just as I had before. I retrieved cash from his wallet, surprised by my haul. He carried about $500. Manhattan indeed. I thanked him by pausing to ensure he breathed and left him lying in the park.

I robbed three more people the same way.

Only one of them did I have to kill—only one. He stood far too large a man for me to take on, far too large for me to knock out without serious injury to either of us.

When I knelt by this particular individual, taking his money and then resurrecting him, I knew I was using something beautiful inside me to fulfill some cruel and inhumane need. Part of me sickened. The other part of me wanted to survive. I chose to survive.

By the end of the night, in a shabby, stained hotel, I counted out the bills—mostly crisp hundreds. Blood stained only a few. I had over $3,000. I sat on the bed, relishing my haul, and closed my eyes. I grew peaceful.

Finally, through all the hell, I found reprieve.

Cyrus would have been proud.

CHAPTER 3
TEST

For two weeks, I slept in different hotels during the day and accumulated just over $108,000 at night. I went to various banks several times and exchanged small bills for large ones. $108,000 in hundreds was easy enough to carry to the apartment building.

I made sure I spoke with the same concierge as before and that when I set the bag of money down, I looked pissed, as though he had slighted me by assuming that I couldn't afford an apartment. I implied that because of that slight, I brought cold hard cash.

"As you requested," I informed him.

He looked at me wide-eyed and open-mouthed. His breath paused, and he seemed ready to reject it, to tell me that they didn't actually take cash for a year's worth of payments on an apartment, and so on. Instead, he took a deep breath, closed his eyes, and apologized profusely.

I waited as he and another man marked each of the bills with a special brown pen to confirm none of them were counterfeit. The concierge smiled at me, perhaps overwhelmed by the cash. I shrugged. "It's Manhattan," I said as I signed a name on the dotted line that I made up on the spot—Sarah Anderson.

I moved into my new apartment, kept an eye on the news, and waited for any mention of my name. Over the weeks, none came. Still, I did not go out unless necessary. I did not feel safe.

To pay for my new life, I continued to kill men, steal their money, and resurrect them, all the while avoiding being noticed by the police who seemed to patrol the city ceaselessly.

While I kept an eye on news reports on my new television, hunger for new experiences tortured me. Ads for shops, restaurants, cafes, bookstores, and theaters deluged me. The world opened, and I desired to fling myself into its gaping maw. *Give me everything you have*, I wanted to say to the city. It required all my self-control to remain indoors, watch, and wait. Nothing was more difficult than hiding, all the while knowing that for just a couple of hundred dollar bills the world would shoot forth new experiences like a bow and flaming arrow. I craved those arrows like a fire swallower. I wanted them to warm and liven me.

In the meantime, it bothered me less and less, and then not at all, that I had to assault people to get what I needed. The whole world seemed filled with assault, in one form or another. That was life. I had not chosen this world. I had been flung into it. Thus, I owed it nothing.

In my apartment by myself, I accessed what I did have. I opened YouTube each night and for hours listened to all the music I had never known existed. I discovered all kinds of poetry in the world and untapped emotions within myself. What artists sang, and how they crooned, pinpointed just who I was and what I felt better than I could. At the first burst of honest emotion, my inclination was to rush into the streets of NYC looking for drugs, as I had always done, but I did not yet know where to find drugs. More importantly, if I muted my emotions, I might always remain a mystery to myself. That was dangerous. All I had was myself.

My unchecked emotions bled into everything, and studying the NYU brochures I found at the New York Public Library made everything worse. As soon as I saw them, I desperately wanted to go to college. But who might see me there? Who might remember me if I was ever exposed as part of Infinitum? How did one build a new identity?

It seemed like my apartment would remain my world.

This central dilemma swirled in me as I readied myself for a night of hunting. I left the apartment armed with my knife and gun, ready to exact my rage on some unsuspecting individual.

I jogged down the stairs to the mail room. I unlocked my tiny mailbox, and the hinge squeaked, metal on metal. I reached inside the dark opening and retrieved the contents, surprised to find a letter. The shoddy envelope appeared handmade. I opened it.

The words on the page inside made me forget the night.

Dear Jack Harper,

I am writing to you, hoping you can help me. The cult claimed that you died, but then Harlowton was talking to someone just a few nights ago, and he said that you were alive and that he had located you at this address.

I almost didn't send this letter because I knew it could be intercepted, that Harlowton might kill me for it, but it's worth the risk. Not just to let you know that you're being watched, but to ask for your help. I hope you think I am worth the risk.

You and I aren't so different. I am trapped in a house very similar to the one you escaped. It is terrifying.

There is something here that turns the rooms white. And Harlowton's followers speak of you. They say you're the One Who Got Away. I, too, desperately want to get away.

Please, if you do not help me, tell me how to escape. Traitors are found and killed here, and I am certain it is only a matter of time before they discover me.

Write to me, please. I'm the one who gets the mail every day, and I will see your letter before anyone else. Or instead, if you can, come to me and take me from here, or at least kill them, like you did Cyrus.

I'd prefer you kill them.

The address of the home is on the back of this page.

I am desperate. Please. I don't know what else to do.

- Annette

I read the letter twice more, completely oblivious to my surroundings. When I came to, I realized someone could have been in that mailroom, in the back somewhere, waiting for me. They would have had me. My back tingled, as though someone watched me, and my eyes flicked to the ceiling fan overhead. It spun helplessly fast, and the blades threatened to fly off.

I returned to my apartment, locked the door, and set one of the kitchen chairs beneath the handle. I checked every room in the apartment, including the closets and under my bed. I overlapped the teal velvet curtains to ensure no cracks between their panels.

When things seemed as safe as possible, I sat and reread the letter.

I inhaled a deep, steadying breath. I lifted the letter to the light and gazed at the paper stock, noting the marble-like appearance. I detected no noticeable odor. Finally, I traced my finger over the signature and traveled the deep mark of the blue pen. The address on the back read 405 BRIMMER.

Two weeks. I had lived in that apartment two weeks, under a name entirely different from my own, and someone had already located me. How? And what was this? A supposed letter from a girl in Infinitum? Wasn't Infinitum dead? Hadn't I caused its downfall? Hadn't Lutin and his brothers saved all the children?

I thought back, picturing the pins on Cyrus's map, the places where the bombings would have taken place had I not intervened. Had those pins not fallen with Cyrus?

I looked again at the letter. Perhaps not. Maybe Alex sent this to scare or trick me. It had to be a trap. Yes, it had to be. I folded the piece of paper and dropped it on my thick glass coffee table. I crossed my feet over the plush, blue living room rug I'd had delivered just a few days before and couldn't get comfortable.

I should leave it alone. I should leave it alone. If Alex wanted me, he could come get me.

Biting my lip, I pulled out my new iPhone and checked to see how far away the supposed house Annette listed was from me.

The maps app said it was forty-five minutes. It was so close. How convenient.

I set my phone on the coffee table. All the possibilities the letter implied swept over me—that Infinitum was not dead, that I had not killed them all, that they had found me.

I wasn't going to visit a house simply because some girl supposedly sent me a letter. It would be sheer stupidity to respond. The best approach would be to do nothing, to stay inside, except at night when I hunted. That was survival.

I slid the letter back into its envelope and placed both beneath the couch. I checked the time, made sure my gun was in my pocket, and left.

CHAPTER 4
BACK AGAIN

ANNETTE'S LETTER WAS AN ITCH that begged to be scratched, but the price of scratching it might be death at Alex's hands in a house only forty-five minutes down the road, whether or not Infinitum still existed.

I turned my attention back to the life I wanted to build. I wanted an education devoid of Cyrus. I yearned to know what real people learned in the real world, outside the grip of a manipulative and power-hungry man. The fall semester at New York University was approaching, and I began researching how to create a fake identity—a proper one, not like the bullshit name I gave the Alexan, knowing no one would attempt to verify my details because they already had their money.

Eventually I dared to venture outside in the daylight, to step between the architecturally gorgeous buildings of NYU. Being outside unsettled me, even more so when I neared the school, surrounded by people whose lives were so different. Still, I became determined. I researched the dark and deep portions of the internet where it seemed anything was available for purchase, including a new identity, a new life.

More letters, though, from other children arrived from all over the country, bringing reverberations of a reality that threatened to swallow me whole. Over four weeks, I received twenty-seven of them, and these letters threw me from my plans. They were magnets, threatening to drag me from my new life in New York.

Three of the letters Annette had signed. The others contained different writing, from different children. I hollowed out a large copy of *Moby-Dick*, and each time I received a new suspicious letter from some child asking for my help, I opened the tome, gazed down into the carved-out pages, and placed the new letter on top of the others.

The style of the letters varied. Some were thin, like business letters. Others were thicker, greeting-card sized. Some were written in black ink, some blue, some red. All requested the same thing—to help them, these children who could not find a way out from the abuse and murder and death, escape.

Always children. Always the same request.

I closed the book and placed it back on my bedroom shelf.

That's not your life, I thought. *At one time, it might have been, but it's not anymore. You take care of yourself. When Alex comes, kill him. That's all you have to do.*

Besides, it's a trap. It's too perfect. You wanted to save the children Cyrus sent out to bomb buildings, and with the help of the ferrics, you did. What better bait to lure you with than letters from more children needing help?

Late at night, though, as I lay in bed, I wondered, was it actually fake? All of it?

Looking around at my new apartment, at the computer where I might purchase a brand-new identity, I knew I should forget the letters. There was no reason for me to leave all that I was building behind. I was becoming more than just anti-Cyrus. I was starting to become myself.

But another part of me, a deeper, animal part, a reptilian part, the part not ready to stop destroying Cyrus, the part that wanted to keep landing blows and slide into familiar old ways, did not like the potential that Cyrus's cult was still alive and well. I felt pure, ice-cold horror and rage at the idea there might be children still being harmed. This part of me was more familiar, and it spoke to me.

It said, Maybe you have more buildings to burn. Maybe it is not yet time to retire.

And that voice, so loud, so deep, tugged at me.

Until I suppressed it, suppressed it, suppressed it, and fell asleep.

⌒

THE FINAL MONDAY EVENING OF October, near Halloween—a holiday I began to assess as particularly useful for someone in my line of work— another letter arrived, addressed to me. It listed no return address. When I opened it, a bulky little item plopped into my palm.

I stared at the little piece of plastic that resembled a Lego. A flash drive.

My breath stopped. I trembled. A curious rage rose inside me.

Don't fucking do it, a voice warned. Don't look.

But it might be from Alex.

I returned to my apartment, staring at the flash drive in my hand. I knew I should burn the thing, smash it, chop it into itty bitty bits, and be on my way.

Still, I entered my apartment, locked the door, and sat at my computer. With a deep breath I slid the drive into the slot on the left. My computer screen woke. A window popped up with an option to open the drive's contents. I reached forward, placed my hand on the cold mouse, and moved the pointer to the drive. I double clicked.

The folder contained only one file—a.wmv. A video.

My mouth became cottony, and chills coursed along my skin. I broke into a cold sweat, and I craved the dulling, sleepy gift of opium.

In near pain, I slid the mouse over the untitled.wmv file, and I double clicked. After a few seconds of a black screen, an image came into view.

It wasn't Alex.

A girl with dark brown hair and a tear-streaked face stared into the camera. She spoke in broken sobs. If I hadn't been listening as though my life depended on the message, I would not have understood her. "I am Annette Canton," she said. Beside her, a man stood. He wore a black, button-down shirt and gray slacks. The camera was positioned too low to catch his face or head.

He spoke next in a voice deep and unidentifiable. "This is the price our followers pay for disobedience."

A knife emerged, shimmering nearly white in the light of the computer. He lifted it up, and, quicker than I could blink, pressed the tip of the knife to the girl's throat, pressing until it pierced deeply. He pulled the blade across, as if cutting a cake. Blood sprayed the camera, reddening the whole screen.

The video ended.

I gripped the computer mouse in my right hand. I screamed, and my voice boomed against the walls of my living room long and hard. *"No!"*

I chucked the mouse against the wall. It exploded into shards of plastic. I shoved the laptop off my desk. It hit the floor and cracked.

I threw everything I had purchased over the prior month—books, ramekins, cups—against the walls. My hands shook, and broken glass littered the entire floor of the living room.

Dropping to the blue rug, I scraped it with hands that had turned into claws. My fingernails bent back. I screamed in frustration, feeling the burn of my muscles and joints.

I had not believed the letters, certain they were a trap. Lutin had killed all of Infinitum...hadn't he? Had the source survived?

This video was proof, wasn't it?

At least twenty-eight children... twenty-seven... had written to me, and more might be seeking me out. And what had I been doing? Hiding!

The letters are real, was all I could think. Agony twisted in my center, grabbed at my throat.

I cursed everything as I flung open the doors to my balcony. I wanted to reach out in front of me and tear the city apart.

Below, the world carried on, as though a child hadn't just been killed, not registering the evil beneath the daily norms.

It never had. Even when the city learned of Cyrus, it learned too little, too late. Already fewer news agencies reported on him and the hundreds of children saved.

My hand gripped the balcony rail, my fingers straining. I suppressed a guttural scream.

I slipped to the concrete floor and shivered. I might have thrown myself off the railing if I hadn't resolved what I needed to do. I was going to kill the man in that video.

Evil may not register in the world, but it registered in me. Unlike others, I did not fear reciprocity.

I stood straight, all of my movements direct, comfortable, liquid. It was like I was slipping into a warm bath. I knew what I would do, and I was ready.

I did not mourn the life I lost. I did not feel anything.

Cyrus would have clapped.

CHAPTER 5
WHITE AND GOLD

THE NEXT MORNING, I CALLED a taxi to drop me off near the address Annette had listed on the back of each ignored letter. I walked several blocks to the tall, bleak house and studied it. Built in Victorian style, with a wraparound porch, it stretched toward the sky like a cathedral. Only a few orange leaves speckled the dark grass of the medium-sized yard. A wrought iron fence at least six feet high enclosed the area. The gate stood partway open, emitting tiny *unnnggs* and *innnggs* as the wind kissed it.

If someone had handed me a blowtorch, I would have burned the place down then and there.

I pushed the gate open to assess the yard. I scanned the grass, with a cold, angry determination in my heart to kill everyone and everything inside, and caught a glimpse of what appeared to be a pink glove—not a winter glove, but an evening glove, like a woman would wear to a formal banquet—near a small shrub by the porch's left corner.

Red stains stretched up from the back of the hand to the elbow. That red might have been an embroidery design or something more ominous, but it lay too distant to tell.

The house reeked of Cyrus. The whole place seemed to be his monument. A house without hope, a building where a missing child might be found, it would swallow one whole. A familiar shiver rolled down my spine. I wished I had brought a blowtorch.

No faces peeked from the windows. No one stood on the grounds. I took a step past the gate. As soon as my foot landed, I stopped breathing.

The door of the house opened wide.

A grainy big-band swing song filtered from inside, distant, pleasant, sweet. Through the doorway, a large, brassy gramophone sat on the floor fifteen feet inside the house. Monstrously large, the shining bell loomed ominously, and, as though it knew I was looking, shifted up. It grew, widened, like a flower blooming. Something white spilled from its center.

My mouth dropped open, and I forgot myself. An invisible energy swept my feet out from under me, and I hit the cement walkway. My teeth clacked painfully, and my lungs emptied.

I slid toward the front door of the Victorian home, towed by some unseen force. The cement caught my coat and dragged it to my chest. I raised my aching head, discovering I had traveled halfway across the sidewalk.

I flipped over onto my stomach, my heart leaping, fear ricocheting through me, and grabbed at a crack in the cement. It slipped from under my fingers, and I spread my arms wide, grabbing hold of the edges of the sidewalk. I held tight. The grass tickled my burning hands. I clenched my stomach and gritted my teeth, trying to crawl forward. If I could get back past the gate, I might be free. The rough surface grated against my skin, peeling off the outer layer. As my knees pressed into the walkway, my kneecaps popped. I barely made it a few inches forward before the magnetic pull overwhelmed me. I slammed down onto my stomach as I rocketed closer to the door.

My feet struck the wooden steps and were lifted. My hands found the rim of the first wooden step, and I gripped it, hooking my right elbow around the jutting corner of the stair. I caught my breath and, for a moment, dangled.

The big-band swing sounded louder. In the midst of the gallivanting trombones arrived the *glop...glop...glop...*of something oozing. The music shifted. Off, out of tune, the melody melted.

The wood of the stair beneath me creaked. I held tight with all my strength. Once inside the house, it would be the end of me.

The stair broke.

Like a champagne cork, my body sailed through the air, and I landed hard just inside the doorway. I jumped forward, attempting to grab the doorframe, but something powerful pulled me further within. The door leisurely closed and locked.

Horrified, I struggled to find anything to hold onto and slow my progress. A pair of shining black leather shoes appeared to my right. A pair of cream heels materialized beside them. Above me, pale and grim faces of not just one man and woman, but many of them, collected. A woman with broadly set gray eyes smiled, one gold tooth gleaming. The man beside her hugged her close, as though the image of me being dragged deeper into the house was comforting. They observed quietly as I slid closer to the gramophone, seeking any crack in the wooden floor to dig my nails into.

My shoe met something not quite solid but not quite liquid either. Gum? Paint, perhaps. Glue. The oak floorboards beneath me bleached. The orange-yellow faded, slipping, disappearing, and a pure white floor took its place. The sleeves of my jacket shifted to gray and then white.

"Fuck," I said. And I thought, This is the end for you. That was your life.

My other foot became entrapped in the thick fluid.

Through the melting music arrived a sudden high, piercing sound, almost like laughter, like people cackling. Anger clenched in my chest. I tried one last stab at the floorboards, and my fingernails filled with splinters of wood and bent back.

The high-pitched laughing continued. The men and women stared at each other, eyes wide, mouths parted, eyebrows drawn down. Afraid. The voices were not coming from them.

The room vibrated, and the cackling overtook the jazz. The cream walls faded to white.

Something dark darted overhead.

A black bird sailed in front of me, followed by another.

The gum-like substance rose to the middle of my shins, but it did not pull quite as strongly as before. I kicked back at the goo as hard as I could, and my left ankle popped free.

Another bird appeared in the room and then ten more, swooping over me, circling, flying dangerously close to the men and women in the hallway. I craned my neck to look upward. Hundreds of birds stormed inside, all screeching.

I slapped my hands over my ears to block out the din.

Both feet free, I achieved some distance between me and the gramophone.

Two women bolted to a room on the left, while the others ran up a staircase on the right. A man fell against the mirror of a tall storage bench in the entryway, shattering it. Shards crashed to the floor, breaking into smaller pieces that reflected the hundreds of birds overhead. The screeching expanded.

I crawled, using every muscle to gain another foot of distance.

The black birds shifted to gray. Several bleached to white. As I kicked and crawled away, all of them turned white.

I managed to gain just a few more feet. The magnetism weakened, and I brought myself to my knees and stood. A tornado of white birds spiraled down into the black center of the huge gramophone, obscuring the bell. The white goo dribbling down slackened. It pooled on the floor limply, white wings and feathers and feet pinned in it.

I sprinted away, leaping out of the living room and through the hall. No one stopped me. The man in the mirror's shards covered his face to protect himself from the birds. Bits of mirror pinned to his face poked through his fingers. Glass speckled both his arms. Several people on the staircase struck at the white birds that swooped over them, dove down, and latched onto their clothes and hair. Everyone else seemed to have disappeared into the recesses of the house.

Tearing open the front door, I jumped onto the porch and raced down the steps. I paused briefly to glance back, witnessing once more the utter chaos of birds, people, and gramophone, before the brown front door gently shut behind me.

I ran.

And ran.

I eventually convinced myself to stop running long enough to call a taxi. I waited for it, focused on making my heart slow, my movements smooth out, my eyes blink. Within five minutes, a car arrived. I got inside, now dressed all in white, and hid my bleeding fingers within my jacket sleeves. To my relief, the driver said little on the drive back to my apartment.

He dropped me off in front of my complex, and I walked through the lobby as casually as possible. My muscles ached, both from the exertion and the adrenaline. The whole world seemed shaky.

I took the stairs carefully, making sure not to tumble. It took me about twenty minutes to reach my floor. As soon as I made it inside my apartment, I pressed myself against the front door and slid to the ground. I waited until my thrumming heart slowed again. When it relented, I rose and went into the bathroom to look at myself. My whole body vibrated.

What an impossible, weird shitstorm. I never should have gone there. The gramophone, the birds, all of it. I had nearly died from some machine that worked very similarly to Cyrus's old box. But I survived. Animals came, had sacrificed themselves, it seemed, and saved me. Right? Wasn't that what had happened? But why? How? Such a thing had never happened when Cyrus attacked his victims.

The people in the house who clawed through the air and flung themselves into rooms to escape the birds obviously hadn't expected that either. Something inexplicable had occurred. Someone, something saved me.

As the adrenaline drained, I stared at myself bitterly and thought one word.

Failure.

They had killed a child; I went there to exact vengeance, and I failed. I wanted to rampage through my apartment, ripping everything apart again, but I didn't have the energy. I simply stood, staring at my white clothes stained with blood.

I pulled a bruised rib muscle as I removed my sweater and winced. The bloody cotton sweater dropped to the floor, and I turned to examine my back in the mirror. A large, raw swath covered the area just below the tip of my shoulder to the bottom of my rib cage. It'd probably need a month to heal.

The tips of my fingers were scraped red and raw, and the blood coating my split lip had darkened and dried. I ran warm water in the sink and brought a cupped handful to my lips and then another. The cut was not quite as noticeable minus the flat black scab.

The bloodied clothes I stuffed beneath my bed to burn later. I found a gray sweater and pulled it on carefully, then a new pair of black pants. I slid my feet into my leather boots and ran a brush through my hair. I pulled my jacket on. My gloves.

In the mirror, I looked normal. Only a slight sheen of sweat coated my pale skin, the pallor emphasized by my black hair and gaunt frame. My dark eyes, no longer sparkling or wide and alert with adrenaline, appeared rather dull.

Normal, yes. That's how I looked. Like I hadn't just been hauled across thirty feet of cement by my legs. Like I hadn't completely failed at seeking retribution for the death of a young girl—a young girl who had sent me three letters in handmade envelopes asking for my help. The same young girl who paid for those letters with a slit throat, her blood spilling across the camera lens. Tears filled my eyes.

A wave of exhaustion washed over me, and I bent over and lay down on the soft carpet. I ran a hand through my hair. It had been a terrible mistake to visit the house alone. I would not make that error again.

The birds had saved me. They had stuffed themselves down into the bell, filling it. Why, I did not know. But if the feathery masses hadn't been there, that would have been the end for me.

No more Jack.

Because Jack was only *one*.

Carefully, I pulled myself upright from the floor. I reached inside my desk, retrieved a black case, and unzipped it. A syringe lay inside. Cotton. A spoon. A tourniquet. Everything clean, shining, in perfect working order because it had been so long since I had used it. I had tried to abstain, to create a new me, but that seemed pointless. Death and I were entwined. What was the point of grasping at purity?

I zipped the case shut and held it above the pocket of my jacket. It dangled in the air for a long while. When I let go, it fell inside perfectly, as though my jacket had been hungry and eaten it whole.

I paused.

And swallowed.

And closed my eyes.

And breathed.

I heard the call of a thousand birds plummeting into a chimney and down into nothing.

I popped my neck and left.

CHAPTER 6
ATEMPORAL HIGH

AFTER I WASHED THE BLOOD from my body and collected my small black case, I focused on erasing the shrieks of the birds and, more importantly, the residue of my failure. I requested a taxi and had it take me to a row of apartments near the edge of the NYU property. I had walked by the place often and noticed evidence of drug sales. The area had been tempting me. I gave in.

A shitty little building loomed before me. Two sad-looking windows abutted a brown door recessed into the apartment face. The blinds appeared cemented shut. An eerie silence surrounded it. Under the one dim porch light, it looked diseased and dying.

I cracked open my gold cigarette case, put a cigarette between my lips, and retrieved a gold lighter. The flame burned hot and bright, and I inhaled deeply. I stood there for a long time.

I began to step forward, but a sound from the road stopped me. Someone cleared his throat.

I turned, glancing at the street.

There she was.

A brilliant and crisp crimson Maserati GranTurismo convertible met me. Top down, beige leather seating, perfectly polished. It was like a silent bang in the night. I felt a swoon, a painful dizziness. I looked around myself, wondering if the world had shifted in the last few minutes. How had the thing crept up on me?

My second thought was that whoever owned that car had a lot of money. The strange, survivalist thought came to me readily, despite the fact I yearned to drown myself in cold, hard chemicals.

"You know, I've been told if you stare too long at her, she'll take your virginity." A very light Irish accent, but there nonetheless. To the left, by the trunk, a young man leaned against the vehicle. His hair, like the car, grabbed my attention. A few inches long and messy, it popped everywhere in spurts like perpetual fireworks. Orange? Red? I couldn't decide.

His eyes sparkled dark green, and his jaw protruded, sharp. Slight dimples ornamented each end of his long lips like a knife had poked him twice. He smiled at me. He held a cigarette, an elbow propped against his side. The other arm hugged his stomach.

When he straightened, he stood tall, probably six foot two, and thin in the way that exaggerates the deliciousness of motion. He wore a nice suit, and the thin black tie hung undone. The first two buttons of his shirt were unfastened. A fuchsia lip print marked his white collar.

In just those few moments I pegged him as the sort who puts on the caricature expected of him to get people talking. As for the personality beneath that caricature, it remained unclear. The waters could run deep or shallow. He could cling to his façade or veer so far from it that it became like a vapor. Either way, he likely had enough hundreds in his wallet that I might not need to kill anyone for a few days, and so I smiled at him. My smile warmed.

"Is that right?" I asked him.

"Yes, it ⊠tis. It's quite magical." He drew on his cigarette, his eyes glued on me.

"I don't doubt you," I said. "I'm sure it practically abducts women."

"No. That's my accent."

I laughed and checked the time on my phone. The illuminated screen showed 11:34—late, and I was weary from the lost battle. Did I have enough energy to pursue this? More importantly, did I have enough energy to do it right?

"This is your first time 'ere?" he asked me.

I looked up at him, adrift on my thoughts. "Why?"

He flicked his cigarette to the curb and walked toward me. "What they sell here... You should know it's shit—watered down or fierce. And I tell you that for your own good. You don't belong here."

I glanced back at the house and knew I didn't really care if the drugs were either weak or poison. "Oh, really?" I sounded uncertain.

"Of course not. You know it. I know it." He shook his head and his whole body moved with the beat.

"Are you a drug dealer?"

He laughed out loud. "No!" he exclaimed as he turned around with outstretched arms. "But I certainly fit the part, eh? But no, no. I am on my way to a party, a party where plenty of the good stuff awaits. The— what do you say?—stuff dreams are made of? You should come. You belong there."

I had no idea why he was putting on such a show. Who was he used to talking to? "Why are you here, then?" I said, flicking my cigarette to the curb and smothering it with my toe.

"Hm?"

"Why are you here if you're going to some big party where drugs are dripping from the heavens above?" I twisted my hand in the air.

"Oh, I'm waiting for a friend. He sells 'is shit here, and then he sells the good stuff where I'm headin'. Same guy." He looked at me soberly. "You should come with me."

I sneered. Taking a deep breath, I thought about shooting him, taking his money, and resurrecting him. But I could hardly think straight, let alone resurrect someone. I was maxed out. For all I knew, it wouldn't work. A man with money like that, I would have to resurrect. People would come looking. No, tonight was not the night.

"Thanks, but no," I told him. I stepped away. I'd return later when I didn't have an audience. But this red-haired stranger started walking behind me, then beside me.

"Why?" he asked.

I shrugged and said the first thing that came to mind. "It's my policy not to do drugs with strangers."

"Well, then, we'll have a few drinks, and we won't be strangers anymore."

"It's also my policy not to do drugs with friends."

"No worries. I'm rich, and the rich never make true friends. A perfect balance between intimacy and total abandonment. Besides..." he hit me in the arm, "what could go wrong?"

I shook my head, bit my lip, and thought of Cyrus, the way he charmed men and women to go with him. "I think the real question is, with the *nouveau riche* what could go right?"

"Lucky you, I'm not *nouveau.*"

"You're not American either."

"So you're holding that against me?"

"No. If anything, it helps."

"Well, that just means you're intelligent, and I'm into intelligence." He winked—a twinkle in his eye that might have been crystal meth.

"Keep talking like that," I said, "and you'll get me all geared up for the worst experience of my life."

He laughed, and his voice echoed against the row of apartments ahead of us like a cannon. "Thank you! Now that your expectations are low enough, I can't possibly fail."

"Nowhere to go but up."

"Exactly."

I smiled. We continued walking. "I'll give you that you're amusing and..." I looked at the Maserati behind us, "bewildering and..." I glanced at the lipstick on the white of his shirt, at the red of his hair, "colorful. But really, today has been hell. I'm on my own tonight. As delicious as it sounds, I don't have a taste for your drugs. I don't want to go to your party. I don't want..."

"Wait. Wait. Look," he said, and he placed a warm hand on my arm, on top of a bruise. I forced myself not to wince. "I'll be straight. As soon as I saw you outside 705, I just had to speak to you. You, I will be pure frank, are a striking person. There's just something about you... Give me a chance an' just, just answer me this.

"When was the last time you were absolutely, extraordinarily happy? Hm? And you have to answer me truthfully." He shook his finger at me. "*And* if that moment turns out to be more than a year ago, you have to come with me tonight. Well, not have to have to, but you should. Fate says you should. Because that's what I'm fucking shooting for tonight. I'm going to this party, and I'm going to absolutely fucking forget this world and live so much tonight that I don't give a shit what happens tomorrow. There is no tomorrow. And you should too. Because you're not like them in there," he pointed to the house, "and you're not like those out there," he pointed to the university, "and you're not like me," he put a hand on his chest. "Obviously. But I think we'll get along together. Just...take a ride with me. Take a high with me. You. Will. Not. Regret it. I swear on that."

The streets were absolutely dead on this side of town. No people, no animals, no strangers, no friends. Just this cinnamon-haired, annoyingly spirited young man. But he did make me curious. And I had to admit, that given enough time and the right drugs, I might just eke out enough energy to kill him, rob him, and resurrect him.

I sighed. "You're honest?" I asked, cocking my head and stepping toward him.

"Of course."

"All right. I will be honest as well. I carry a loaded .38 revolver. I take it with me when I walk alone on dark nights. I do not have a concealed handgun license. The serial numbers are scrubbed away. *If* you accept that I have this, I will proceed with you on this insane and hopeful adventure of yours. Because..." I scanned him from toe to head, "you're at least a little right. And you, too, are 'striking'... What is your name?"

"Patrick."

"Patrick. You accept the fact I wouldn't think twice about shooting you, and I'll follow you to Oz."

"Fantastic!" He shook his head insanely and looked to the sky. "Excellent!" He beamed all his teeth at me, and he held out his elbow as would a nineteenth-century gentlemen. "I have one more condition. You cannot look in the trunk of my car."

"No problem."

These were the kinds of decisions that got people killed. I was used to making them. So, it seemed, was he.

In little time, we arrived on the other side of campus, dropping his drug dealer off at his own car. Then we entered the highway. Patrick drove ninety miles an hour, then one hundred or more, as he wove in and out of traffic.

"What's your name?" he yelled out above the moaning wind.

"Sarah," I said, and I looked at him.

"Sarah what?"

"Sarah Anderson."

"It's a pleasure to meet you. Will you do me a favor, Sarah, and open that glove box?"

I steadied myself by gripping the passenger door as Patrick swerved to the right to avoid hitting a white Honda Accord. When he drove straight again, I reached down and opened the compartment. A cobalt blue bottle, about the size of a flask, surprised me. The blue was so deep it practically glowed. A tan-colored cork kept its brownish liquid contents from pouring out. Impossibly, the bottle stood upright.

"Drink it," he said. "You won't regret it."

"You keep saying that." I peered into his green eyes, and he smiled at me with a devil's grin. He waggled his Clementine eyebrows back and forth in a wave.

I picked up the bottle, noticing little raised imprints in the glass that looked like latticework. I inspected its contents. A large air bubble sloshed around inside.

"What is it?"

"What do you think?"

I opened it and put my nose close, took a whiff. Despite the wind, the smell came to me. Sweet and earthy. Strong. Impossible. I looked at Patrick, somewhat shocked, somewhat impressed. In my hands was what seemed to be laudanum. The scent took me back to the first time Cyrus brought it to me, after I had killed a man named Havinger—my first true victim. He had been a large, burly man who unexpectedly attacked Cyrus.

"My friend Derrick has been doing some research," Patrick said. He nodded to the bottle. "*That's* supposed to be the closest thing to laudanum as is possible to create, based on what we know. He, and only he, makes it. Enjoy it as much as you want. You won't get it anywhere else."

Even without the spell of Patrick's words, my nostalgia for a deep and alluring power drew my lips to the bottle. I downed a long, healthy swig. The liquid tasted sweet, floral, and medicinal, just like it should, and it rekindled a sense of childlike certainty in me. After that swallow, I knew everything was going to be okay. It didn't matter if the girl had been killed. I could bring her back. It didn't matter that the cult had nearly killed me. They hadn't. I would find a way. In just a few minutes, the night dazzled.

There were no cares in the world.

There was no world.

There was no me.

But there was Patrick, and there was the night, and the air, oh the air. The cement road turned to water, and we swam through it.

The road shifted up and over me, and I knew that soon we, too, would be upside down. And, God, ecstasy was in everything. The red lights on the cars in front of us appeared as glowing, thrumming hearts that I could hold with my mind and feel warm again.

I looked to my right, at a white semi with SCHWAY on the cab. I neared it. I reached out, effortlessly, and touched it—or almost did—before Patrick glided us away. A car horn blared.

"Shit! Motherfucker! That was close, right?" Patrick yelled.

I just laughed, and then he laughed.

Patrick turned music on, and a fast, deep bass, a techno-ish sound, surrounded us. And it made me feel like I was God with a violin.

I felt into my coat pocket for my .38. I reached in to touch it again. Again and again. Each time my hand left the cold metal, it seemed as though it had vanished.

I unbuckled my seat belt so that I wouldn't have to scream to be heard—screaming then seemed impossible—and I leaned over to him. "Thank you for that," I said, and then I relaxed, sinking into the leather.

He laughed. "It will make you believe in God, won't it?!" he yelled.

In mere seconds, it seemed, we arrived. He pointed straight toward a house. "Where all is but a dream," he said. Patrick parked in the nearest slot. His emerald eyes twinkled, and he straightened the red strands of his hair, mussed by the wind.

In front of us a stout, singular building towered, surrounded by dark green grass amid crisply manicured trees. The postmodern house was all glass, as though constructed of ice or some witchy, clear fairytale sugar. I saw into the living room, bedrooms, and kitchen, where all of New York danced to the bass of some fast-paced music. The home had probably never experienced a crack or smudge on the shine and polish. It invited us to join in and mix in. The windows allowed the permeation of infinite beauty, wildness and art inside, as floor to ceiling, seducing everyone without caution, nature and art equaled.

We arrived at the front of the house, and Patrick stepped onto the patio. On each of his shoulders there was nothing but air, driving backward care's twisting spirals, which I imagined rolled in billows, leaving him alone in front of the red door. With a crooked smile, he twisted the gold knob. He beckoned me with certainty, like a jester, toward chaos.

Inside, Patrick led me around. He introduced me to Monica. Then Bryce. Then Steven. Matt. Carl. John. Felicia. Dujan. Sarah. Bryan. Javier. Two Jessicas. Mark. Young. Carla. Others known by their last names. An O'Malley who wasn't Irish. A Wolfe. A Fields. I soon lost count.

At one point a guy named David stripped. Jessica removed her shirt and handed him her pink bra, and he did push-ups on the pool table while the players continued their game. He threatened to remove his red boxers, and the guys shoved him from the table. They let Jessica on instead.

After this, all the lights turned off, and a girl undressed and held two flashlights under her massive breasts. They lit up like giant jack-o-lanterns from the implants, and a collective silence dropped over the crowd, either from disgust or awe. I could only stare at the veins.

Around two in the morning, someone set off a firework in the kitchen, and it shot throughout the house like a demon. It took ten pitchers of water to quench all the fires, leaving black spots behind. At that point I concentrated on looking for orange juice.

A boy named Jared had dropped acid. He wrote in Sharpie on all the stainless-steel kitchen cupboards, the floor, the dishwasher, and the stove about the meaning of life and the connections between spiderwebs and iPhones and pumpkins and erasers and the Higgs boson particle. He talked to me while I searched for juice, and I could neither agree nor disagree with him. It made sense at the time. When the firework went off, he thought his graffiti truths had made the known universe explode, and I had to calm him.

At another point, a man revealed his balls to Patrick. I can't remember why. Patrick jokingly prescribed him penicillin.

A few streakers and skinny-dipping followed. A couple of guys produced miniature bombs from the pool's hydrochloric acid and balls of aluminum. Beneath them, clumps of grass burned and blackened. All waxed lovely beneath the watery gauze of laudanum, or, as Patrick had said, as close to laudanum as his friend could get.

Nothing special, and yet all so lovely.

Patrick played one of the pianos, a jazzy number, and he sang along. A couple of girls stripped and danced on the piano, pulling at their hair and breasts, before we all got tired of being away from the frantic activity in the other rooms and returned.

One of the girls whispered to him that she wanted to make love to his accent. He shot a smile at me. "See?" he said. Then I wanted his accent.

At last, we danced, and someone taught me the salsa, and the rumba, and the fox trot, and the west coast swing. Finally, the east coast swing. Then I swayed and moved with Patrick and the others to club music. We crushed so many pills beneath our feet, the table looked like a chalkboard.

Patrick slipped his arm around me for just one moment, and the bruise on my back vanished.

There were no cuts on my fingertips. My lip did not bleed when I smiled. My bloody clothes lay beneath someone else's bed. My scrapes, bruises, and scabs adorned someone else's body.

And the white birds were not calling.

Nothing special, and yet all so lovely. Dear God, I was happy.

When I reached into my pocket, feeling for my revolver, I felt nothing. I stared down into my pocket, elation shifting to horror; it was empty. My .38 was gone.

CHAPTER 7
MILES TO GO

Shit. I shouldn't have come here.

I jumped off the coffee table and looked around the room at all of the people laughing and dancing, snorting and inhaling. I slid my raw fingers into my hair and pulled it back from my face. What was I going to do?

"What's wrong?" Patrick, suddenly beside me, asked. His face shone with sweat.

I grabbed him by his shirt and pulled him close. "What did you do with it?" I yelled.

He covered my fists with his hands, his orange eyebrows dropping. "What are you talking about? Calm down."

"Where's my gun, Patrick?"

"Your gun?" He couldn't have faked the shock on his face. I let him go. "It's gone?" His words were soft and concerned.

I clenched my hands, ready to attack anyone and everyone in the room. Patrick grabbed my arm and tugged me. "Come on."

"What are you doing?" I asked, jerking free.

He held his hands up and nodded. "Just...come on." He strode away with a determined step, leading me to the back door. "Let's try out here."

We came to stand on the lawn beside a gigantic cement swimming pool. With the door shut, silencing the music, gunshots echoed in the distance. The staccato reports could have been mistaken for fireworks, but they were not.

I swiveled and zeroed in on a distant bonfire, a clump of four guys standing around it. The tall one with short, blond hair wore a baseball cap, and he cocked his head at an object in his hand. The others faced it. A muzzle flashed. A gun. I bolted forward.

Behind me, Patrick called my name. I raced toward the group of four, arriving at the bonfire in less than a minute. Breathless, I immediately slipped my right foot behind the baseball-capped blond's left leg and landed a quick, efficient punch against his neck. The man collapsed hard, his head impacting with the ground. He looked up, dazed, and I planted my foot emphatically on the hand still holding my .38. He yelled.

"Jesus Christ!" someone said, and a hand grabbed my arm.

"Get back!" Patrick ordered. Whoever's hand held me released. I bent down, retrieved the gun, and inspected it in the bonfire light.

All of them watched me, the three other strangers slack-jawed.

"Is it yours?" Patrick asked.

I looked at the familiar scrub marks and areas where the metal shined and dulled. The weight of it and the way it rested in my hand confirmed it was mine.

"Yeah." A huge, trembling sigh escaped me. Patrick held two guys back. Now he pushed them and took a few steps toward the house.

"You shouldn't take shit that isn't yours," Patrick shouted.

"Fuck you!" yelled the shortest one.

Suppressing an urge to fire a shot in their direction, I turned and left the circle without saying anything.

Patrick's steps crunched beside mine. He placed a comforting hand on my back, and I pushed it away.

"Don't do that. I don't know you."

He swung his hands to his sides. "It was a shitty thing they did," he said. "Fucked up. But you need to calm down. You need a drink."

"I don't want a drink."

"All right, then *I* need a drink."

When we reached the porch, I wove, weary and dizzy. I leaned against the brick wall and bent forward, my hands on my thighs. I took a deep breath.

God, what a day.

God, what a night.

"Where'd you learn to punch people like that?"

I shook my head. It was all I could do. "It doesn't matter."

After a long pause he smiled, his breath slowing, almost in sync with mine.

"I'm going to go get myself two drinks. If you decide you want one of them, you can have it." He disappeared into the house.

I needed to go, to get away from all this. Nothing good was going to come of being there. I tried to move, but my muscles and my will gave out. I stared at the ground, confused, uncomprehending, dizzy, muted. I could take only so much. I wasn't going anywhere, and I knew it. I didn't really have anywhere to go, and I didn't have it in me to head toward another nowhere.

CHAPTER 8
BOND

WHEN PATRICK RETURNED, HE TOOK my wrist and slid a drink against my palm. I managed to balance on my own two feet. After a few sips, I followed him to the edge of the swimming pool. He briefly put his hands on the sides of my face and touched his forehead to mine. "Your ears ringing?" he asked.

I nodded and sipped. It tasted like rubbing alcohol with a little lime.

Patrick laughed. "I always tell myself it's just ferrics singing."

I opened my eyes wide and stared at him, hundreds of little hairs on my arms, my back, my neck lifting. "*Who?*"

He spoke like the answer should be obvious, like my sudden interest surprised him. "Fairies."

I paused, stared into his drunken eyes. I released a deep breath, still wary. Perhaps it was his accent. Perhaps not. "What an imagination."

His thumb barely grazed the cut on my lip. Still, the area burned from the salt on his skin. I pulled my head back.

"Don't do that."

"I won't. I'm sorry. I'm just…soused." He stepped backward in the soft grass. "Sober me a little. Tell me about yourself, Sarah."

I spoke efficiently, carelessly, hardly considering the words I said as I made them up. "I am from Florida," I told him. "I moved here for college. Grew up on a lot of land with my mom and dad. Didn't grow anything on that land, though. Had llamas for a while when I was younger. I have a brother. His name is Jason. He's going to the University of Maryland. He's studying aeronautics."

Patrick's head moved up and down as I spoke.

"Listening to Jason talk about the shit he does," I continued, "makes me want to put a bullet through my head…or his. It's so boring." I shook my head back and forth. "Came to NYU to study biology. How about you?"

Patrick nodded one more time, pointed his beer at me amiably, and smiled. "That's complete bullshit. What you just said."

I offered more bullshit, and he waved an arm at me and shook his head. "There's no need to lie. Not here. At four in the morning. After all that," he said motioning to the bonfire, "near some stranger's pool and some…" he eyed something close to the ground, "purple thong in the grass. None of that shit matters anyway." He turned away, walked toward the pool and leaned dangerously toward it. "There are other ways to get to know a person. You don't have to tell me about your past if you don't want to."

I stared at him for a long while, and then I simply said, "I have had the shittiest day. I can't even think of anything to tell you."

He looked at me sideways and bit his bottom lip. For a minute, only the beat of the nearby music sounded. He came to stand beside me.

"Times like this," he said, "are when I think of pleasant things in my life. Can you think of anything pleasant?"

I shook my head, and looked out into the night, bone tired. A few stars twinkled at me. If only I could lie down somewhere quiet. Then, strangely, a memory did come to me, unbeckoned.

"Hm," I said.

"Hm?" Patrick asked. "That sounds promising."

"Don't get your hopes up." The memory filed into my head rapidly, despite myself. When I spoke, my voice did not betray my exhaustion.

"One day," I said, "when I was about seventeen, I had the worst day of my life. It made me run from home. When I did, I met a stranger, and she asked me one of the most intriguing questions I have ever encountered. It kind of woke me up. The question I was asked," I said, meeting Patrick's green eyes, "had to do with art."

"Art," Patrick said, as though revealing something provocative.

"Yes." I sipped my drink. "This…woman—her name was Margaret. She explained to me that some art is for beauty's sake. Some isn't. Some art exists for the…swoon. A painful, pleasurable dizziness that occurs when something can't be fully comprehended. She said, if art is capable of eliciting that dizziness, then everyday items could do the same thing. She asked, 'What, in your everyday existence, could present the soul to you?' What could I look at that said *soul*?"

"What was your answer?" Patrick asked, his lip lifted at the corner, like he enjoyed watching me bring this memory to the surface.

"I said glowing blue liquid. If a soul could bleed, *that's* what it would bleed. Something brilliant. Striking. Like hot magma."

"Hmm." Patrick spun around the grass, looking this way and that, "I wonder what I would choose." He stopped suddenly, lifted his glass, smiled, and spoke as though the answer was obvious. "Oh, I know."

My eyes narrowed. He couldn't have come up with an answer just like that. "What?"

He bit his lip. His green eyes slipped to the grass, and he appeared serious and honest.

"I think what says *soul* to me is what says *home* to me. And that would be an opal rosary I had when I was younger."

"A rosary?"

"Yes. It was my mother's. Looked like there was blue lightning in the stone, and there was also some green and red. And it glowed. Like that blue liquid you talked about." He nodded at me and drew a ring around the rim of his glass. "She gave it to me when my father had a heart attack. When she placed it in my hand, she told me, 'Everything is going to be all right. Even when it's not all right, it's all right.' I don't know. I guess I've clung to that ever since. Even when she died a few years later. Even when I accidentally broke the damned thing." He shook his head. "The rosary says *soul* to me, and it always will, even though I broke it. But I lost it."

"You lost it?"

"Yeah," he said, a bit of mystery at the edge of his pupils. "Well, sort of. I know where it is, but I can't get it…yet. It's in a house I used to own and live in." He gazed at me, only one eye open, as though inferring I knew what he spoke of from my own experience. "You know how meth makes you paranoid?"

"Yes," I said, my mind wandering to the few times I had used it. They were dark, grisly, bloody nights that would make the young man in front of me shrink away and scream.

"Well, back then I was really fucking paranoid. I'd hide things—in the yard, taped to the back of the toilet, in the loose fireplace bricks.

"One year, my father got tired of me and came with two men to get me. They forced me in a car, took me to a rehab center, and wouldn't release me.

"They got me clean in half a year, enrolled me in college, got my life back on track. I'll admit that. But while I was in rehab, my dad sold the house. I didn't know until later."

"So it's still at the house," I said.

"And not just that." He chuckled, and the chuckle died. "There's probably about fifty grand hidden around that fireplace. Some of the bricks pull out. I carved out a few pockets inside the fireplace wall. I don't know if any of it is still there. But I don't want to risk tipping off the new owners that there's something worth my returning a year and a half later to get. If I were to tell them exactly what I'm missing, they certainly wouldn't let me have it. So I'm waiting, keeping an eye on the house in case it goes up for sale again."

I stared at him, and he stared at me, and I wondered why he had told me. Did he know the words "fifty grand" would set off a ringing bell in my head? Did he know I would go after it? He looked at me as if he might indeed know, but then that look disappeared.

"You must have been pretty fucking out of it," I observed. I finished my drink.

"I was," he replied quietly.

"And where is this house exactly?"

He smirked, but he didn't respond.

I thought about fifty large and considered how many people I would have to steal from to acquire that amount of money. Too many. If he had that kind of cash just lying around, it would be a mistake not to see this through, one way or another, despite the feverish ferocity of the night.

"You look tired, Jack. How about I drive you home?"

I took a deep breath and agreed. Yes, of course, whatever you say, Patrick. Let's talk about tiredness, not about money in some house probably not too far from here. That sounds like a great idea.

We arrived at his car in less than a minute. I sat in the passenger's seat, thinking that nothing compared to the hum of a hundred-thousand-dollar car that caressed my body. The seating was made from the softest slaughtered cows. Patrick adjusted the rearview and accelerated away. On the highway, he raced no one at a hundred and twenty. And, in the single second when Patrick nearly killed us both when a semi cut across our lane, I reached down and opened the glove compartment, pretending I needed another swig of laudanum. Instead, I quietly slipped Patrick's car registration into my pocket. He drove so erratically he didn't notice. Soon he returned me home. Noticing how much I coveted the drug, he offered me the blue bottle of laudanum, as well as his number, in case I wanted more. I thanked him, and he winked. We said good-bye.

Inside the apartment building lobby, I retrieved Patrick's car registration, hoping that it would reveal his second-most recent address. I looked at the date, longer than six months ago. That meant it wouldn't offer his most recent address.

I looked up the address on my phone and discovered the location was about an hour and a half away—when he had described the house, he said it was about an hour away.

Damn, I thought. *It might be the right one.*

I called a taxi.

CHAPTER 9
DEBT

AN HOUR AND A HALF later, I looked upon a house, far more energized than I could have expected. I realized I wasn't as played out as I'd thought I was.

It sat like a tiny sugar castle in the night, its light blue paint twinkling in the moonlight. If this operation went smoothly, I resolved to buy a box of sugar cubes and eat them all. When I had a job to do, everything and everything else seemed delicious. Tinges of adrenaline crawled into the crevices of my neck.

We don't have to do this tonight, a voice inside said.

That was true. Then again, I didn't have to do anything.

The fireplace chimney rose from the back of the house, rather than the center, and I released a breath I had been holding, pleased I wouldn't need to travel deep within. I would be in and out. "In and out," I whispered.

In about three minutes' time, I picked the lock, and I slipped through the back door. I waited, listening. No alarm beeped. The dark interior cloaked me as I stole one last glance at the yard that shone in the bright moonlight. I shut and locked the door.

I switched on the tiny but effective flashlight I carried in my pocket. Half the size of a tire gauge, it resembled a coffee stir stick.

The brilliant light hugged the walls, revealing a ruby couch, a full bookshelf featuring a clear beer stein that shimmered like water. Beside the bookshelf stretched a slim closet door, and then, finally, neighboring the back door, the fireplace, a mouth without a tongue. I was eager to put my hands inside.

I sat in front of the brick face and shined the flashlight around until I noticed a set of bricks out of place. As I attempted to pull them free, my raw fingers slid against them painfully, and I nearly cursed. I retrieved my apartment keys from my pocket, and I dug at the mortar, cringing at the scratching sound, like chalk on a blackboard. At first, I worried I had chosen the wrong place to chisel; there was so much mortar. I scraped my fingernails against the brick hard enough that they bent back. "Fuck!" I hissed.

I glanced around again. No one was there. But I needed to hurry.

A crack appeared, a little black amid the white. I shined the thin flashlight at the crevice, leaning in until my bruised stomach muscles screamed, and I scraped more of the mortar away.

When I tugged the brick free, money immediately erupted, like feathers exploding from a slashed pillow. I snatched the cash, pushing green bills and gray ash into the black bag I had brought with me. The few that I missed dropped into the center of the fireplace, and I grabbed those too.

The night improved, finally going the way it should. My heart swelled, feeling whole again, rather than fractured and in desperate need of rest. I relished the energy, closed my eyes, and smiled.

Click.

That wasn't me. The hairs on the back of my neck lifted. I had been privy to that particular sound many times before. The cocking of a gun.

I inhaled one steady breath before the lights beamed around me.

"What the *fuck* are you doing?"

The voice boomed deep. His words rumbled firm and controlled, but they did not conceal his fury.

. I raised my hands and turned. I studied him. He loomed large and stout. Silver streaked his hair and beard, and he wore a white undershirt. He resembled a truck driver. Tightly, he gripped a shotgun. I stared at the barrel. In less than a second, if he wanted, he could end me. My shitty night would disappear, and the world would vanish, if his right finger moved barely an inch.

"Hitting the fireplace jackpot," I said as a cold sweat flooded my entire body. "Would you like some?"

"What are you talking about?" He raised and aimed the weapon. I lifted my hands higher.

"You broke into my house!" he said, his volume and fury growing. "You are breaking into *my house!*" His face reddened; his chest pumped up and down like a piston. I shook my hands at him to interject.

"Let me show you," I said. I looked up at him, my expression inquisitive and soothing.

The man cocked his head, narrowed his eyes, and waited.

Slowly—cagily—I reached into the bag and retrieved a handful of bills. I dropped them, allowing them to slip to the floor, each a paper airplane. I grabbed more from the fireplace and let the ash and green drift to the floor like snow. Hundreds of dollars. Tens of hundreds.

Tens of thousands.

The man's expression shifted from fright to surprise. His blue irises glimmered in delight.

"It's all yours if you let me go and promise you won't call the police."

He looked at me, his gray wife beater stretched across his protruding belly. He asked, intensely curious, sounding more human than predator, "How much is there?"

"Fifty grand."

He steadied the shotgun against his shoulder and adjusted his stance. Eventually, he seemed to make a decision. He suddenly swung the shotgun up on his shoulder, the muzzle facing the ceiling.

Breathe deep. Aim well.

Without hesitation, I reached in my pocket and withdrew my .38. I shot the man five times. His body jerked with each shot, and he collapsed to the floor, inert and bleeding. Death would follow.

With a deep breath, I returned to the fireplace and collected all the money from within its walls. As the man bled out, I retrieved my knife. Now that I had time, I dug into the mortar and removed more bricks. I reached inside the hole I'd created, felt along the back, and discovered the other item Patrick had mentioned. The rosary was cool against my hand, like the skin of a snake, and I wrapped my fingers around it and freed it from its cage. The odor of brick dust arrived with it. I coughed and slipped the rosary into my pocket.

I searched the cubby again, discovering a few other small items inside. I brought those out as well and tucked them into my other pocket.

I picked up the full bag, swung it over my shoulder, and left. At the edge of the door, I searched within myself for my power. It bloomed in my veins, and the true me returned with it, like the night had never been, like my childhood had never been. Like I had never heard of Infinitum or Cyrus or even Patrick. My mind was all resurrection. All the dents in me that the world had made didn't exist. I reveled in the sensation like I was swimming in liquid lightning. I smiled and thrust the surge of power out to the body.

With hardly a shiver, the homeowner lived and breathed again, healed—the blood-soaked floor the only residue of his death.

In a few short seconds, I departed the house, walking on the stiff grass in the night, dreaming of sugar cubes.

A safe distance from the old home, I called a taxi and waited. I withdrew everything from my pockets and peered at the fragments in the light of my phone. The rosary necklace was in two pieces; a few stones had fallen out. Even broken, it put other jewelry to shame. Blues, reds, and greens streaked and shimmered within the white stones. The colors tasted like candy. I wondered why Patrick had ever hidden it in a fireplace to begin with, how he had broken it.

When I looked into the rosary beads, I didn't hear the word *soul*. The glow reminded me of mountain goats that are so white they are rumored to practically glow, and something about the soft pallid color illuminating the night brought to mind something beyond, unfathomable. A red box with a golden shelf. A gramophone with a gold bell. White from skin to core. A white war. I shivered.

I knelt and set the rosary pieces down. My own necklace hung safely beneath my gray cotton shirt. I lifted the long chain without opening the clasp and held the necklace out, beneath the light. Then I placed it on the ground beside the rosary. It swiveled, threatening to plummet down the sloping concrete, before it finally stilled. It looked like a shriveled windowpane, so black and charred that it appeared absolutely worthless next to the opal beads.

Like Patrick, I knew what it was like to live with a cross.

I knew what it was like to miss the one who had gifted it.

Sitting there, waiting for the taxi, examining the pieces of jewelry, one from a mother, one from Roland, I realized it was kind of nice to view them as a pair.

THE TAXI ARRIVED AT MY apartment. I swung out the bag with fifty grand happily, eager to secure it in the small fireproof safe I had recently purchased and already drilled into the floorboards of my closet. The day, which had started off so miserably, had a good ending. I took a good swig from the blue bottle of laudanum, and it seemed to kick in. I was sleepy and glowing.

I quietly shut the taxi door, and it drove away. I crossed the street toward my building, absentmindedly fingering the rosary in my right hand, the bag of money in my left.

The air wafted, crisp and cool, across my skin, and I shivered and smiled, despite myself. The empty lobby beamed back at me through the clear glass windows.

As I stepped up the curb, something brushed against my face, and then a sharp pain jabbed my throat. My head jerked back so quickly I thought my neck would snap. I fell backward and hit something hard.

I grabbed for my neck. My fingernails scraped against thin wire. Panic pierced me.

Something shoved itself into my mouth and cut into the corners of my lips. It wound around my head. My hands were jerked and pinned behind me. I opened my eyes and gasped.

I saw three figures in the dark before my vision went black, my eyes covered in cloth. The strangers carried me some distance and dropped me. I didn't hit concrete, something slightly softer. My bruised back reignited in pain. Hands pushed my legs toward my chest, and then I heard a thud. I was in the trunk of a car.

Soon we were silently moving. I thought of Cyrus. Of his followers. My kidnappers must be them. They had emerged from their Victorian cave, away from the safety of their gramophone.

There were no cackling birds to help me this time.

CHAPTER 10
A DIFFERENT BREED

IN THE TRUNK, I BEGAN to imagine in excruciating detail what would happen to me. The next moments felt long, horrible.

I tried to pull the cuffs up, but they bound my arms to my waist. I feared I might suffocate from the cord in my mouth.

When the trunk finally opened, I psychically reached out for cool air as hands seized me and dragged me out. They grabbed my hair and held it, pushing me forward so that I walked. They jerked me to a stop. Footsteps echoed against close walls. I had entered a room—a small one. A finger pushed me backward, hard enough so that I fell. I collapsed into a chair.

The bag over my head lifted off, and the gag left my mouth. I tasted blood.

I looked wildly at them, peering into eyes, eyes, everywhere. Five pairs of them, none I recognized. They were cold, numb, experienced eyes. They were unfeeling, but they were not Infinitum's type of unfeeling.

I relaxed and looked dead center.

A square dark wood table stood between me and a trim, graying man. He registered as older, maybe in his forties or fifties. His face was heart-shaped, his perfectly cut hair wavy. He looked crisp, more solid than the table. A black leather jacket zipped to his throat. He laid his hands on the table, like a card reader. A file lay between them.

"Manage your breathing," he said.

I noticed my heaving breaths, and I tried to control them, deepen them, slow my heart. I looked at the floor and leaned back against the chair, attempting to return my perception to normal. The floor didn't help, so I glanced at the ceiling and noted exposed pipes.

One of the men walked forward and unbuttoned my jacket. He slipped his hand inside my left inside pocket, searching, and he retrieved my.38. He popped the revolver open and removed the bullets in one quick motion before he laid the gun and bullets on the table in front of the man across from me.

From my bottom left inner pocket, he retrieved my cigarettes in their golden case, as well as my gold lighter, my cell phone, and the bottle of laudanum. He placed these items to the right of the weapon.

The man continued to search my pockets. He retrieved Roland's cross and Patrick's mother's rosary. His hand returned and grasped the several remaining rosary pieces and placed them on the table. Finally, he found my keys.

He tapped my jean pockets and checked my shoes.

While he worked, warm liquid ran down the center of my bottom lip and chin. It dripped into my lap, onto my black wool coat. I barely registered the red tinge before it disappeared into the fabric.

The man patting me down finished. The one who sat across from me scanned my face. "Your lip is deeply torn. Not us, though, was it?" He resumed his scrutiny. "That bruise on your cheek is old."

Roland's withered cross stopped rolling and found a sturdy position near the point of a bullet.

After glancing at the items on the table, he nodded to another man, who set down a full pack of cigarettes and a lighter. "Would you like a smoke?"

I gave the barest of nods. "The whole pack."

His laugh thundered velvety and deep. "We have liquor too."

There was a thump, and sure enough, a glass appeared in front of me, as well as a very small unopened bottle of whiskey.

"James, remove the cuffs. I don't think we'll have any problems with... you go by Jack?"

I nodded.

I leaned forward, and, with a little effort, James unbuckled me. I pulled my hands around to the front and lit a cigarette that had appeared alongside a lighter. Blood from by lip soaked into the cigarette tube. I wiped away as much as I could with my palm.

I smoked and smoked. The man stared at my scraped hands.

He finally said, "You didn't scream."

I nearly laughed. Of all the things for him to say. "No."

"Why?"

"It never occurred to me."

"Hm," he said. "Are you sure that's why?"

"What else would it be?"

He said nothing. Then, "You should learn how to scream. It might save you one day."

I didn't respond.

"Jack, do you live at the Alexan?"

I glanced at the deep lines beside his eyes. "Yes," I said tentatively.

"Expensive place, isn't it?"

I looked at him and the other men. "I manage."

He smiled but did not press me. "And...you are friends with Patrick Flannigan?" He glanced up.

The silence between us seemed impenetrable until I responded, "I just met him tonight. How do you know about him?"

"I try to be someone who knows everything about my targets."

That set a million questions buzzing in my brain. I inhaled another drag.

"I'm a target?"

"Yes."

"For what?"

"You'll soon find out."

I tried to swallow, but my throat burned, sticky, and saliva refused to come. "And you know all about me..."

"Well, not all. But some, yes. And what I do know makes me want to know more. You...interest me. When I was first told about you, I Googled every story I could find about Cyrus Harper and Infinitum, searching for any mention of you, but none arrived. The oddity, though, the sheer oddity, of what I was told about you made me want to meet you. Now that I have, I find you just as intriguing as I'd imagined."

As I stared at the man before me, reality landed its blows, left and right. Someone had contacted him about me, perhaps because they needed his help in dealing with me. Apparently they had told him everything.

Perhaps it was even worse than that. Perhaps this was another cult of some sort, a rival cult. "Who are you?" I said, an unwelcome hint of fear in my voice.

"Let's keep the focus on you."

I took another shaky drag.

He slid the folder from his side of the table to mine. "I want you to read this."

I took it.

On a white sheet of paper, black print outlined a set of instructions. A recipe of sorts. "Take her. Behead her. With black charcoal, draw Xs on her eyes and an upside-down cross on her lips. Place her head on a pike..."

I didn't read the rest. I didn't need to. I knew what came next. Dismemberment. I had seen it before.

I looked toward the man in front of me.

"We were supposed to do something very similar to you tonight," he said. "We were paid two hundred thousand to do so."

My mind returned to the night at the dark Victorian home, where I had been dragged across the cement, up the stairs, nearly eaten alive by some white, gooey tongue climbing out of a gramophone. People like that would want this to happen.

"Are you going to read the rest?" he asked.

"I know what it says."

He said, "Yes. So you are familiar."

I waited for him to say more, but nothing arrived. "Are you going to do it?"

"No." He said this simply, and as he did, he closed the file. The way he pursed his lips reminded me of a college professor who had decided not to fail me out of his class.

He picked up Patrick's mother's rosary with the tips of his fingers. He held it carefully up to the light, gazed at it as though it were a kaleidoscope, and then set it back down. He spread the stone fragments out on the table.

"Why not?" I whispered.

"Our employer is far less interested in who these instructions were intended for and far more interested in who gave them."

"You don't know?"

"Why would we? Jobs like these are anonymous. Always anonymous. We defend that anonymity."

Jobs. Anonymous jobs. He wasn't part of a cult, at least not in any ordinary sense. His job was to kill people, just like mine had been when I worked for Cyrus. But I was betting that he made a lot more money and had a lot more freedom; he did not serve some man who called himself a god. For some reason, that made his choice more respectable in my eyes. No manipulation. Simply death.

"I would expect you to...have some resources," I said. "To find out about me."

He flipped his hands toward the dank walls beside us. "These are our resources." He smiled.

I paused, crushed the cigarette out on the table, and lit another one.

"Do you know who wrote the letter?" he asked.

"Why does your employer want to know?" I doubted he would answer.

"Someone he knew was murdered this way. Recently." The man tapped the table such that he pointed to the file before me. "We are having trouble finding out who is responsible. This, you understand, was lucky...for you. Very lucky. It means you get to live, at least for a little while. And if we do kill you, it won't be so ornately."

Ornately. The word reverberated in my head and made me shiver. I took a drag off my second cigarette and held in the nicotine until I sweated.

"So do you know who wrote it?" he asked.

"Yes," I said. "I know."

"Who?"

"A very sadistic blond-haired, blue-eyed boy by the name of Alexander Harper."

"Cyrus's son, then?" the man asked. "The one who tortured animals in the woods, including the old family pet?"

I peered at the man through the cigarette smoke. "How do you know all that?"

He smiled serenely, but he did not answer.

Closing my eyes wearily, I could come up with only two answers. "You are either in a rival cult or you know someone who followed Cyrus. That person knows about me, has told you all about me and my brother."

I opened my eyes and waited for an answer. All he said was, "We are not part of any cult."

"Then what do you care?"

"I told you. *You* interest me, Jack."

I swallowed against the dryness in my mouth. "But why?"

"Because you killed a man no one else was able to, and, despite what I understand was a rough upbringing, you are not insane. You are not a follower. You were raised your whole life to be one, and yet you are not. You took down someone the police now believe was the greatest terrorist threat to the nation. And you are what? Eighteen? So you are young, and a killer and not insane. And, perhaps, you have respect for life, or at least for children. You didn't kill Cyrus to take over. You killed him to save lives. All of this means, to me, that you are perfectly on the border."

The amount of information he knew about me stunned me for a few minutes. Once I accepted this violation of privacy, I took a deep breath. Cocking my head, I said, "What do you mean, 'on the border?'"

"In my experience, there are, *usually*, only two types of people in the world. Those who, if you will kindly excuse the biblical reference, take the apple from the snake. And their bites are hearty. Their chin is always dripping with the juice. And that juice, over time, turns to blood. Yet they keep on eating. They learn to like it.

"On the other hand, there are those who run from proffered power. They never look back, and they never try anything that even remotely looks like an apple. They have no taste for it. They recognize a jug of blood when they see it.

"But every once in a while, I come across someone like you. Someone who, if they were left in the garden and the snake tempted them, would never eat, yet never run. Rather, they'd say to the snake, 'Keep talking, because this moment is *the* moment. I'll never say yes to you, I'll never say no. Just let me sit here, right here. That is my pleasure.' Where you get pleasure is in the border that divides between life and death. Not many get it, get you. But I do."

I wouldn't respond to that. It was too strange. The way he stared at me, he didn't expect me to.

"What kind of a person are you?" I asked.

He chuckled. All five men in the room laughed. "My dear," he said. "I have been eating for a very, very long time. You are in a room full of people who live under the apple tree. Just like you always have."

He smiled at me. "But you can appreciate that. After all, it comes with the border territory."

I sensed a hint of wonder. He was no imbecile, but I wasn't sure what he was. I asked him, "If you truly know anything about me, about the number of people I have…" I didn't finish the sentence. I didn't need to. "I wonder how you could ever believe that I was on the border."

"That's a good one," he said. "But the question, you'll learn with time, is never 'What have I done?' or 'What have I been taught to do?' The question, instead, is 'What would I have rather done?' Or, perhaps more aptly for you, 'Why am I not Alexander Harper?' You were raised the same way, after all. Or trained the same way. So why are you Jack and not Alexander?"

I did not answer the question, or even begin to consider it, for the time required would be far too great. I had to admit I'd never wondered, and I didn't know why.

The man held Roland's cross in his hands and dangled the little ball at eye level, examining every contour. He set the cross down on the table carefully. It rolled only slightly and then settled against the butt of the gun.

"From that bruise on your cheek and the split lip, it appears that you were in an accident of some sort. Would you care to elaborate?"

"I'm fine."

The man rose from his seat. He took the three strides to reach me and simply placed his hand on my back. He pressed hard with his fingers, and I winced.

"Hmm," he said. "That's what I thought."

He pressed my side, and again I grimaced. He took my scabbed hands into his and looked at them, as if a doctor.

My mouth dried again, and I took a long drag on my cigarette. My eyes never veered from his, but behind my gaze, my brain reeled, racked with surprise and confusion.

The man took a few steps, as though pacing through his own mind. "There always seems to be something new with you. Odd little inconsistencies. Strange slips of reality unaccountable in the numbers. Like how you afford the Alexan on your own, at the age of eighteen. Or how you brought down a man like Cyrus Harper. Why you have with you a bag with, what? Fifty thousand in it? It makes me wonder what the explanations could possibly be. As for your wounds... I was unaware you had been attacked. Who harmed you?"

"It was just a small accident."

His gaze bore into me with an intensity that would have made anyone else relent, but he freed my hands and returned to his seat. He asked me quite suddenly, "Is there anyone else it could be?"

It took me a second to realize what he meant, and I said, "Oh," then, "No," then, "Wait," then, "Yes."

"Who?"

"Anybody remotely related to the old group."

"I thought Cyrus's following was dead."

"I thought so, too, for a while. But now, I suspect, there might be thousands of old followers spread across the country. Infinitum... well, it could have regrouped. Alex would be with them, probably leading them, if they have. Anyone in Infinitum would want me dead as much as Alex would. Still, this," I tapped the folder, "reeks of Alex."

"Why would he want you to die this way?" the man asked, scanning the file.

"It's a ritual."

"What ritual?"

I thought of his employer, how this might upset him, even though I found all of Cyrus's old rituals meaningless. "It doesn't matter."

"Tell me."

I sighed. "It's not important."

"I will not ask again."

This wasn't worth losing fingers over. I said, "It's to cut off the line. The biological line. The idea is that, somehow, if this ritual is done, there will be a domino effect. One by one by one, the family dies off, so that no more roots are set down in the world. The line can't continue."

The man eyed me with what seemed like curiosity.

"Your employer shouldn't believe it," I said. "It's just the Kool-Aid talking."

"Why would Alex want to destroy your biological line?" he asked. "Is he not your brother?"

He hit upon something I'd been wondering for a long, long while— whether I was actually adopted, whether Alex was Cyrus's son, whether I was Cyrus's daughter. "I don't know," I said. "But I don't think that's what the message is here."

"What's the message?"

I pursed my lips. "Alex selected the children who went into Infinitum. Did you know that?"

He shook his head. There was at least one thing he didn't know.

"Well he did. And he chose children who looked like me. That's what I discovered, as soon as I met them. Alex has a proclivity toward looks like mine. This," I said, motioning toward the file containing the instructions for how to kill me, "is just more of the same. He doesn't just want me dead. He wants everyone who looks like me dead. The biological line, I think, has to be read metaphorically. And I'd bet, though I might be reaching here, that whoever you know who was killed like this looked like me."

The cogs behind his eyes worked. It was obvious in the way that his head tilted back so slightly that I had hit upon some truth. The realization shone like a tiny psychic light behind his eyes. He seemed surprised that I had connected the dots and pressed his thumb to his bottom lip. This was my only chance to state what was on my mind.

"If it is Alex, I want to be the one to kill him."

"You don't get a say." He didn't look at me.

"You have no idea how much hell I have been through over him."

"No, I know. I know everything. Besides, we can do a much better job of killing him. A longer job. A more ornate one."

Again, that word. Ornate.

Of that I had no doubt, but it was the principle for me. I opened my mouth to argue with him, but he held up his hand.

"Here it is," the man said, "the rules of our engagement, so to speak. If you talk about us to anyone, if you go to the authorities, we will kill you and your friend, Patrick. If you leave town, we will kill the both of you. You are to stay in the city, in your apartment preferably. You are to go about your days like this never happened. Eventually, we will contact you again. The plan is to set up a meeting with the person who hired us, who told us everything about you—or at least someone representing the person who did—and when we do meet, we want you there to identify him to the best of your ability."

"And I have no choice?"

"Of course. You have no choice."

He slid my keys, my cigarettes, lighter, and phone back to me. When he touched the broken rosary, however, he paused and prodded the jewels. He held the broken chain up to the light and said, half to himself, "Beautiful little piece." He blew on it, releasing a bit of fireplace grit. The dust danced and dispersed beneath the fluorescent lights. He pocketed the rosary and then each little piece.

"In the meantime, we will hang onto these items." He collected the shriveled cross and placed it in another pocket. Then the laudanum. Finally, he picked up my gun and the bullets that went with it.

A wave of anger ran through me. Roland had given me that gun.

"We will return them, and your money, when you have sufficiently assisted us. That should provide adequate motivation."

I crushed the cigarette out on the table, furious. I glanced at the others in the room. "What would you do if I took something of yours?" I asked angrily. "How would you react?"

"Why should we debate things that will never come to be?" the man across from me asked contemptuously. He stood from his seat and straightened the arms of his coat.

"Nevertheless, what would you do?"

He sighed and gazed at me as though I were an afterthought. "If I were you, I'd do my best to convince the people who had granted me life that I deserved it. I would be forthcoming with information."

I shook my head. "I am not convinced that tactic would be the most effective."

"Then that is *your* problem.

"And Jack," the man said, "in the future, try to keep your balance. It looks like you took quite a fall. Don't want anything happening to you in the meantime. For Patrick's sake. Hm?"

His expression conveyed a stern warning before he walked away. Another man hooked his hand under my arm. We made our way out of the room and back to the car.

The bag once again covered my head.

CHAPTER 11
PULSE

WHEN MY ABDUCTORS DROPPED ME off at my apartment, day had already broken. As soon as I walked through my apartment door, I slammed it, locked it, and collapsed against the wall. I slid to the floor and drew in a shaky breath. The night's events would require careful dissection, but my mind, as rusty as my limbs, refused and protested. Sleep was the only cure. I crawled into bed and fell unconscious in mere seconds.

When I woke midafternoon, I stood in front of the bathroom mirror, inspecting my wounds. The large bruise was starting to yellow. The purple had faded, even with my being thrown into a trunk. The raised scabs on my palms and fingertips had shriveled slightly. Tiny and round, they tickled my palms when I rubbed my hands together to warm them. The cut on my lip had once again crusted over. A small bruise on my cheek was now a slightly paler shade of gray. My body erased the minor catastrophes with ease.

It had only been one day since I had returned to my apartment bloody and sore before heading back into the night to seek chemical solace and encountering Patrick. One day since my near death. I was healing quickly.

I dressed and brewed a pot of coffee. As I waited for it to finish, I retrieved the mail. Something had arrived, and I knew what it was before I slid my finger beneath the seal and ripped the envelope open.

It was the only thing in the world that could have torn my mind from the previous night's abduction.

It was a letter from Annette.

Dear Jack Harper,

By the time you receive this, I will be dead.

Harlowton is sitting beside me, and he is making me write this letter. He knows about the others I have sent you. I am going to be punished. He wants you to know that you did this to me. And he wants you to know that he knows about the other children who have been writing to you.

He says if you give yourself up, no one else will need to be punished. I will be the only one.

We both hope you will listen this time.

Please help the others, even if you cannot help me.

Give yourself to Harlowton. Perhaps he will grant you mercy.

Mercy is better than death.

- Annette

An intense rage expanded in my chest, blocking every other thought.

I resisted the urge to grip the paper in my hand, to rip it to shreds. Harlowton should not be worried about granting mercy. He should be worried about receiving it.

Though tears came to my eyes, my mind followed an analytical train of thought. On my own, I had managed—and always would manage— my own way, surviving, succeeding. But only up to a certain point. There were places now that I needed to go, and I could not travel the path alone. Four-zero-five Brimmer had taught me that lesson with a cut lip, enormous bruise, and scraped fingers and stomach, and I had not even stepped inside the house. I had only stood outside of its fence and barely, just barely, dabbed a toe past the gate's threshold.

And WHAM! I had been pulled to near death.

My bruised back twinged as I reached for a pillow from the couch and plopped it on the floor. I rested my head on it, cleared my thoughts, and ran my hand through my hair.

I yearned to know the realities of Infinitum. How had it evolved? What did it do with its children? What did it desire? What was it planning? How did it function without Cyrus?

Infinitum wasn't yet dead, and I readied to finish the job. I had walked away too soon, underestimating their resilience.

Receiving letters from the children of followers and seeing the homes of believers shocked me; nearly being pulled to death, though, enraged me. And the video. God, the video. I had not believed there was ever a possibility the followers could hurt me again, that they could best me. Not after I had killed their leader and left them far, far behind. I was wrong.

The evil I left behind not only remembered me. Its teeth remained quite sharp, like fishhooks. Time and distance did nothing to dull them.

If the birds had not intervened, I would be dead.

Stupid, Jack, I thought. *Stupid.*

I lit a cigarette and cut the bitter memory with sweet nicotine.

I replayed the image of the man across the table inspecting Roland's cross and the broken rosary in the light and slipping both into his pocket.

I decided I would play along, just as he had advised: "Go about your daily life. Act as though this never happened." I gave into their wishes to keep things agreeable between us. Eventually, perhaps I could slip in a request, maybe show them the letters, the video. The man had said I interested him. Maybe I could cultivate that interest.

I jumped when my phone sounded. Someone texted me.

It was Patrick. I shook away the horrid memory with a shiver and sat up.

Though we had exchanged numbers the previous night in case I wanted to buy more laudanum, I hadn't expected to hear from him.

"Call me when you can," his text read. "I want to hang out."

The screen went black. I paused to stretch my sore muscles, enjoying the serene silence. Roth and his men had taken fifty large from me… And here was this young, careless red-haired man, who would be so easy to kill. It might be good to return to him, lift whatever was in his wallet or confiscate whatever he might have stashed in, say, the fireplace of his new apartment, and be on my way. I did not have my gun, but that didn't mean anything.

I got up, showered, and changed into running clothes. When ready, I called Patrick and agreed to get together. I asked where to meet. He said he would pick me up. We settled on eight. He never said where we were going.

I tossed my phone on the couch and made a cup of coffee. I carried the mug out on my balcony and smoked a cigarette, preparing myself for the inevitable kill. Then I left the apartment to go for a run.

While I ran among Manhattan's pedestrians, I noticed two men in a black car, the same two men, the same black car, at least six times.

If I stole from Patrick, it would have to be inside, away from the prying eyes of such men, if that kind of place existed.

PATRICK ARRIVED AT MY BUILDING on time. When I got into his car, I smelled liquor on his breath. I looked him up and down, eyeing his jacket pockets. "Would you like me to drive?" I asked.

His red, bleary face scrunched in a fake contemplative expression. Freckles on his cheeks stood out. He rubbed his nose with the back of his gloved right hand. "Not a bad idea," he said. We switched places.

"Where to?" I asked, checking the rearview mirror. Taxis and cars passed. I didn't recognize any of them.

"Well, we could go to dinner," he said. "Or..."

"Or?"

"We could go where I go every Tuesday. To the grave."

"The cemetery?"

He nodded.

That surprised me. Looking into his glazed eyes, I wondered if he only asked because he was very, very drunk. "I can do that," I said, smiling. I glanced once more behind me and then pulled onto the street.

That seemed to please him greatly, and he cheerfully gave me directions. It was about half an hour away.

There was no howling wind. No radio. No drugs on the dashboard. We spoke to one another in the quiet, in the calm, traveling along on an almost empty highway. I relaxed.

I thought about my trip to his former house, how I had discovered and claimed the money and the rosary, which I planned to return to him but had failed. These thoughts lent the night a wistful and disappointed air—I had almost given him something, but fate had stopped me; he had almost given me something, and fate had stopped him.

Patrick told me to park a few blocks away from the cemetery, and then we walked quietly through the night to a place where the fence reached a tree line. The bars bent just barely wide enough for us to pass through. He angled his tall frame between them, and I did the same.

Patrick had seemingly completed this ritual often enough to reach his destination in his sleep. We passed through moonlit patches of grass until we arrived at a large grave guarded by an angel. Patrick bent to his knees and kissed the base of the statue. I drew closer, and when he rose to his feet, I read the name DEIRDRE FLANNIGAN.

"This is...?" I whispered.

"My mother," he replied. He removed a flask from his inner right pocket and took a swig. "She's in a good place." He waved at himself. "And I'm in a good place." He pushed the flask into my hand. "Now we're all in a good place."

Patrick flopped on the ground and leaned against the tombstone. Around us, hundreds of headstones and angels stood watch, rising on a hill in the distance. Where the hill dipped, they disappeared, leaving just a surrounding black veil.

"She isn't buried in Ireland?" I took a sip of what tasted like bourbon.

He shrugged, and I sat beside him. "My father said if we were stuck in the US, then she would be too."

I snorted, leaned back, and lit a cigarette.

"She was murdered, you know," he said.

In the middle of a drag, I stopped to stare at him.

"Sorry. I don't know why I said that." He laughed nervously, playing with the lid of his silver flask. "I've never told anybody that. If it's too much for you..." he swiped his hand through the air, "you can literally just get up and leave, and it won't hurt my feelings."

"Why *did* you tell me?"

"I don't know." He placed his hand over his heart. "I feel in here you are safe to tell things to, you know?"

"A person who carries a gun with her? Who said she wouldn't think twice about shooting you? Right."

"Sometimes genuineness feels like that. You know, that gravitas."

"I know." I smoked my cigarette quietly before I asked, "Who was the fucker that did it?"

Patrick lit his own cancer stick. The two of us swooned in the night, neither of us afraid to speak of death. A tightly coiled spring in my center released. I sighed.

"That's a long story."

I didn't press him, but he offered in his lyrical voice that made everything sound as though it wasn't a big deal, "I was the one who found her. I've never told anyone that before either."

"Shit."

"Yeah. I was *nine*."

"Nine," I repeated softly. "Young."

"Would it have been better if I were older?"

"It might have been, yes."

The tip of his cigarette fluoresced in the dark. "I don't know... Something like that. Maybe we're always nine when we see the harsh stuff. Always children." His eyes met mine. "Something like that ever happen to you?"

The wind brushed over me. The soft, dark night seemed to speak to me, and all the dead beneath the ground. They all advised me to be careful.

"You don't have to tell me, if you don't want to."

I cleared my throat. "I think most of us have experienced something terrible. Not necessarily at nine years old, but at some point."

"Sets the tone, doesn't it?"

"Tone?"

"For your whole goddamn life."

I passed the flask to him, and he swished a mouthful down. "So tell me something about yourself," he said. "Are you going to the university here?"

"Yes, I am," I lied.

"What are you studying?"

"Biology," I said wistfully.

"Why?"

"I want to uncover the elixir of life." I winked.

Patrick chuckled. "Well, then you certainly wouldn't major in basket-weaving."

I smiled.

"And why here?"

"I have free rent where I'm living," I said. "It's a nice place."

"Where at?"

"The Alexan."

"Holy shit."

"I know."

"For free? How'd you manage that?"

I shrugged. "I know someone who knows the owner." Another lie. It didn't matter if I kept up with them. I had no intention of spending much more time with this individual.

"That's a hell of a person to know."

"I know a hell of a lot of people."

When he laughed, I smelled his alcoholic breath, and the smoke, and his cologne. He pointed to my hand holding the cigarette. "So what happened to you? Why are your hands scraped?"

"You sure do ask a lot of questions," I said, wondering for the first time if he had shared his mother's death with me as part of a quid pro quo.

"Last one, for now. I promise."

I inhaled deeply on my cigarette and peered at him through the darkness. "I fell."

"Is that right?"

"That's another question."

Patrick laughed.

After a beat, I said, "What was she like? Your mother?"

"Beautiful. Smart. And honest... She'd hate me, now, for doing what I do to my body."

"Then maybe you should stop."

"And feel something? Are you mad? Anyways, losing three teeth isn't losing a life. And I don't mind losing them." He sighed. "It's frightening to me. The idea that she'll never be here to yell at me, help me, forgive me, set things right."

"No," I said. That made Patrick turn. I smashed my cigarette into the dirt. "That's not so frightening."

"No?"

I shook my head. "What's frightening is knowing that it wouldn't matter if she did return. That if she came walking in through the door tomorrow, it wouldn't be enough. That miracles aren't miraculous enough."

I looked at Patrick. He remained quiet. Then he whispered, "Why would you say something like that?"

"Happened to someone I know. He thought his father was dead, blamed all of his problems on his father being taken from him. It turned out his father wasn't dead. He showed up one day. In the end, it didn't solve any of his problems."

"That man's an idiot," Patrick said. "Just stupid. I swear to you, if it turned out my mother wasn't murdered, if she walked through the front door one day, I'd be finished with all the shite in the world. I'd be whole again. I'd be fine."

"He said the same thing."

Patrick shrugged. "We're different people. You cannot compare one person to another. Maybe he was lying. To himself and to others. About the reason behind his addictions."

"Yes, he was lying," I said. "And my point is that we're all lying, all of the time."

"Jack," he said, "you go down that path, and it all becomes hopeless."

He took a drag and exhaled. "Besides, didn't you say that in the end things didn't change? So that means they changed for a while?"

"Yes," I said. "So?"

"So maybe it did work, just as well as most anything does. Temporarily."

I shook my head. "I don't understand."

"*Maybe*, if every three months another dead family member turned out to be alive, again and again and again, the guy would never return to his problems. Maybe the miracle needs a rhythm to work. It needs to pulse."

"How terribly disappointing that would be," I answered. "What is the difference between a miracle and a drug if a miracle also has to be administered?"

He laughed abruptly. He laughed loud and for a long time, leaning against the angel. "That's the question, isn't it?" he said, moaning in glee, his soft red hair crunching against the stone and then the grass as he tumbled over, chuckling. "Welcome to my world. Where *miracle* is spelled H-E-R-O-I-N."

And because he kept laughing, I couldn't help but chuckle too. Watching him forced me to laugh.

From up in the trees came a low *hoo-hoo*. Patrick and I both peered up and noticed an owl sitting on a limb ten feet above us.

"Well 'ello," Patrick said, still chuckling, as he rolled into a sitting position. He saluted the owl. "Someone else wants to laugh."

As I looked up at the feathery being with bright gold eyes that returned my stare with a judging scowl, Patrick shifted beside me.

"Were there...flowers here, before?" he asked, pointing to my left, where a full bouquet of red roses rested in a stone vase by the angel's feet. They had been dead. When Patrick wasn't looking, I released a little of my power into them. They bloomed fresh and vibrant.

"I guess," I said and shrugged, turning to look back at the owl. The tree branch swayed, empty.

"Huh... So drunk I don't remember them being there. Wonder who brought them."

"I've got an early day tomorrow," I told him, and I rose. "I need to go." He nodded.

"We should do this again," I said.

"No," he replied, smiling. "We should do more. I'm going to a party Friday. You should come."

"All right," I said, brushing the dirt from my clothes.

"Promise me." His thin lips stretched into a smile. "For your own sake."

"My own sake?"

He half-bowed and momentarily slipped into a high British accent. "My company has been known to cure all ailments, frustrations, and failures. Or at least make you forget them for an evening." He lifted a hand as if to situate better a monocle beneath his brow.

"That's quite a phenomenon," I said.

He shrugged. "P-A-T-R-I-C-K. That's how you spell *miracle.*"

"Your narcissism knows no bounds."

"Promise me," he said.

I promised.

⌒

ON OUR WAY BACK INTO town, Patrick drifted off. He dozed against the passenger side door as relaxed as a child rocked to sleep. When I arrived at his apartment, I let the engine idle and watched him for a moment in what seemed a rare peaceful state.

Eventually, I slipped my hand inside his jacket and retrieved his wallet. Inside were over a thousand dollars. I stared at the money. I looked at his apartment. Perhaps it might be better to walk him inside. Perhaps he would fall asleep quickly. That would give me time to search his home. As long as he didn't have any surveillance cameras, and something told me that, based on the drugs he consumed, he would not, I might discover more than a thousand there.

After replacing Patrick's wallet in his jacket, I clasped the front of his coat and shook him a good three times before he woke.

"Time to go inside," I said. "Time to go to sleep."

He nodded, and I turned the car off and handed him his keys. We each stepped out of the car. As soon as we'd shut the doors, I glimpsed a man sitting beneath Patrick's front porch light on the concrete steps. Shit.

My hand reflexively dove into my pocket, searching for the gun that wasn't there. I inhaled, ready to tell Patrick to get back in the car.

At the sight of the man, though, Patrick instantaneously brightened and laughed. "Derrick!"

The long-haired man stood. They walked toward each other and met on the lawn, where they briefly hugged.

"Jack, meet Derrick Willoughby."

The stranger plucked the cigarette from his mouth between his thumb and forefinger and smiled. A curtain of brown hair framed his face in the shadows. An aquiline nose poked from beneath dark eyes. His smile widened.

"Haven't met you before," Derrick remarked.

"Jack's a new friend."

"I see. Welcome to the insanity that is..." He opened both his hands toward Patrick.

"I'll bet you need a couch for the night," Patrick said, brushing past him. He went to the front door and unlocked it. We all moved inside, and the man named Derrick collapsed on the sofa.

Patrick brought out a decanter half full of amber liquid. I took a seat, and he poured us each a drink. I glanced at the time before I picked up the liquor and decided I could stay for just a few minutes.

I took a sip, and the whiskey burned my throat.

Derrick nodded at me and said, "So how do you know this devil?"

"We met at a party."

"Of course," Derrick said.

"That's not quite correct." Patrick grinned, replacing the crystal top on the decanter. "But I'll let it slide."

"Oh?"

Patrick slid a glass across the coffee table to him, and it landed against his hand perfectly. Derrick brought it to his lips.

"We met at Levi's house."

Derrick laughed as though that meant something uproariously funny. He looked at me with curious eyes. "I see. And I'd guess you're a student too?"

"Sure," I said.

"Yes, yes, a student." He rolled his eyes. "They're all students around here."

"And are you?"

Patrick turned some music on. The volume low, it elevated the mood.

"No, no. Not for a few years. Now I deal," he said.

"Ah, like Kevin," I replied.

"Kind of." He set his glass down. "The difference between me and Kevin is that I have a day job."

"Why?"

His wet lips glistened beneath the track lighting. "People can get just as addicted to selling as they can to buying. I cut that addiction with a normal full-time job."

"He means he has to claim revenue from somewhere," Patrick said.

Derrick briefly presented his middle finger.

I set my glass on the table and snugged my jacket tighter around my torso. It was cold in the apartment.

"And what's your day job?" I asked.

Derrick shot a look at Patrick, who rested against the kitchen bar, glass in hand.

As they stared at each other, Patrick's face broke into a smile. "You brought another one, didn't you?"

"Yep." Derrick bent to his bag on the floor and unzipped it.

I looked between them. "Another what?"

"You can't tell anyone," Derrick said, smirking. He retrieved something from the bag—it looked like a ball—and he tossed it to Patrick. "And if you do tell someone," he said, pressing me with his eyes, "don't mention my name. Or his."

I shrugged. "Whatever helps you sleep at night."

Patrick set his glass on the kitchen counter and gazed at the white orb. "Is this...?" Patrick smelled it.

"Yes."

"They create the coolest fucking things."

"What?" I asked.

Despite his apparent exhaustion, Patrick's red eyes twinkled. He tossed the ball. It landed in my hands with a familiar sound and weight, and I took a good look at it.

"Prepare thyself." Patrick grinned.

It wasn't a ball. It wasn't plastic or glass. Nor was it perfectly spherical, as it had appeared from a distance. There was an obvious top and bottom. Ridges, almost like little feet, adorned the bottom.

Though it didn't look right, there was no question about what it was.

"Holy shit," I said.

"Yeah," Derrick replied, shaking his head and lighting a cigarette.

No, I almost said. *You couldn't possibly understand.*

A pristine, pure white apple sat in my hands. The skin glistened white. The place where the core began glowed white. Every aspect of it shined colorless. I held it in my hands and thought its existence impossible.

The guys laughed, but I sat voiceless. The very sight of it brought to mind old and recent memories—a red box with blacker-than-black stones on a gold shelf, fire deep within. The brilliant, blooming bell of a gramophone that shifted and turned and made the whole world seem to pivot about its axis, a white ooze flowing down it.

The room began to tilt. Deep inside, I remarked that the impossible white I had seen throughout my life ran through my memories as though bits of my mind had sat in the sun too long or been washed in bleach.

Someone was working demonic magic with another box. Some new elite member of Infinitum had put an unearthly contraption within a secular city. I was sure of it.

Shit, oh shit. My muscles tensed. Derrick hadn't taunted me with the apple. He hadn't threatened me. Yet panic and cold rage deluged me.

Proof that Infinitum had oozed into the real world of normal people with normal lives. In an apple. A fucking apple.

My insides quaked.

"*Where* did you find this?" I asked, using every ounce of energy not to pounce on Derrick and threaten him if he didn't tell me.

"I made it," Derrick said. He smiled at me and crossed his feet on the coffee table, completely ignorant of my torment.

"You look shocked," he said, laughing. "God, I love shocking people." He pointed at the object. "The company I work for has a mechanism. It makes white paint. That's, basically, what my job is. I load the paint cans onto the shelf. Then I make my way back to the control panel." He walked his fingers through the air. "I pull the lever, and the walls of the mechanism close. I wait five minutes, and when it's done, everything is that perfect white."

"Everything?"

"*Todas las cosas,*" Derrick said. "Even the cans themselves." He shrugged. "So, of course, one day I decided to try it out on something else. I had these grungy old sneakers I wore to work one day and put them inside. Thought I'd try to whiten them, even if they weren't liquid. I thought maybe all it requires is a bit of moisture? Boom! It worked. As good as new." He smirked. "Well, not new...but white."

"*Holy shit,*" I muttered, ready to collapse.

"I know, right? If I ever spill ketchup on a white shirt," he shrugged, "no problem."

Wanting to ensure that this was undoubtedly Infinitum's work, I retrieved my knife from my coat pocket and flipped it open. While the others watched, I dug into the apple with the tip of the blade and peeled back a chunk of flesh. Beneath the skin sparkled juicy white fruit. It shined moistly in the light.

I gazed at the piece on the blade. After smelling it again, I lifted it to my mouth.

"Whoa! Whoa!" Patrick said, and Derrick shot forward, holding his hand in front of me. "You don't know what sort of chemicals..."

I slipped the piece of apple into my mouth and chewed. It didn't taste like an apple, but it didn't taste like chemicals either. It was tasteless in the same way the apple had been odorless. I swallowed.

"If you die," Derrick said, throwing his hands up in the air and standing, "not my problem. I wasn't even here." He took the remainder of the apple from me.

I wasn't going to die, and I knew it. I slipped into my seat.

"You all right?" Patrick asked. He came near me and sat on the edge of the coffee table.

"Yeah."

"I can't believe you just did that. Here." Patrick poured his whiskey into my glass. Derrick sniffed at the apple and checked out the missing portion.

After he'd poked and prodded the apple and confirmed I wasn't getting sick, he seemed a little incensed that I had been more daring than he. He held out his hand for my knife, and I handed it to him. Both he and Patrick chewed small pieces.

"Weird," Patrick remarked while chewing. "It's like...potato. But not."

"Where did you say you worked again?" I asked.

"I didn't," Derrick replied, setting the apple down on the table. He used the back of his hand to brush his long brown hair from his face and handed my knife back to me. "I work for Lucient Laboratories, up on the turnpike. They're mainly into pharmaceuticals. I happen to work for a creative sector of the business that dabbles in the new and innovative."

"And you help a pharmaceutical company manufacture...*paint*?"

"Yeah." He looked at me and then threw his hands in the air, as though trying to apologize. "Well, they're known for pharmaceuticals, but Lucient is an expert in fluid engineering. Chemicals, pharmaceuticals, paint—they all require precise mixing processes, nanoparticle dispersion, emulsification. Believe me, they've got the process down. There's never been a paint so white. And never any paint that *stays* white. Nothing stains it.

"They'll move it to the pilot plant soon. If that goes well, the production plant will be next. Do you know how much money they'll make?" He whistled. "Think of it. A car that never has to be washed, a house that never needs to be repainted."

"Fluid engineering." I rolled the words around in my mouth. What a fantastic cover. "So you help engineer the paint?" I asked half to hear what his answer would be and half to see if he actually believed it.

Derrick shook his head. "Not personally. The paint arrives," he explained. "I transfer the cans to the shelves inside. I pull the lever. The walls of the machine close in. I wait five minutes, and..." he motioned toward the apple, "it comes out perfect. Crazy, huh?"

Attempting not to sound as insane as I felt, I agreed. "Crazy does not even begin to cover it."

He pointed my own knife at me. "Not a word."

I shook my head side to side. Words had nothing on this. Destruction was the only recourse.

Derrick tossed the apple up in the air and caught it. "Man. If we don't die from eating this, I'll experiment on the coke. See if it loses its bang. Make it odorless. Tasteless. Whiter than white. Get that shit pristine."

CHAPTER 12
CONTEMPLATE

I SAT AT THE TABLE in my apartment with a cup of hot coffee, its steam twirling up and disappearing. In the steam, I pictured a gray building.

A place named Lucient Laboratories possessed a contraption very similar to the gramophone, similar to a box that Cyrus had owned. An item I had tried my best to forget.

They used it on *paint*, of all things.

Infinitum was sending me letters, a group of men hired to kill me by Infinitum had abducted me, and now this. I couldn't believe it. The whole world, it seemed, was spinning out of control.

My phone suddenly rang. Caller ID indicated an unknown number. Nevertheless, expecting something like this, I tentatively pressed Answer and lifted the phone to my ear. "Hello."

A familiar voice spoke.

"We were able to set up the meeting. Be downstairs by the curb in two hours."

"I will," I said. I glanced at the USB drive on the edge of my desk, the one with the video of the young girl being killed. I grabbed it and slipped it into my pocket.

"Who knows? You do this well, and maybe I'll give you your gun back."

"That's very kind of you."

He chuckled. "We will see you soon."

I returned my phone to my pocket and stared at the coffee again. I thought on what I needed to do.

CHAPTER 13
YOU'RE WELCOME

I SAT BETWEEN TWO MEN in the backseat and glanced at the back of the driver's wavy salt-and-pepper hair. It was the man who had slid the folder across the table to me.

The car hummed, and the tires carried us smoothly over the asphalt. The blues played at low volume on the radio; at the sudden entrance of a tenor sax, I pressed my lips together. The wound on my bottom lip, which had nearly healed, broke open again. I slipped my tongue across it, tasting the metallic flavor of blood.

I flashed back to when I first learned to play the alto sax with Roland, when my teeth had cut into my lip one evening. The mouthpiece reed had turned slightly pink, and I tasted raw flesh. The developing callus smarted in a way that only old wounds could.

Roland had smiled and squeezed my shoulder. "The skin learns not to bleed after a while." I had looked up into his exceedingly kind face, and the pain had left me.

In the car, I wiped away the blood, comforted, if only slightly, by the memory.

The man in the passenger seat leaned forward and pressed several buttons on the stereo screen. The radio flipped through different stations before it stopped on a classical broadcast.

About an hour and a half passed before we arrived at our destination. I became conscious of the two men on either side of me. These individuals had not covered my eyes as we approached. They did not mind me seeing the route, and that meant something far weightier than if they had blindfolded me. I fumbled with the USB drive in my pocket.

The driver pulled into a driveway and parked, and we emerged from the car.

We stood among the thick trees of a large forest. Strangely, though, smack dab in the middle of the dark woods stood a large metal building— it had to be at least five thousand square feet—a gravel road leading to it. It was more suited to a location in a city full of restaurants, businesses, and people blushing in the cold. We were far, far away from any city, though. We were nowhere.

The large bald man who had sat to my left opened the building door, and the driver and another man entered it. I followed, feeling the dark presence of another man behind me.

The high fluorescent lights in the building shed very little light across the stark, concrete floor. One man sat at a table in the middle of the vast space in a folding chair. He had blond hair, and when I spotted the back of his head, hope and rage bloomed fully in me.

The man turned in his seat. My heart sank. I stopped walking. It wasn't Alex.

The shock and disappointment on his face was as great as my own. I came to myself and walked toward him carefully, ensuring that the table remained between us. "You," Julian said. "You're supposed to be dead."

An image of a large mound of children's toys three times as tall as me entered my mind. Then, Julian bolting into the night, away from Cyrus's red barn. The sound of police sirens. I had not even considered what had happened to him until that moment.

I opened my hands out, indicating the empty building and silence and the foreign men. "Perhaps you'll get your wish soon enough."

Julian smiled, but abruptly his smile faded, and he looked at the leader of the group, the man who had questioned me one-one-one several nights ago. "Jasper, you told me she was dead."

Jasper. The man with salt-and-pepper hair, a face like a mutt. The one who had taken my gun, my money, who was so "interested" in me. Now I had a name.

Turning to me, Jasper ignored Julian and asked, "Is this him?"

I shook my head. "No. But with enough pressure, he might be able to give you the man you want. The people you want."

Behind me, feet shuffled, and all eyes veered to the sound. I turned.

A tall man dressed in black from neck to toe entered the building. His black hair swooped, framing his face. Lines began at the bottom of his nostrils and curved down below his cheeks, ending near his mouth. These lines looked almost as intentional as tribal scars. His eyes appeared harder, more scrutinizing, than any I'd ever seen.

He walked to Jasper and leaned toward him. I couldn't hear what he whispered or read his lips. Then he approached me. He held out a hand, and I shook it.

"My name is Jonathon Roth." His voice was deep and cultured.

"It's a pleasure to meet you."

He nodded, seeming both austere and sure of himself. He gazed at Julian.

"Would you excuse us for a moment, Jack?" Roth asked. A man with a buzz cut walked to me and motioned for me to exit. Roth wanted, perhaps, to shield me from what they intended to do. The request was unnecessary, but nevertheless I went.

Julian began to protest, but his words didn't reach me, and they didn't reach the others. The thing to be decided had been decided days, weeks, months, years ago. It was decided before Julian was ever born. This was the way it was always going to be. His death, in this building, as a result of what he had asked them to do to me, had an air of fate.

I slipped out into the night and lit a cigarette. A young man with dark hair stepped outside with me, and he pushed the door to. He introduced himself as Asher, adding nothing more.

Julian screamed for a long, long time, his yells slipping through the crack of the door and its jamb. As he screamed, I sweated. He swore he had no information as to the whereabouts of Alex perhaps twenty times. Finally, the screaming ended, and the men inside mumbled, discussing. A conversation took place.

A gunshot echoed. Then silence.

The door behind me opened. The men walked out, and one of them told me it was time to go.

I clenched the USB drive in my pocket.

A cigarette perched on my lips, I gazed around at the forest. I said to Roth, who stood in the doorway wiping blood from his hands, "Julian is not quite like the others. Julian is a hard man to kill." With that, I allowed a little of the power to come alive within me—the power that felt like circulation returning, like I swam in lightning, soaking in liquid opal— and I directed it behind me.

Roth's brow wrinkled.

A strange rattling emitted from inside the metal building and then hurried footsteps approached. Jasper's head poked through the door. His eyebrows raised, his breath quick.

"He's not dead," he reported.

Under the doorway light, Roth stared at him like he had never heard a stranger sentence uttered. "What are you talking about?"

Jasper glanced toward me, Asher, and the man with the buzz cut. "There is no wound, Roth. He is bloody and impeccable."

Roth grunted and disappeared back through the doorway. The others followed. I let them go, remaining out in the night, watching the swaying trees, taking in the beautiful full moon. I listened to their confusion, Julian's stammering and pleading, and then several shots. Again, silence.

"He's dead now," a man at the edge of the doorway asserted confidently, with satisfaction, as though a bug that had eluded him and made him chase it all over the building had been squished.

The others did not leave the building immediately. Several minutes passed before Roth appeared. Halfway through my cigarette, I stole a glance at his expression. "Strange," he remarked. "So fucking strange."

He inhaled deeply, as though finally breaking the odd scene's spell. He stepped toward me deliberately, looked me in the eye, and clasped his hands together in front of him. "Are you ready now to discuss the terms of our relationship?"

I smiled, thinking to myself that we were doing just that, though he didn't yet realize it. I let more power trickle into the corpse beyond the door.

More commotion erupted inside, including screaming this time. Roth frowned, his dark eyebrows slanting over his brow. Abruptly he turned from me, as though irritated. In the light that emanated from the doorway, I observed the look on his face. It was a look he likely hardly ever expressed anymore.

Surprise.

The men strode back into the building, leaving me outside alone. The wind played with my hair, and the moon shone on the hand that held the burning cigarette.

They shot him again, and they waited. They did not reappear. Most likely, they desired to watch it happen, see him return, and, sooner perhaps than they expected, I gave them what they wanted and resurrected him yet again. At his revival, several voices questioned why he wouldn't stay dead. Julian had no explanation, except that perhaps some sort of higher power must be protecting him.

"The ferrics must be close by," he announced loudly, proudly.

My skin prickled.

"Who?" Roth asked.

"The beings with fire in their veins. The enemy."

Roth said he had no idea what Julian was talking about, that no higher power would protect a man like him. Several guns went off, sending a horrible racket into the night.

In my left pocket, I found a pack of Cloves, and I released a black cigarette from its resting place, held the cinnamon tip to my lips. I lit it; it tasted like candy dipped in a chimney. After a few more minutes, Julian returned again.

It went on like that for a while. I smoked the Clove. They killed Julian. They killed him until they had no bullets left. They killed him until blood leaked from beneath the door. They killed him until I felt bad for Julian, who by then surely just wanted to die.

They killed him again.

I peered inside the building and observed fear in their eyes.

Jasper killed him one more time before I entered.

The previously solid men hunched raggedy, breathless, terrified. Roth pointed at me and yelled to wait outside.

I didn't. Instead, I finished the Clove. "I'm the one doing it."

Roth yelled, "Get the fuck out of the building," and stopped. He scrutinized me. "What?" Beads of sweat collected in the tribal-scar crevices along his mouth.

"I can resurrect the dead. I brought him back. Again. Again. Again." My voice grew softer with each "again."

The men looked at me as though seeing me for the first time.

I threw the cigarette on the ground; it hissed in blood. "If you would like, you could bring me that girl," I said. "The one who was murdered, like you were hired to do to me. I can resurrect her." I stared at their haggard, slouching forms. "Or," and I stretched my arms wide, enunciating each word carefully, "you could bring me your dead mothers, fathers, sisters, brothers, victims, enemies, comrades, lovers, wives." I let that thought sit with them for a moment. "Bring me anyone you want, and I will resurrect them. Just as I did with Julian. No holds barred.

"But first..." I said, as I considered Roth and Jasper, the young man with dark hair named Asher, the older man with dark brown hair and wide set eyes, the short, squatty one with a thin black tie, and the big bald man who had opened the car door, "tell me again. Who does Alex belong to?"

Silence.

CHAPTER 14
THE BRIM

AFTER WITNESSING JULIAN'S MULTIPLE DEATHS, Roth wasted no time in finding out if I was capable of more.

The woman who was killed in the same way that I was supposed to be murdered was named Emily. Roth said he wanted her resurrected in a cathedral, and I immediately replied I had never resurrected anyone in a church. He said there was a difference between a cathedral and a church, and I told him that wasn't the point.

Very late in the evening we arrived at said cathedral, and I rested in one of the pews and asked Roth where the body was. He told me, "There is no body." He gestured toward a plain table on the chancel supporting a silver cup with a lid. He said "Sam" had brought it and met us there.

"Ashes," he said. "Emily was cremated."

I gasped.

"What's wrong?" Roth asked.

"I've never been able to bring a cremated person back from the dead." I thought of Roland's burned body. Cyrus had told me that not even Lutin could bring Roland back after that.

I watched as Roth's heart dropped. It was odd, seeing that, in a man who betrayed nothing.

"Who is this girl?" I asked. "How do you know Emily?"

Roth shook his head and didn't answer, and that was enough for me to guess.

I cleared my throat. "Don't worry. I'll figure it out."

"Didn't you just say..."

"Yes. And now I'm telling you I'll figure it out."

I rose from the pew and walked to the table. I opened the urn and dipped my hand into the ash, trying to hold a handful, but the sandy grit and bits of bone slid through my fingers. The ash would not hold its shape.

I faced a gap I had been wanting to close—not just for Roth, but because I *wanted* it. It would mean I would have no boundaries. Nothing and no one could hold me back. I yearned to resurrect a person from gravel and dust, then just half of that gravel, half of that dust, and then from there a mere a teaspoon, a speck of bone, a hair. If I could get it down to just one hair, I'd be happy. And maybe, just maybe, I could return to Cyrus's mansion and find a particle of Roland and return him. I could move on from there—find specks of all the children Infinitum had killed over the years and resurrect them.

But in that cathedral, with killers all around me, the ash would not heed my call.

I began to sweat.

CHAPTER 15
RISE

AT HALF PAST FOUR IN the morning, I crawled up on the table and lay down beside the beautiful silver cup. I looked at myself in the reflection and closed my eyes.

I had been trying to resurrect her for hours. Even the men seemed to feel the vibrations, the waves of each attempt, like earthquakes in some other dimension. Each time I tried to resurrect her, they looked around themselves as though something swept through the cathedral. First they sat on the floor, then they reclined, a couple of them in pews, and I tried to ignore them.

What if you're not able to do this? What will they do to you?

These thoughts drifted in and out as I maintained my power, humming close in the dim light, before sweet nothingness took me and I fell asleep.

Patrick and I sat together, and he laughed so hard his face reddened with the strain. He doubled over on grass so very dark and green. I looked behind me and saw the name DEIRDRE FLANNIGAN engraved in light gray stone; flowers filled the stone vase next to the angel's feet.

"What is the difference in dosage," Patrick asked me, "between a miracle and heroin? None. There's none." He took a deep, heavy breath, and his face relaxed. About two seconds later, he began giggling again. "You might as well be shooting up, Jack, for all the good you're doing. Drugs solve everything, and you know what's best about them? They're real. You can count on them. No one can count on you." He turned over on the grass and looked at me, but suddenly I wasn't staring at Patrick. I was looking at Cyrus, and we weren't on Deirdre Flannigan's grave anymore.

He sat in the hospital room on the first night he decided to show me what his red box—what the ferrics called an *arca*—could do. The yellow lights above us buzzed like flies. Meredith, the daughter of one of Cyrus's followers, slept in the hospital bed. Cyrus's eyes focused on his book, a hot cup of tea in his hand. His silver hair fluoresced impossibly in the light. A black wool jacket draped his tall frame. His gray eyes flicked to me, and my heart felt like bees had swarmed it.

"Go home, Jack."

"What?"

"Shoot up. Get the soul back in you. These nights, heroin is surprisingly heroic."

His expression pressed upon me, like he was laughing at me, too. A strange noise, a loud static, overtook me. The hairs on my neck and back and arms stood on end. Hundreds of birds cackled overhead. Their cries were deafening.

I woke with a jolt.

I lay on the table, next to the urn, and my flailing arm nearly tipped it over. I caught it, set it straight, and sat up.

Silence.

The men lay all around me, sleeping. Dawn had not yet approached, the world beyond the windows still dark. Whether moved by my dream, or mad from it, I reached into my jacket pocket. I retrieved a small black case and unzipped it, revealing a small bag, a piece of cotton, a spoon, a tourniquet, and a fresh syringe.

Not knowing why I was doing it but sensing I must, I retrieved the empty syringe as if I were a marionette controlled by the dream. I found a blue vein just barely raised over the skin, and I pressed the needle to it.

I broke the skin and felt the bite. With that bite came a strange, unearthly sensation, as if the whole building quaked. I gasped.

I removed the needle and a dot of blood rose.

"Holy shit," I said. Blood trickled down my arm toward the urn, as though magnetism existed between the iron and the silver. I lifted my arm above the container. The blood descended.

Jonathon Roth stood and walked toward me, and I thought, Don't stop me. Not now. Something is happening. Finally.

As he neared, the blood on my arm cooled.

Roth stood at my left, warmth radiating from him. I saw his dark form, could picture those tribal-looking lines on his face. *Just don't say anything*, I thought. *Just don't say a word.*

The drop fell into the center of the ash, and something in my core loosened. A sweet peace rushed in through the cathedral doors and overtook the whole room. There was no more strain or fear. The problem was solved.

I looked up at Roth. "Can I have your knife?"

His right hand slipped into his jacket, and he retrieved his knife. He opened it and asked, "Where?"

Turning my left arm over, I pointed to the vein at the bend in my elbow. He nicked me with cool expertise. Blood dribbled, and I moved the arm directly over the urn. A psychic boom resonated. The blood dripped into the cup, and the ash drank it in. When the blood stopped flowing as freely, I poured the now-bloody ash on the table. I slid down and landed on the floor, a tad woozy.

Roth steadied me, and I said, "Are you ready to meet your daughter?"

He trembled, shaky, and I held his arm fast. He whispered, "Yes."

I blinked and thrust a final vibration from my center out. It shook the table and the pews.

She lay on the table. Naked and young, her brown eyes open.

She looked at Roth and sat up. After looking at me and the others, she spoke. "Dad?" she asked. "Where am I?"

Without a word, he wrapped her in a wide embrace, his face scrunched, his eyes pained. I stepped back, but his hand caught my arm, and he pulled me toward them. After he kissed the top of her head, he kissed mine and squeezed my arm firmly. His hand shook.

A couple of men roused the others. Jasper came and slipped his jacket over the girl's back, covering her nakedness. When I separated from Roth and his daughter, Jasper stopped me, threw his arms around me, and kissed me.

"Welcome to the Outfit," he said.

I shivered.

CHAPTER 16
PHOENIX

IN THE EARLY MORNING, JUST hours after I had resurrected Emily, we sat in Roth's office. "Is there anything you need?" he asked from across a solid mahogany desk topped with black and gray marble.

I relished those words. His offer was why I had done all of it—shown him my power, proven that I was irreplaceable, that I could help them—whatever the latent consequences of doing so might be. In the meantime, between his being shocked by me, not knowing what else I could do, and potentially locking me up, I could use him to my benefit. There were people that needed killing, and I didn't have the resources for the job.

· Roth's office, on the fifteenth floor of a high-rise in the dead center of the city, towered over Manhattan. Shiny dark wood floors stretched to every corner; expensive paintings and gold-rimmed mirrors decorated the walls. Behind his desk, two expansive bookshelves stretched to the edges of the room. The main colors seemed to be black, cream, and chocolate. The curtains, though, added mint green.

Brilliant sunlight poured in through the open windows. The fresh air from the city was cold but uplifting. I inhaled, rejuvenated. Perhaps my sense of renewal was also part of what I had accomplished, something I had wanted to achieve for a while—I'd resurrected someone from ashes. I felt powerful, tremendously powerful.

Roth smiled warmly and presented me with a gift enclosed in a long robin's-egg blue box wrapped in a white silk bow.

I accepted the box and lifted the soft strand of silk until the bow lazily unraveled. It felt like water sliding against water. Impatient, I slipped the tips of my forefinger and thumb beneath the strands and pulled. Both ends of the silk flopped lazily free.

Lifting the lid, I peered inside to see a beautiful silver chain, spotless, so smooth it seemed fluid. I traced my finger down the chain. At the end was a red stone feather, sparkling silver lines delineating the downy barbs and veins.

The pendant fastened itself to the strand horizontally, connected at both the calamus and tip. I drew my hand over the tiny soft feather.

The meaning of the feather was not lost on me.

"Red jasper," Roth said, "overlaid with crimson silk and platinum."

"It is beautiful," I told him. "Thank you."

"No. Thank you. Even though 'thank you' will never, *ever* cover it."

I looked up into his eyes.

"Is there anything you need, Jack? Anything I can do for you? Something, perhaps, that needs doing now, before we negotiate details? I obviously cannot repay you, but I'll do my best."

How austere and driven this man looked. I could picture him maturing from his early twenties, one step ahead of all the rest. The one who ran the marathon at night while the others slept. The one who sought specificity in an imprecise world. The one who would have mastered calculus using a piece of coal on the back of a shovel, if need be.

I peered down at the tiny feather.

"Your business is killing for hire, correct?" I asked.

"That is one portion of our operations, yes."

"Just how good are you?"

"In detail, that would take some time to explain. In general, I can assure you that you will find no group as experienced or varied in their expertise as this one."

Spoken like a true businessman, whether or not accurate. I supposed that what I was about to ask of him would certainly make that distinction clear.

I met Roth's eyes. I knew—not with my heart, but with my head—I could trust him for the time being.

The truth was, a version of Jonathon Roth would always be inevitable in my life. There were certain alleyways I could not successfully travel alone. The importance of traveling those antechambers had increased. Roth was a welcome addition. I couldn't have planned this better.

"There is a house nearby, at 405 Brimmer Lane," I told him. A spearmint curtain danced in a light wind as I spoke. "Approximately a week ago, I stopped there because I suspected it was a base for members who are still part of Infinitum and once followed Cyrus. I was dragged inside and nearly killed.

"I considered going back alone and attempting one last battle, but I realized how stupid that would be," I said. "There are likely many houses similar to it across the country. I am probably not lucky enough to survive that battle."

"That would be very stupid," Roth agreed, but not in a demeaning way. He retrieved a pad of paper and a pen and noted the address. "Continue."

I gazed through one of the bright windows onto a spotless balcony and bit my lip. "They sent me so many letters." I sounded like someone truly in need. Pride bloomed in me. It was the truth, but it was more. It was a truth I told because it allowed me to act helpless. I needed Roth, but I also needed him to feel needed.

"Who did?"

"Some…children all over the country who are unable to escape the abuse and horror they are dealt in these homes. I received almost thirty letters, from California to Colorado and North Dakota to South Carolina. And here, of course.

"The letters," I said. "I thought they were lies. That is, until a USB drive arrived with a video on it."

Roth cocked his head, narrowing his eyes.

"The video is of a girl crying. Beside her is a man who then slits her throat."

"Jesus Christ," Roth exclaimed.

"I want them dead. All of them. And I want all the children in their custody rescued. These are likely the same individuals who killed your daughter. They are taunting me, either by pretending to threaten children or by actually threatening and killing them."

"Where's the video now?"

I reached into my pocket and retrieved the USB drive I had brought with me. I set it on his desk. He stared at it and then slid it to the right. "Tell me what else you know."

"I'll tell you what I think," I said. "I think one of those letters is real. Maybe two. The others have been sent to pile a haystack onto the needle, to trick me into believing there is no needle. The girl in the video might have been the Annette who was writing me, or she might not have been. Either way, it doesn't matter. They have proven that the followers are still alive, still active, and I want them all destroyed. I want Infinitum destroyed. Alex is lucky. He has only one person to get rid of. I have, perhaps, thousands."

"Well," Roth said, "people have succeeded under worse odds and been bested by better."

I smiled, running my hand along the silk, jasper, and platinum feather. "This challenge requires all of my attention. I've had my vacation." Roth made another note. I remarked, "You will need *a lot* of people."

He nodded briskly. "As many as you think are necessary. There might be children inside 405 Brimmer?"

"Maybe. Maybe not."

"If there are, I'm guessing you want us to…"

"Hand them off to the authorities," I said. I looked up at Roth. Almost absentmindedly, I said, "Most of the children in Cyrus's care were beaten. Most of them were brainwashed to be mindless, not threats. Everything but a threat."

"And," Roth said, "what if they are dead?"

I paused, thinking. "Bring them to me. Every single one. Then they won't be dead anymore."

We stared at each other for a long while.

After a few twitches of his lip, he stopped ruminating and said, "All right."

"One more thing…"

He looked up from his notes.

"Can you look into Lucient Laboratories?"

He wrote the name down on the same pad of paper. "Of course," he said. "What for?"

I opened my mouth and paused. Death teetered on my tongue. It dissolved. "Find out what it is they're producing all that paint for."

I WAITED FOR A TAXI near the lobby door in the afternoon sunlight when Jasper approached. No one occupied the lobby, except for us and a man behind the counter.

Jasper carried a familiar-looking black bag and a plastic box in his hand. He walked across the sunlit floor, and when he reached me, he opened the box. My .38, the bullets, Roland's cross, and Patrick's mother's rosary rested inside. The rosary had been repaired. My mouth dropped open when I saw it.

"Nearly forgot." Jasper pointed at the cross. "Mr. Edward Matthis knows what he is doing. He works at the Gold Connection on 21st and 7th. I took it to him myself and paid for the repairs. You will never see such superb work, and you will never get it as fast as from Matthis." The opal stones shined impeccable, the silver gorgeous.

Jasper pointed to Roland's cross. "There's no mending *that* without melting it down," he said. "Matthis told me he had never seen anything like it."

I carefully lifted each free and slipped them into my pockets. The rosary had earned a special place in the left inside pocket. "Thank you for returning what's mine."

He handed the heavy black bag to me. "All $46,500."

"There was supposed to be $50,000," I said.

"I figured, but there wasn't. That's why I am adding *this*." He lifted a white envelope from his jacket pocket and handed it to me. I took it, wondered for a moment if he had lied to me simply to provoke in me trust or gratitude. I placed it unopened into the black bag and zipped it shut again.

"You brought Emily back. You're a part of us now. I'll do what I can for you."

I cocked my head at him inquisitively. "Only because I'm useful?"

He shrugged and gazed out at the drive. "Isn't that why you helped us?"

CHAPTER 17
RED

WHEN I ARRIVED AT MY apartment, I heaved a sigh and began to relax. I grabbed a partial bottle of vodka from the freezer, slid to the floor, and took a few swallows. My phone vibrated, and I checked the ID. Patrick.

His image popped up on the screen, along with the option to accept the call. I set the phone on the floor and drank from the bottle while the call went to voicemail. Now was not the time. But he called again. Then again. The fourth time, I picked up.

"*Yes?*" I hissed.

He told me he had missed me, wondered where I had disappeared to, and then immediately invited me to a party that evening.

"Not tonight."

"I can't go alone."

"Yes, you can. You'll survive."

"Normally, I'd agree with you," he said. "But my father is making me go to this one. It's some twentieth anniversary celebration or something at Lucient Laboratories."

A chill ran down my spine, and I sat straight up.

"What are you talking about?" I said. "I thought Derrick worked at Lucient."

Patrick laughed. "How do you think he got the job, Jack?"

My mind reeled. What was Patrick saying?

"My father owns Lucient. I put in a good word for Derrick. I *always* take care of my friends."

I licked my lips with my dry tongue and attempted not to sound too greedy. "I guess I could go with you."

"That was quick."

"Yeah, well." I retrieved the rosary from my pocket and gazed at it. "I've got a gift for you. Now is as good a time as any."

"*A gift*," Patrick enthused. "Be still my beating heart."

I laughed. *I'm thinking the same thing.* Patrick told me when he would pick me up and thanked me repeatedly.

I hung up and got ready.

When six came around, his car appeared in the driveway. I slipped into the passenger seat. Patrick's hair and clothes were impeccable. Not a wrinkle, not a red hair out of place. His appearance was striking. I wore black pants, a nice black button-down shirt, and the red feather necklace that Roth had given me. My coat rested in my lap, and the shoes I wore were comfortable enough to run in. My outfit was classy enough to get by without hindering me.

A car honked behind us, and Patrick drove down the street. "Just so you know," he said, "I'm only going because I know that's what my mother would have wanted."

I looked at him. "You don't need to explain yourself to me."

"That's why I like you, Sarah. I never feel the need to."

We arrived at Lucient, and I discovered Patrick had not exaggerated. For Lucient's twentieth anniversary, the large convention area included curling archways, gray walls, a white floor, and soft pink roses at all the tables with crystal candelabras and white candles.

At every oversized round table silver trains carried crystal decanters of liquor round and round, through the candelabra and pink roses, in figure eights. The splendor absorbed me.

My red-haired acquaintance progressed among the tables and large gatherings of human beings. I followed him. Near the podium, we approached a dark-haired man just slightly over six feet tall speaking with a couple. Patrick gently circled the man's arm. He turned around; his flat face featured a pointed chin.

Patrick shook the man's empty left hand and said, "Congratulations." He smiled nervously.

The bewildered-looking man must be Patrick's father. He gazed at Patrick and nodded at his son, the smallest smirk on his lips.

As Patrick said, "I'd like you to meet..." his father leaned back and scanned Patrick's eyes. It wasn't a look, a gaze, or a glance. It was scrutiny, as though instead of Patrick Flannigan standing there, he was studying a walking, talking glitch. He touched Patrick's chin, and Patrick jerked away. Then he straightened and looked around.

His father squinted. "Your cheeks are thin. Your eyes are red. Are you using again?"

Before I could blink, Patrick had turned away. He did not wave for me to follow him but crossed the expanse of white carpet alone, as though embarrassed beyond what he could stand.

The man with the flat face and pointed chin turned back to the man he had been speaking to and drank from his glass. He said, "I know. I know," softly and looked at his retreating son. I observed him for a moment, intrigued, thinking to myself that this man might have connected with my brother, if he produced something at Lucient that turned paint and apples white.

I stared at his uninterested brown eyes and decided to introduce myself. I held out my hand. "Hi, I'm Jack Harper. Patrick's friend."

He rotated toward me and stared at my hand for one dismissive second. He began to turn back, but then he took a second glance at me, and his eyes narrowed. He cocked his head. He searched my face, as though rifling through a yellowing old photo album, and frowned.

"Do I know you?" His eyes danced quizzically over my face.

I released a big smile. He had just given me everything. Someone had mentioned me to him. Someone had shown him my face. "Congratulations on your twentieth anniversary. It was a pleasure." I turned and left.

He called "Hey!" in a deep voice.

Not glancing back, I strolled among the tables, aiming toward the only bright redhead in the crowd.

When I arrived, the words, "Ready for a drink?" were already on Patrick's lips.

"Yes," I said, checking that Bryan Flannigan had not followed me before we settled at an empty table away from the crowd. Patrick began medicating.

He didn't speak much, and I didn't press him. I crossed my legs and relaxed against my seat. In the distance, Mr. Flannigan turned around and spotted me. He stared then turned away. That was all. It was enough.

The stark differences between father and son struck me. Patrick remained but a child. In Cyrus's black and white world of leaders and followers, he was a follower, specifically of pleasure. Unlike his father, unlike me, he was led by all things that provided relief. He was subject to emotion, surrounded by people who existed in a world he could not see because he did not understand personal reliability. Someone like me or Roth or his father would eat him alive. It was only a matter of time.

The crowd became quiet. A woman took the stage and summarized, using a PowerPoint presentation on the screen behind her, the past twenty years of accomplishments the various teams had made. A new antipsychotic with far fewer side effects and far better effectiveness had entered the market because of them. She spoke about an anti-inflammatory medication that caused fewer gastrointestinal issues and two new antibiotics their company had helped produce.

Patrick turned to watch and listen.

This was the moment. I reached into my coat pocket and retrieved the shimmery white rosary and set it on the plate in front of him. Patrick straightened and noticed it.

He did a double take. His face revealed a combination of shock, astonishment, and disbelief. For a long while, he froze, stuck in time. When he found his wits again, he looked at me.

"Holy shit!" he exclaimed. He picked up the rosary. "Is this... This can't be..."

"You're welcome."

He slid his hand over the stones. "I don't believe it." His expression looked almost pained. "How did you..."

"You don't want to know," I said. "And I'll never tell you."

A grim look momentarily crossed his face, and he nodded. "I don't know how to thank you."

I beamed. "You know what would be really cool?"

"What?"

"If you could show me that machine. The one that turns things white. Is it around here?"

Patrick furtively looked around and said, "Shhh... Not everyone knows about that." Satisfied no one had noticed us, he placed the rosary in his pocket. He grinned at me like I had just become his best friend in the world and nodded intimately. "Yeah, it's here." He rubbed his chin. "I think I could do that. It'd certainly be more interesting than this."

I smiled back, just as intimately.

He stood, plucked a pink rose from the vase, and led me out of the room.

We marched out into the night. He held the rose in his left hand and looked at me with mischief in his eyes. "This way for a *white* rose." He reached into his back pocket and retrieved a rectangular plastic card, a UPC code on it. His eyebrows wiggled back and forth. "A few sentences with my father was an easy price to pay. I palmed it off him."

The night quieted as I stood there, not comprehending.

"So you can see the machine," Patrick explained. "The one that bleaches the paint."

I remembered Patrick leaning in toward his father, apparently becoming insulted, and walking away. But he had stolen the card then. I had underestimated him, after all. He was a child, but he had a few tricks up his sleeve.

"You think I didn't figure out you'd want to see that machine? You think I thought you came all the way here just for my company?" He chuckled.

The tiniest sense of awe swept through me.

"You look so concerned." He laughed, beckoning me. "Come on. It's fine. I don't care." He sauntered off through the darkness.

I smiled. A few tricks indeed.

I followed.

CHAPTER 18
BUILDING 1C

WE WALKED PERHAPS TWO HUNDRED feet before we arrived at a tall, windowless cream cement structure. Patrick was a few steps ahead of me. I glanced around to ensure we remained alone. The asphalt sparkled, empty.

Patrick led me around the right side of the building, pausing at a side door between one corner and the other. It was locked.

He inserted a silver key on the same ring as the white card into the lock and jiggled it. It would not turn. He cursed the key amiably, kicked the door, and tried it again. This second time, it revolved perfectly. He turned to me with a smile. "It's a finicky lock." He opened the door and held it for me. I stepped inside. He shut the door behind us and locked it.

We stood in a long, dim corridor with white plastic floor tiles, cream walls, and fluorescent lights. Half of the lights brightened. Half of them remained black. Patrick headed to the right. I followed.

"When we open the main room," he said, "the alarm will go off. Derrick gave me the key code, though. Should be fine."

I glanced at the end of the hallway and noticed two small black surveillance cameras on either side, positioned directly at us. My heart leaped. I pulled my jacket over my face. Tapping Patrick on the arm, I pointed to them.

He shrugged. "Nobody watches those unless they have to."

I sighed, closed my eyes, and told myself that what was done was done. Even if I turned back, I couldn't erase my image. More importantly, I didn't want to turn back. I was too close to the machine beyond. I boldly peered up into the camera and made my decision.

I jogged to catch up with Patrick.

We followed the corridor approximately twenty-five feet. A glass door perched at the end. Through the glass, a dimly lit office. The flooring transitioned from light tile to dark carpet.

Patrick waved his key card in front of a small dark gray box, and the red light beside it turned green. The door unlocked, and he pulled it open. We both entered.

Patrick stepped between two desks, toward another door with a large window. Beyond the window, a massive, dimly lit chamber stretched high and wide.

"All right, so, I'll open the door and we'll walk inside, quick," he said. "The alarm will go off, so I'll have to run to the panel on the left and enter the code. If I memorized it correctly, we'll be fine."

"And if you didn't?"

He shrugged. "What are they going to do to me? My father owns the fucking company." He bookended the statement with another shrug.

So close to seeing Mr. Flannigan's machine, I didn't particularly care either way. It would be enough to get inside, see the thing, figure out if it was a box like Cyrus's, and get out.

Patrick waved the key card in front of another gray plastic rectangle to the right of the door. A loud, heavy click sounded. The red light blinked green, and the door unlocked. Patrick inhaled a deep breath, as though about to dive into a large, deep pool of water and swim to the bottom. When he thrust the door open, the alarm immediately blared. The high-pitched wail cut through the air as all the fluorescent lights in the area illuminated brilliantly. Patrick bolted inside, and I followed. The door closed behind me, and the lock clicked automatically.

Patrick jogged along the rail to the left, his footsteps clanking against metal. He halted at an illuminated panel and entered numbers. As he did, I surveyed the place.

The ceiling stretched three stories high. The walls extended approximately ten car-lengths wide. The polished cement floor beneath the grated balcony on which I stood shined beneath the bright lights. To my left, a set of stairs descended.

Immediately, I looked for the contraption of which Patrick and Derrick had spoken. Across from me on the first floor, pallet upon pallet of uniform paint cans stretched along the back wall. The cans and the labels glared pure white. Near the cans sat a yellow forklift, and beside it a table supported stacks of paper.

Patrick yelled something. The alarm still shrieked, and its shrillness, initially a minor annoyance, increased. Pain bit deep inside my ear. Then, it cut off abruptly.

At last, blessed silence.

"Thank God," Patrick said. He pressed a finger to his ear and bent over. The pink rose in his left hand lost a petal as it flopped forward. "Damn, that's loud." His voice echoed inside the facility.

I pointed to the petal beside his foot.

He smiled, bent gracefully, picked up the petal, and stuck it in his pocket. "This way," he said.

I made my way across the balcony, my shoes clanging against the metal grating, and then we walked to a small alcove in the left corner of the room toward a doorless entryway with two glassless windows on either side. Inside, two swivel chairs sat across from a control panel.

A series of buttons and lights speckled the panel beside the door. Patrick's right hand fluttered over them before he selected a lever on the left and flicked it up. The board illuminated, and a series of tiny beeps signaled as the system woke. Patrick pressed a button. From the center of the facility came a pop. I peered through the glassless window as a large rectangular structure just below the balcony opened like a claw, releasing what it grasped.

My mouth dropped. It was so...massive.

I stepped out of the alcove and stared. This was no clarinet-sized case. This was no gramophone. It loomed dark, minimal, wide, and tall, without decoration. No handles protruded. When closed, I noticed no seams. The edges of the doors looked sharp enough to cut wood. It was a simple structure, like a giant coffin on end, and it easily melded into the background behind the machinery.

I took the set of stairs nearest me down. Patrick trailed.

"So you just put whatever you want whitened in there," he explained, "and then you run back to the control station and press the button marked B. The doors close. You wait five minutes. Then you press U."

"Why five minutes?" I asked from the bottom of the stairs.

"Just because."

When we reached the mechanism, I estimated that ten pallets of paint could potentially fit inside at one time. The open doors spread wide enough.

As I inspected the contraption, I noted there were no hoses inside. There was no drain, no electrical wires, no technology of any sort on the walls. In fact, it appeared to be simply four metal walls and a door.

"And *how* does it work?"

"I don't know. Here..." He stepped inside and placed the pink rose on the floor of the contraption. The petals on the floor side flattened, and the others remained bowed on top. Patrick retreated a few steps. "Watch."

He jogged back to the stairs and sprinted up them. As I stared at the rose, I sensed the slightest tingle of a distant emotion-laden memory. In my mind, Lutin's dark face appeared in the night as he stood outside of Cyrus's burning mansion. He smiled at me knowingly. And disappeared.

Patrick pressed the button labeled B. The walls closed in, and the structure sealed with a gentle puff. I stepped nearer and listened. No sounds emanated from the metallic structure—not a *whirr* or a *beep*.

I pressed my ear directly to the left wall. No hum.

During the five minutes we waited, Patrick remained in the control station, and I walked around the facility, glancing at the various stackers and other equipment. On my right, stacks of pure white cans and pallets towered.

It had been a long time since I had seen anything like it, except for the apple Derrick had shown me. Before the apple, my encounter with such unforgiving whiteness had been the rooms of Cyrus's mansion that his red box had bleached. I felt both terror and nostalgia. I began remembering things I had stashed away. The dead rose I had first brought to Lutin. He had returned it to me, slipping it beneath the door where he had been locked and hidden away to be used by Cyrus. What had I brought him after he had resurrected the rose? A blanched piece of a curtain I had cut from one of the white rooms. And what had Lutin done to that piece of fabric? He had turned it blue and gold again.

I stood by the stacks of white cans and let my glance roam over them. I held my hand up and gazed at my fingers. After the rose turned white, could I make it pink again? Had Lutin given me that ability as well? I didn't need to wait for the rose to find out.

Placing the tip of my finger on the edge of a can of paint, I released from within me a tiny shred of the power that let my body feel as though it were actually alive.

The paint can was no longer white. It beamed silver, and the colorful label announced deep crimson paint inside. Curious.

I marveled, my mouth an open O as I ran my fingers over the silver, over the red, over the black lettering and the cream background.

I tilted my head and retrieved a set of keys from inside my pocket. Glancing up the stairs to make sure Patrick wasn't peeking over the balcony edge, I popped the lid open. It wasn't the red of a perfectly mixed can of paint, but it certainly would be after a few swirls of a paint stick.

Oh, Mr. Flannigan, just what do you think you are doing?

"Nearly finished!" Patrick yelled from the alcove, waking me from my trance. I popped the lid down. Realizing how obvious the can would now be among the stack of white cans and white labels, I looked around for a place to hide it.

Something stopped me.

A small but definite sound whispered behind me, not unlike a piece of paper dropping. I turned.

Near the mechanism a small black hole appeared that had not been there before. A gap carved out the concrete, a tiny shadow that might lead to a bottomless chasm. I approached it, replaying the sound in my head, noticing the perfect symmetry. As I touched it, I discovered that it was not a black hole, though it appeared to be. On the floor rested a very *dark* piece of paper.

I searched the balcony overhead, and then the ceiling. I found no place from which the piece of paper could have fallen.

Cautiously, I retrieved the object. The weight of it was odd, the black darker than black. My thumb nearly disappeared into it. I flipped the slip of paper to its other side and noticed something written in gold, the gold shimmering from the page like a hologram. It reminded me instantly of the stones from his living machine Cyrus had shown me. Those stones had also featured gold lettering—the names of traitors.

The paper didn't contain a name but an address. BLDG 1C concluded it. It was the place Patrick and I were.

Patrick yelled, "Stand back!" and I slipped the piece of paper into my pocket.

I stepped away from the mechanism, noticing for the first time that the left wall wasn't completely smooth. On the left door I located a small opening, large enough for a piece of paper to slip through.

With a hiss, the machine doors unlocked and swiftly opened. On the concrete floor inside the machine rested a rose, the color of milk from the bloom to the tip of its stem.

Behind me, Patrick bolted down the stairs, his shoes clinking. He arrived at my right. He exhaled, smiled, and stooped toward the flower.

"Not just any rose for not just any woman," he said as he presented it to me.

I swallowed and leaned forward. I sniffed it. The petals brushed soft against my skin, so white they almost glowed, but I detected no fragrance. The lack was grotesque.

"So," as he stepped between me and the contraption. I looked up into his green eyes. "You went back to that house, and you found my mother's rosary."

I nodded, swallowing. "I did."

He pulled the rosary from his pocket and looked it over. "You had it mended too."

"Yes."

Without warning, he leaned forward and kissed me, a soft brush of warm lips against warm lips.

I jerked back. "Whoa!" I said. "No." I shook my head. "No, no, no."

Patrick's expression revealed absolute shock. He dropped the rose. It fell to the floor soundlessly. "Oh, I thought... I thought, since you... I thought you wanted to..."

"No," I repeated.

"Shit. Sorry." Patrick turned away. His boot landed on the rose, grinding some of the white petals into the cement. They looked gooey, like gum or glue. My whole body went cold.

Patrick walked a few steps, turned back, and steepled his hands, the tips of his fingers touching the bottom of his chin.

"Can I ask why?"

"Why what?"

"Why you...don't want to kiss me?"

My eyes darted around the room. I wasn't going to lie to him. I had no need to, and so I told him the obvious truth.

"Because you're a child."

His eyes narrowed. He looked certain he had misheard me, that I had made a mistake. "What?"

"People like me..." I shook my head, realizing it would sound much harsher aloud.

"Go on. Say it."

Should I? Patrick stared at me in earnest. He opened his hands toward me, like *Come on. Get it out.* So I did.

"I could only hurt you."

For a long moment, nothing. I took a step back, away from the bloom now ground into the cement. Patrick interpreted that as me stepping away from him.

"I see." He turned his back to me. His head drooped low, and he said something softly. I couldn't tell if he was questioning me or trying the words out himself to see if they fit. "I'm a child..."

High above us, a door swung shut. My gaze instantly lifted to the balcony.

Above us stood two men, both in dark suits. Exact opposites, one boasted a full beard and thick dark brown hair, while the other was bald and clean-shaven. The bearded one grasped the hand rail, and they stared down at us with unblinking eyes.

Immediately, I worried about the full-color can of paint among the others. I hadn't hidden it. I nearly groaned. There were, as well, the black piece of paper in my pocket and the white rose on the floor.

"Heeyyy..." Patrick said, his tone like a wilting joke. "I was just showing Sarah the place, and um..." He took two very small steps back.

Without a word, the bald man walked across the balcony to our right in an automated fashion; the other man followed behind him. They descended the stairs and arrived at the first level.

The bald man tilted his head to the right, his eyes moving back and forth between ours. "What are you doing down here?" His gaze shifted to take in the entire room. I couldn't see the stacks of paint cans from where I stood, but I knew immediately when the man's focus settled on it. He frowned. He walked to our right as Patrick began his explanation.

"Just looking around. I swear."

The man with the full head of brown hair nodded toward the white rose on the floor. "Then why is the machinery on?" He clasped his hands before him and stared at Patrick penetratingly.

Patrick glanced between the man and the rose. His temper got the best of him.

"Well, why the fuck are *you* down here?"

I stopped myself from slapping my palm to my face.

"We monitor the place," the bald man said. "The alarm went off." He turned and pointed to the red paint can beside him. It stuck out against the pale others like a bloody thumb. "What's this?"

Patrick's eyes narrowed as he stared at the can. He shrugged with genuine indifference. "I don't know. Must have been here already. We haven't touched any of the paint."

The bald man walked over to the machine and scanned the cement floor, sweeping his foot across the exact spot where the slip of paper had fallen. He inspected the side of the machine. I forced myself to breathe easily and not think of the black sheet in my pocket.

When he finished running his hand along the left door, he said, "You need to come with us, Mr. Flannigan." He walked to the rose on the floor and picked it up. "Your friend, too."

Without question, we followed the bald man up the stairs, the second man following close behind. My heart jackhammered, and I had to assure myself they couldn't hear it.

They led us down several hallways to an empty room; the dark-haired man remained with us when the other left.

I stared at Patrick. But he did not look at me or say anything, so I crossed my arms and perched on the small desk. Nervous sweat filled the tiny nooks and crannies of my neck. I had the .38 in my pocket, but there were how many men, how many witnesses, how much road between me and my exit?

Eventually, the door opened. Of all people, Bryan Flannigan entered.

Patrick stopped pacing.

His father walked into the room without a word. When he reached his son, Patrick began to stutter an explanation, until Mr. Flannigan held out one open palm and said, "My key card." Patrick stopped speaking. He fumbled, patting his pockets until he came up with the white card from the right back pocket of his slacks. He handed it to his father without a word, not meeting his eyes.

The card disappeared into Flannigan's jacket pocket. Behind his top lip, he ran his tongue over his teeth.

"Dad, I'm sorry. I just..."

Patrick's father punched him the face. It happened so quickly that neither Patrick nor I had time to react. Patrick reeled. He tried to maintain his balance, but he fell. His head hit the cement with a smack.

My eyes locked on Flannigan's. I waited for him to reach down and help his son up, but he didn't. Patrick laid there, shaking his head, before he pushed himself up from the concrete floor, wobbling just slightly when he straightened. A speck of blood bloomed above his temple.

His father placed his hands together and pointed them at Patrick. Patrick flinched.

"Never again do you steal from me. Never again do you come down here. Do you understand?"

His son nodded. "We'll just leave. I swear. We'll leave."

"Not yet." Flannigan's eyes flicked momentarily to me and then back to Patrick. He pointed his right thumb at the hall behind him. "How did you know the alarm pass code?"

I wondered what lie Patrick would come up with. Instead, Patrick simply denied it. "It shut itself off."

Flannigan's jaw muscles tensed visibly in the light. "You're lying to me."

"I'm not lying."

"And what about the can of red paint? How did that get there?"

Patrick shrugged, his hand pressed to his temple. "I don't know."

With a deep inhale, Flannigan's eyes cut to me. He paused. "What is your name?"

I swallowed. I had told Patrick my name was Sarah, but as I looked into Flannigan's face, I wanted him to remember me correctly, especially if he explained this to Infinitum and Alex. Meeting him at the banquet apparently hadn't been enough to sear my name into his memory.

"Jack," I said pointedly.

Patrick's eyes hovered on mine in confusion.

"Jack what?"

"Harper. Like I told you before, upstairs, when your son lifted that key from your pocket." I smiled. "You don't give him nearly enough credit. He's been too accommodating to you." I stepped toward him and crossed my arms. "*I* wouldn't put up with this. Not like he does. You hit someone like me, you don't come back from that."

Flannigan's gaze probed my face. The man stepped closer to me, taking in my dark hair and my eyes. He looked like a demon dreaming, thinking many things I would never be privy to. "Go home, Jack Harper," he said.

Of course. I didn't mind. I had the sheet of paper in my pocket. I had seen what the machine could do. I needed nothing else. I took a few steps back and passed him. Patrick followed, but his father stopped him with a hand on his chest. I turned.

"You stay here. I need to talk to you," he said.

Patrick shrugged free. "All right. All right." He threw his hands up and backed away.

The way that Flannigan placed his hand on Patrick's chest made me suspect this episode would not end quickly. I blinked a few times, wondering if this situation required my attention or any drastic action. I decided I couldn't risk it. Not then. With evidence of the machine secure in my pocket, the sooner I could get it out of there, the better. Besides, Patrick had survived a good two decades without me. One more night wouldn't hurt, would it?

I paused.

"Come on, miss," the tall man with dark hair said. He tapped my arm. I stared at Patrick's bleeding head, thinking of Annette, of all the trapped children. Here was another trapped child.

You can't save everyone, I told myself.

The stranger tapped my arm a second time, and I tore my attention away. I could not handle this alone. The timing, the place—all wrong. I would bring this problem to Roth, and I would do that as soon as possible. With a small nod, I followed the man up the stairs and out of the building. He called a taxi for me and refused to go back inside until I had entered the car and left.

The ride seemed longer than usual and frayed my nerves. The whole world vibrated.

An image of Flannigan hitting his son kept returning to me. In my visualization, as Patrick fell, the rosary in his pocket fractured against his hip. I could practically hear it crackling, all the precious stones loose, the sterling breaking bones. I thought to myself, of course. Those bones were weak. They had been broken before.

Lucient Laboratories possessed some evolved version of Cyrus's box. That meant that Patrick's father was somehow connected to Alex's group, which seemed to be expanding, becoming more public. When the threat was only Infinitum, it was already too much for me to sweep alone. But that large black machine in the middle of 1C? I was in way over my head.

Roth seemed the answer to all of this. Whether or not I wanted to, whether or not it made me uncomfortable, our fates seemed entwined. I had resurrected his daughter, killed by someone in Infinitum. As I had helped him, he would help me. He wanted to find Alex and would undoubtedly want to investigate Lucient.

Not only was I slowly but surely investing in Roth, I had to.

As soon as I reached my apartment, I decided to call him. If I could persuade him to visit Lucient that night, that might save Patrick some pain.

I called the number Roth had given me. On the third ring, someone picked up. I almost said, "Roth, I need to talk to you." But it wasn't Roth on the line.

The grainy automated voice of a woman told me the number I dialed couldn't be reached.

I hung up, confused, and dialed again. Still the same woman, still the same automatic message.

What the hell was this?

CHAPTER 19
SLIP

I NEEDED TO REACH ROTH. I needed tell him everything. This sudden and inexplicable block sent a rush of adrenaline surging through me.

I possessed no other number for him. Back inside apartment, I dialed again and listened to two rings. Mid-ring the third time, a strange sound, some sort of blip, preceded the same automated monotone voice. It was a prerecorded message, an intercept, telling me the line had been disconnected. Undeterred, I hung up and called yet again. I frowned when I got the same message.

"We're sorry. You have reached a number that has been disconnected or is no longer in service. If you feel you have reached this recording in error..."

I hit End Call and stared at the bright screen. *Yeah. Right.* I cocked my head and considered that his group could likely turn the numbers they used on and off at will; I wondered why they might do so. It seemed strange. But the discovery of another box at Lucient Laboratories made me nearly panic. I had to contact Roth.

I texted Jasper several times with a simple question mark. The texts wouldn't go through. I drew my arm back to heave the phone across the living room. Then I sighed and dropped my arm.

If I had to wait for Roth, what could I do in the meantime? I leaned back on my couch, running my fingers across the microsuede fabric, thinking. It occurred to me that it would be important to know exactly where, on a map, Building 1C was located. I left the couch and walked to my desk. I pulled the leather rolling chair out and sat. I opened the web browser on my laptop and moved the mouse to hover above the search bar in the upper right. I clicked, and my eyes swept down to the keyboard, but something made me pause.

My browser sat open on the main page of my e-mail, just as it always did. But my eyes had swept across Roth's face. I swallowed.

Impossible.

I looked again. The list of top news stories had shifted, moved on to the next one. A picture of a child standing with a dog just as tall as him replaced the picture I had seen before.

I moved my cursor down and pressed the button that took me to the previous article. As I leaned back in my chair, the world dropped away.

There he was, suit and all, his dark hair swooping down and framing his forehead, deep-cut lines in his face. He veered away from the camera, looking just to the right. The headline read JONATHON ROTH ARRESTED FOR MCFADDEN DEATH. In shock, I stared at the words, wide-eyed. My hand moved automatically.

My fingers positioned the cursor over the picture. I clicked the mouse to open the article and skimmed the lines, absorbing as much information as possible on the first read through. After wrapping my mind around the immensity of the information, I read the article more closely.

Roth had been arrested. That was clear.

So, it appeared, had two other men. Whether they were Roth's coworkers, I didn't know. I looked at one man's beady eyes and another's pointed chin and did not recognize their faces. Their names were unfamiliar. After the first two paragraphs, plenty of information on the victim followed—three-quarters of the article. I barely recalled having heard about his death previously.

James McFadden was a mathematician turned hacker who had been suffocated in his apartment six years before. Police ruled his death a homicide, but there had been little evidence found at the crime scene—no fingerprints, no forced entry, no murder weapon. They discovered several types of DNA that didn't belong to McFadden on the door handle of his bedroom, but none could be linked to anyone in their database at that time.

That changed yesterday.

Police became suspicious of Roth because a previously overlooked e-mail of McFadden's mentioned a man named JR. McFadden's cell phone tracker placed him near Roth's office building shortly before his disappearance.

They'd retrieved DNA from a Kleenex in Roth's trash. It matched the DNA found at the crime scene.

That didn't necessarily mean that Roth had committed the crime. Several other types of DNA remained unaccounted for, but they had arrested him. The article stated he had been allowed no bail.

I gripped the sides of the desk, staring at the article. As the realization hit of what it might mean for Roth to be gone, even for a short period of time, I squeezed my eyes shut and whispered, "No no no."

If he had been arrested just a few days before he found me, it would have been fine, but he hadn't. He had been arrested just a few days after I had revealed to him and five other individuals my power. By that point, any number of people could know about me. It could have escalated to ten or fifty or five hundred.

Roth might have told someone. Everyone who had been at that warehouse when I resurrected Julian could have told others. I had put on that little show to make an impression on them, to sway them to let me live. I had played my best hand then, but now my best move was my worst.

Even if it turned out to be just a short absence, someone beneath Roth might choose to rise above him. The room around me felt strange, foreign. Thoughts of what might happen in his absence made me sink to the floor. If Roth was weak and his men revolted, whomever took advantage of the power might have other plans for me. The agreements Roth and I made might be null and void.

Reality had shifted in mere seconds.

Looking back at the screen, I doubted Roth had even done the murder. It seemed a job his employees would be more than capable of handling, unless there was something personal in it. This might be a power play by another individual in his world. But, then again, could he have made a mistake? Had I overestimated him?

It didn't matter. Not one bit. The ifs made no difference.

I crawled back into my chair and rubbed my face. My heart raced, and I willed it to slow so I could think.

This development must be why I couldn't call him, why I couldn't get hold of any of them. Things had gone horribly wrong.

Soon, someone would come find me. If Roth never returned, someone would rise to the top, whether by right or by force. This new person wouldn't share the same motivations as Roth. He wouldn't have a daughter who had been murdered by Alex. He wouldn't share the desire for vengeance.

Shit. Shit. Shit.

For the first time, I realized how closely this man and I were linked. I had to work with Roth. It was Roth or no one.

Patrick disappeared from my mind. So did Alex. This required immediate action.

My phone vibrated against the desk.

I checked the screen—no name appeared at the top of the message. I had never seen the number before. The message held just two words. "Sit tight."

I shook my head.

Fuck that.

CHAPTER 20
RUSH

MY FIRST FEVERISH THOUGHT AS I closed Jasper's message was that I needed to get out of town. Several men might be on their way to my apartment right now. I rose from my chair, walked to my closet, and pulled a black duffel bag free. After I opened several dresser drawers and started pulling clothes out, I paused.

Long term, what good would running do? I was only one individual. I couldn't elude Alex's group, or Roth's group for that matter, over a long period of time. Either would eventually find me, and I wasn't sure which one would be worse.

I cursed profusely and shut the dresser drawer again. I returned to my chair and sat, my back rigid, hands on my legs. I opened the desk drawer, retrieved my .38, and tucked it in my coat pocket. I forced myself to swallow, and my mouth felt full of cotton.

I knew what needed to be done.

Roth had to be freed from jail—not temporarily, either. Permanently. The answer became obvious.

You've got to be careful, I thought. You've never done anything like this before.

The potential repercussions from the solution that came to mind were too extensive to analyze in a short period of time. I had to act as soon as possible, move things back into the correct position, ensure all the players remained snug in their spots, so that the game could commence as it should.

My hands moved to the keyboard, and I opened a new tab. I typed "James McFadden" into the search bar and pulled up as many articles on him as possible. I read through each of them, learning about the crime scene and McFadden's life. In the fourth article, I came across exactly what I searched for—the story of McFadden's family and, more importantly, where he had been laid to rest.

Galloway Cemetery.

Patrick and I had journeyed to that cemetery recently to visit his mother's grave. I remembered the directions. As long as the roads were clear, it should take me no more than thirty minutes.

I felt like I slid backward in time, that reality crumbled around me— that something, somewhere, pulled me away from my goal of stopping Alex. I wasn't having it. My plan was insane, but I had to try.

I did a Galloway Cemetery grave search and located where his body was buried on the tiny map on the screen. I memorized the location.

You've got to go, a voice inside me said. *Now.*

I closed my web browsers and shut my laptop.

My thoughts raced feverishly, like arrows dipped in poison. From the small toolbox in my closet I retrieved a long flat-head screwdriver and dropped it into my pocket. I left my apartment, locked the door behind me, and rode the elevator down.

I scanned the lobby, half expecting to see men waiting for me, and breathed a small sigh of relief when I found none. When I stepped outside into the night, I ensured a clear path before I crossed the gray pavement.

I walked about fifteen minutes to a communal gardening center I had passed several times that belonged to a small apartment building. I walked through the gate to the shed in the middle of the rows of established vegetables and herbs. Inside, I found several gardening tools, among them a large shovel and a spade. I grabbed both.

I shut the shed door behind me and continued east. I needed a car, preferably a car built in the eighties. I began my search in a secluded area of the city. I checked several alleys before I found a car that would do. Between two buildings, beside a thin black fence, sat a 1988 Acura Integra.

I broke the driver side window with a rock, used the rock to clear the shards, and opened the door. I unlocked the backdoors, threw the shovels in, and then took my seat in front of the steering wheel. Pieces of glass crinkled beneath me, but my thick coat protected me from the shards and covered them so that no one just looking in would see.

Using lessons Cyrus and Roland had taught me, I retrieved the screwdriver from my pocket and jammed it into the ignition. I turned it, and the start cylinder moved. The car came to life. One obstacle down. I pressed my forehead against the wheel and thanked my luck.

After a moment to steady my nerves, I took a deep breath and drove the car from its parking space.

On the highway, the lines of the road slipped past, the engine thrummed in my ears, and the blank canvas of the road stretched before me. Complications of my plan began to enter my mind.

You really think you will be able to dig McFadden up in one night? You, Jack? Alone? What are you going to do? Scare the soil from on top of the coffin? How are you going to get into the fucking burial vault? You didn't bring a crow bar.

I shook my head in defiance of these huge flaws. I had to try, even if that meant trying and failing. No, there was no failing. Even if it took me two days to get that coffin open, I'd get it open. I wiped sweat from my forehead and cursed. Why did Roth have to get arrested? And now? Was he not better than that? Above it?

Who do you expect him to be? An interior voice asked. Cyrus?

I brushed it away.

By the time I reached the cemetery, dark had fully descended. The gates were closed, but I remembered where the fence split. I parked a few blocks away and retrieved the shovel and spade from the backseat. I walked in the twilight, one tool in each hand, to a place where the trees met the fence. Finding the familiar gap in the fence, I tossed the tools through. I ducked and slipped inside the opening.

Stooping low, I collected the shovel and spade and quietly bolted across the cemetery, making my way to the opposite end. I had to hurry. It would take me all night to uncover the coffin, and this would be my only chance to get the job done.

When I approached the right area, I realized I had forgotten exactly which row of the northeast corner McFadden was buried in. In the dim light, I scanned the names of every fourth headstone of the rows. Spurred by adrenaline or luck, I found him. A sparkling gray granite headstone poked up through the grass and faded fake flowers. It shimmered in the night, the dark letters wishing peace upon the man below.

I tossed the shovel to the side and pushed the spade down into the earth, broke the solid soil. It had been six years since McFadden's death, six years since the soil had been laid down. It was compacted, more than I expected. Toiling in it felt like digging up rocks and stone rather than dirt.

As I broke open the old earth, my mind hearkened back to when Alex had killed Shakespeare, our family dog, and Cyrus forced him to dig a proper grave. At just eight or so, Alex had mined quite a large hole for a boy of his size.

It seemed to me that that moment and this one were connected.

That was something, it seemed, the two of us were good at—digging down, working through the fear, using our thrumming hearts as extra pistons.

I licked my lips and tasted soil. I blinked my eyes as dirt puffed into their corners, scratching them. I breathed it in, imagined my lungs coated in the grime. My back muscles began to ache, and I thanked myself for every day I had worked out—running, pushing myself to my physical limits in preparation for when I might meet Alex.

Over the next half hour, only the large round moon kept me company. Occasionally, the sound of feathers arrived as claws released tree limbs and owls swooped from branch to branch or branch to ground.

The piles of dirt on either side of me loomed like mountains. I stood in the valley wishing for water. I had brought no food, no drink, no sustenance of any sort. I yearned to accomplish the inhuman, and only humans needed sustenance.

You're not immortal yet, a voice within me mocked.

After another hour of work, sweat coated my entire body, despite the cool air. My muscles ached beyond cramping.

I straightened and took a deep breath, letting my arms rest. I gazed over the edge of the earth that surrounded the hole. It met my hip. I still had plenty to go.

McFadden might not even be down there, another voice warned.

That was true. He might not be. For all I knew, James McFadden didn't even exist. He could have been conjured up by a group of intelligent people I knew nothing about to entrap Roth. It all could be one giant hoax. The grave might be empty.

I dropped to my knees and placed my hand on top of the soil. I willed the power in me to seek out the dead, asking if anyone rested beneath. The tingling in my core slipped to my hand and then down into the soil, and I waited, breathless, fearful.

After a while, I did feel a magnetic pull, like the beckoning of an instinctual act, and I immediately lifted my hand from the soil. Someone was down there. I would have to trust it was McFadden.

I stood, grabbed the shovel again, heaved it into the dirt, heard the metallic clink of the soil connecting with it, and dumped the next load over my shoulder. My mind reduced down to just the act itself, hands on a wooden handle, metal plunging into the dirt and casting it away, soil increasing the mountains on either side of me.

Another hour passed before I slipped, nearly too tired to continue. My whole body ached. Half of the night had burned away with still half the depth to go. Then would come the slow, arduous process of opening the concrete vault. After that, I would have to return McFadden to the living. And then...

I paused. A new question entered my mind.

Who was this man? Was he a killer? It was certainly possible. I would need to wound him as soon as I resurrected him. And then what? Haul a fully-grown man up and out of the grave, across the cemetery, and into the backseat of a stolen car?

Shit, I thought. That wouldn't work. The plan was fucked.

My strength shrank. I could not ensure Roth's release from jail within the next few days. I could not foresee who next would come for me.

Emotion welled in the center of my chest. I placed my hands on either side of my head and clasped my tangled, dirty hair. Though I grew weary, my chest felt like it housed a thunderstorm. I had traded my identity for nothing. I had given them everything for nothing.

I slipped down to the dirt and leaned against the wall that rose high over me. My hands gripped the soil beside me like talons, and I shut my eyes. Grit coated in my teeth, covered my tongue. I grimaced as the particles broke under my bite.

My breath caught in my throat, and my eyes shot open. A sound arrived, as soft as owl feathers brushing the grass. The noise emanated from right above me, and every question inside me suddenly collapsed, put on hold.

I looked up.

A man's shoes perched on the edge of the grass, between two mountains of dirt. They shone in the moonlight. His hands were in the pockets of a nice pair of black slacks, supported by a black belt. He wore a dark button-down shirt and a jacket.

It was Jasper.

"I thought I might find you here," he said.

I swallowed the grime down and leaned my head against the soil. I breathed in the smell of the dirt and caught just the barest whiff of Jasper's perfumed scent.

The man with a face like a mutt turned slightly to his left, slightly to his right, to survey my work. His hands remained in his pockets, and I wondered if I could reach my pistol before he reached his. After digging for four hours, I doubted it.

With very little warning, Jasper lifted one foot forward and hopped with his other. He landed in the hole beside me. I leaned back when he looked down at me and smiled. "These are tumultuous hours. If I were you, this is exactly what I would have done."

Behind him six other individuals surrounded us, all similarly dressed in equally dark clothes. Most of them were bald or nearly so. Several of them I recognized from the warehouse, but others were foreign to me.

"Come on," Jasper said, and he grabbed me by my arm and pulled me upright. Without saying anything else, he stepped behind me and lifted me up, his arms beneath my shoulders, while another individual grabbed my hands and pulled me from the hole.

When I stood outside the grave, they released me. Those who wore jackets wordlessly took them off. Four individuals picked up shovels from the ground and jumped into the grave. One of them threw a shovel to Jasper. They all began digging.

I watched.

Slowly, I realized they were not there to kill me, nor were they going to kidnap me or take me back to their building. There had either been no coup against Roth or these men were not involved.

They were not going to try to take over and replace him. They were, rather, doing what I was.

They were going to get him out.

CHAPTER 21
CLOSE

IT WAS ODD SEEING THEM work so effortlessly and quickly when I was so drained. Their presence comforted me.

Several of them had brought flashlights. They pressed them into the sides of the hole so they pointed down, providing enough light to illuminate the area while they perfected my work.

The grave's sides became crisper, the hole deeper. Sooner than I expected, metal clanked against concrete. They had reached the burial vault.

Near the headstone, their dirt-covered hands swirled the soil on top of the concrete and then pulled it away. For a little while, they dug just to the right of the casket, low enough that they would be able to access the vault lid and open it.

Steadily, they completed this work.

Several of them jimmied crowbars between the top of the burial vault and its core. With some effort and maneuvering, they leveraged the lid open. It swung like a hinge until it rested against the wall of dirt on the opposite side.

Within lay a dark wooden casket.

Several of the men climbed out. I made my way to the other side of the grave to see better.

The four remaining men undid the casket latches and prepared to open it. Jasper told them to stop. He turned his head and looked up at me. I knelt and then swung my legs over the edge. He held up his hand, suggesting I stayed where I was.

"Can you do what you need to do from up there?" he asked.

I looked down at the casket, a mere seven feet away.

"Yes."

"Then stay up there. Don't do anything until I tell you to."

He and the others freed handkerchiefs from their pockets and pressed them to their noses. They opened the casket. A foul stench immediately filled the air. I looked away from the interior of the coffin, where black body fluids stained the fabric.

I saw bones.

Jasper and the others put gloves on. A man across from me tossed some black cloth and a set of handcuffs to Jasper. Jasper caught them effortlessly and laid them beside the vault.

He looked up at me and withdrew the handkerchief from his nose. He grimaced at the stench.

"I don't want him to be able to see you when you return him."

I looked down at my legs dangling over the edge of the grave and realized what he meant. I nodded. With a small effort, I pulled my legs up and positioned myself so that I lay on the ground perpendicular to the hole, between two piles of dirt. I stared up into the night sky at the multitude of stars. I relaxed, content with a bit of rest, and wondered how long it had been since I had last gazed upon stars.

The dirt crunched beneath me as I turned my head and peered into the eyes of a man I had never seen before. Is this his first experience, I wondered, of seeing what I can do? Does he already know what he will witness? How will he react?

The man returned my gaze. He seemed unmoved.

"All right." Jasper's voice rose to me from deep in the ground.

I closed my eyes and, as I breathed in, felt out the death.

Deep within my core, I sought the familiar warmth and released it. It flowed through my limbs, warming me like returning circulation. It drifted through the top of my head and down into the hole below me.

After just a second came the sound of a quick intake of breath. Jasper said, "We've got him." My eyes shot open. The man who had been standing to my left leaned away. He recovered from his shock and shut his mouth.

Below, in the grave, there was the sound of handcuffs latching, and people exchanged muffled words. Jasper said, "We're good."

I stood and peered below.

Whereas there had been four men, now existed five. One coughed, gagged and blindfolded, covered in a rotten suit. He would have to shower and be given fresh clothes. Jasper had likely already thought of that.

Four men remained behind to deal with the coffin and the vault, promising to fill in the hole before dawn broke, which would be soon. I joined those above ground. Jasper held a finger to his lips, motioning for me to be quiet, and then he pressed his hand against my back to urge me forward with them.

Jasper and one of the bald men steered McFadden through the cemetery.

For about fifteen minutes, we walked through the tombstones to the southwest, towards the entrance. Though the accomplishment of resurrecting McFadden sent a release through me, part of me still surged with adrenaline. The stress felt positive, though, for we had accomplished what we needed to.

When we reached the entrance, a black car immediately pulled up. The trunk opened.

They maneuvered the handcuffed, gagged, and blindfolded McFadden to the trunk and pushed him in. He fell with a thud and struggled against the cuffs. Jasper retrieved a small case from the trunk and unzipped it. At first I couldn't make out what he held, but when it glinted in the lamp light overhead, I recognized a syringe. Jasper carefully slid the tip into McFadden's neck. The plunger descended, and McFadden stopped struggling. He lay in the trunk, inordinately still, as though dead again. Jasper replaced the syringe in the case.

I looked both directions along the road, hoping no one would drive by as Jasper shut the trunk and opened the passenger door closest to me. He motioned for me to get in. The other man slipped into the front passenger seat.

I approached Jasper, leaned in, and whispered that I had left a vehicle several blocks to the west.

He nodded. "It has already been taken care of." He pointed again at the empty seat awaiting me. My mind still puzzling over what his words meant, I stepped forward and dropped my weary body on the leather. Jasper shut the door quietly, calmly walked to the other side of the car, and took his place beside me. When he shut the door, I took a deep breath, and the car drove off.

The quiet ride calmed me. The trees passed silently, and the sun began to light the world around us, the road before us.

The tension in my muscles faded.

Jasper nudged me. He held a bottle of water.

I thanked him, accepted it, screwed off the top, and drank deeply. I downed the bottle like I was inhaling fresh air. The liquid refreshed and cleaned my mouth. It cooled my stomach. I capped the empty bottle and tossed it to the floor. I would have happily had another, but it would do for now. I would find a glass of fresh water wherever we ended up.

I smiled. McFadden was alive and on his way back to the city, proof that Roth never committed the crime police accused him of. Roth would soon be released, as would the other two men they had jailed.

The whole case would be turned upside down. Police would return to the grave and find it empty. The laws of reality would appear violated. It would become one of the great mysteries of science, of crime scene investigation. Paranoid theories would take the place of logic.

Simply because I had done what I had done. And Jasper had done what he had done.

I looked over at him, at his smashed-in nose, his thin lips, his salt-and-pepper hair. He had almost immediately figured out my location. He could have kidnapped me if he had wanted. He could have driven there alone, found me in the dead of night, and abducted me, but he hadn't.

Instead, he had selected a group of men and drove to the grave to help me…or, rather, Roth.

At least that's how it looked from the outside.

"I know what you're wondering," he said. He looked over at me.

"What?"

"If I am on Roth's side or my own."

I felt grit against my eyes as I looked at the floor, then at Jasper. "So what's the answer?"

"Roth's side *is* my side. He would have done the same for me."

Jasper faced the road before us. I inhaled deeply and also faced forward. I closed my eyes. Jasper's answer was the best he could have given.

These were, admittedly, men who had already kidnapped me—and would have killed me if I had not proven useful. But considering that Patrick was potentially in trouble, that Alex had eluded me, that Infinitum had nearly killed me, this was as good as it was going to get. We had done everything right; we had McFadden. Roth, Jasper, and the others had useful skills that I could exploit, and perhaps, in just a little while, Alex and the rest of Infinitum would be dead. There would be no resurrection for them.

I relaxed, weary, and observed the man in the passenger seat. He had sandy, buzz-cut hair and wore a nice suit wrinkled and riddled with dirt. He had been standing beside me when I sent my power below to McFadden. His eyes had widened when he witnessed the short, impossible miracle. Then he silently helped the others.

I took a deep breath, relaxed more fully, and turned to Jasper. "Is Roth waiting for us?"

Jasper nodded and opened his mouth to speak. Then the man in the passenger seat turned and looked at me swiftly. With his sharp look came an equally sharp pain in my stomach, so quick and effortless I seemed almost not to feel it. My body froze. My lungs wouldn't take in air. The sun beamed off the steering wheel and the steel weapon in his hand.

The man shifted to aim the gun at Jasper, but Jasper already pointed his own weapon into the passenger seat. He shoved the man's gun away while simultaneously shooting him three times through the back. The well-dressed man vibrated in his seat, as if rattled by an earthquake. His gun discharged, hitting no one. The driver raised his hand, a pistol in it, and turned toward Jasper.

Jasper had already moved. Far quicker than could be expected, he shot the driver three times. Blood exploded from beneath his right cheekbone. Teeth flew out of his mouth to rattle off the windshield.

The car violently veered left, jerking across the median. I bounced back and forth in my seat, my body rigid and unyielding.

"Fuck!" Jasper said. He dove forward, grabbed the wheel, and jerked it to the right, just as we began to cross into the other lanes of traffic.

As Jasper crawled into the front to regain control of the vehicle, I took off my seatbelt. The car interior filled with black dots. Every time I blinked, they multiplied. I fell over, prone on the seat. I reached for my gun, but I couldn't feel my hand anymore. I couldn't feel anything.

"You all right, kiddo?!" Jasper yelled. "You all right? You all right? You all right?"

I couldn't seem to speak. I forced myself to look down. The bullet had blown the cloth of my shirt away, and blood covered my stomach. The wound was in my center, where Lutin had once cut me to put the piece of himself. Had the bullet killed the part of me that was Lutin?

"Holy shit! You're all right! You're all right! We're gonna get you to someone we know! Shit! Shit! Shit! Shit!" Jasper sounded very far away, like I were listening to him through a long tube.

I forced myself to inhale, and through the dots, through everything, I said, "No hospital." My voice weakened, and my mouth moved on its own, as though I were a fish out of water.

I was fucking dying. Right there and then, in that car, I was dying. Too quick to feel fear. Consciousness slipped away. Trying to hold on, I clenched my teeth and shrieked.

"Goddammit!" Jasper yelled.

My awareness went black.

Two men stood over me, pulling me out of the car. A garage stretched around us. "Shit," one of them said. Red hot fear radiated from his face.

Black again.

A bright white room. Five people stood over me, one of them in a white coat. My skin was bare, and an incredible heaviness weighed on my stomach. I couldn't breathe. I tried to scream. "Blood pressure is 72 over 52," someone said.

"You're going to be fine! Can you hear me, Jack? You just got to hang on!" Blood on someone's hands and face. Sound flowing in waves.

Nothing.

For a long, long time, nothing.

I AM STANDING IN A liquid pool like molten silver. The pool stretches into black infinity, as still as glass. A moon or sun is high above, illuminating the nothingness, but not an actual moon, actual sun. Infinite black surrounds me. I am not alone.

Something new appears in the silver pool in the distance. It is large and white, like a white block of wood drifting in the black. The white block splits and moves. Frisson, nausea, chills. It is alive. I should run. Instead, I watch and hope it does not see me.

I try to run. I can't. I'm frozen. There is no possibility of me moving.

It has no face. It's a white block with white plastic limbs. A bendable doll come to life, an artist's doll that maintains poses. It is pure white, sleek and shiny, like it is made of white goo.

The block doll is bending over a table that is as silver as the surface beneath us. A man is on that table. His dark jeans and shoes poke out to the left of the white monster.

The creature rises, its strange, white feet gliding over the top of the metallic pool, as though the two never meet. Now I see the face of the man on the table.

Alex.

Blood dribbles off the table. His eyes are unmoving, his whole body stiff. He does not look like my brother.

The creature glides to the other side of the table. Its blank face is as featureless as a block of cheese. It faces me. It does not know I am here.

The creature leans over my brother and holds its unformed hand over his stomach. The hand shape-shifts into a knife. The blade drops quickly, violently, slicing open Alex's stomach. The barest red is visible as the creature lifts the knife up. Its other shapeless arm becomes a hand with a thumb and five fingers, as if form follows need. The hand grasps the blade of the sharp white knife and breaks off a piece. The monster rolls the shard of itself between the two fingers of its left hand until it becomes soft and spherical. A little ball of poison dough.

It pushes the dough through the wound in Alex's chest. The creature reaches inside, up to its shoulder. Impossible. It fiddles. Its white, plastic hand emerges bloody. The blood soaks into the white and disappears like smoke evaporating. All is white.

My heart pounds. The incision in Alex's chest closes itself like a zipper. Life lights Alex's eyes. His body brightens, lightens. He pales. His hair is whiter than white. He sits like an automaton on the table, bending perfectly at the hip, and smiles.

He lifts his face to the creature in awe. "Thank you," he says. Alex does not sound like himself.

God help me. I gasp.

The creature jerks its head up to look straight at me, although it has no eyes. In the place empty of a mouth, a mouth now forms. "Ferric!" The voice is nonvoice. The void of sound forms the word.

Alex looks toward me, then through me.

The creature's right hand shoots forward to encircle the throat I didn't know I had. It is crushing me, absorbing me into itself, like I am one drop of dye in an ocean of milk. I cannot scream. I cannot do anything but dissolve.

And then I wake.

CHAPTER 22
CRACKED

I LAY ON A METAL gurney in a dark room, my torso naked, surrounded by tables full of bloody metal tools and gauze. My chest rose as I sucked in air. I looked around, frantically searching for the shiny white creature.

"Holy shit," someone said, invisible in the dark.

A man sat in a corner. Shadows obscured his features. He held something black in his hand. He pressed a button, and a beep sounded. "Roth," he said, "get down here."

I jerked and slipped off the gurney, hitting the floor hard. Breath exploded out of me. I felt no pain though. I scrambled away, leaving bloody smears on the tile. I managed to stand and bolt to the other side of the room. A pair of arms trapped me, and I screamed.

I braced myself, anchoring one foot against the wall, and kicked as hard as I could with the other, propelling us both backward. He fell, and I landed on top of him. Some instinct activated, and I reached around his jacket, found a holster, pulled free his gun, and rolled away. I aimed the barrel at him, and he raised both hands and called, "Jack! Jack! It's me."

Inches from the muzzle was Jasper's face.

"It's okay, Jack. It's okay." His voice purred calm, soothing. His eyes maintained contact with mine.

I looked around, searching for the white creature. The memory of it sent shivers rolling through every cell. The whole world felt wrong.

"You're okay, Jack. You're okay."

I backed away from Jasper, and he slowly stood.

"Come on," he said. "Let's get a shirt on you."

I stopped at the other side of the room and looked around. White tile divided the floor like gridded paper. A row of silver gurneys stretched to my left. One very bloody gurney stood to my right. Four trays of bloody tools and gauze surrounded it. A light in the back right of the room flickered. "Where the fuck am I?"

"At Purdom," he said. "Roth's building. We thought you were dead."

I caught sight of myself in a silver mirror to my left. Blood covered my chest—more than just blood. I nearly dropped the gun. The chills began to roll again, and I almost laughed at the sheer impossibility. Beneath the blood, across my pale skin, large black lines, the width of a small sword's blade, traveled over my stomach, chest, breasts, and arms like sprawling tree limbs. I looked like myself, but cracked.

Shaking, unable to believe the image in the mirror, I lifted the gun and pressed the muzzle into the counter beside me and dropped it. It hit the counter with a *bang*. I walked to the mirror, gripped the chair in front of it, and stared at my reflection. My black hair stuck to my body in congealed bits of blood. Pockets of it swooped out in multitudinous places. A large black mark dipped across my left clavicle; when I ran my hand over it, I expected to feel a deep impression, but the skin only registered as slightly more velvety than normal.

Jasper appeared in the mirror behind me, his mutt-like face alive, especially around the eyes. He seemed to want to calm me, and yet his own face did not appear calm. He lifted his gun from the counter and return it to his holster.

"You weren't like that before," he said, in his deep voice that reminded me of gravel and silk. "Right before you woke, they crawled across your body. You screamed. What happened?"

I shivered again, wondering if the monster lurked near. "How long have I been down here?"

"A week," Jasper said. "But you weren't deteriorating. That's why Roth had you kept out. We didn't know if… if you could bring yourself back."

My memory returned to the white monster reaching for me, pulling bits of me into him, then to the cracks. Perhaps they were related. Lutin and his brothers looked exactly like this…except their lines had been different. They had been filled with fire that fluoresced when they moved or even breathed. I had no fire. All I had was black.

The door behind us opened. I turned. I met Roth's wary gaze. He appeared shocked, the tribal-like lines beneath his cheekbones emphasized under the overhead light. His black hair swooped over his staring dark eyes. "You're alive." He took several steps forward, his eyes flicking between Jasper and me. He abruptly stopped. "You look…what happened?"

He seemed to be waiting for a response, but the image of one of Roth's men in the passenger seat of the car turning and shooting me entered my mind, and I decided I had none to give him. I turned to Jasper and held out my hand. "The shirt."

He handed me a large gray T-shirt, far too large for me. It resembled a sack when I shrugged it on.

I looked at Roth with an anger that made me feel like all the new lines in my body *should* be filled with fire. "*Your* man. Fucking. Killed me."

Roth shook his head. "He's not anything anymore. Gone. Trust me. I apologize. Endlessly. He could not handle what he saw when he saw you."

"Oh? Is that what it was?"

Roth nodded, entering the room more fully. "If I had put him up to it, we wouldn't have tried to save you. And we wouldn't have let your body rest here. We waited, hoping you would return. Besides, why would I do such a thing? You saved my daughter, and not just that. You saved me from a very long trial and possible imprisonment."

I inhaled a long, deep breath. That was true. Despite my rage, I knew it was true. "You need to vet your men better."

His eyes drifted to the floor, and he nodded. My anger demanded vengeance, but my mind determined that Roth was not the right one. Reality sank in, and in this reality, no white monster prowled, just men. The nightmare scene distanced itself, caught in the thread of a dreamcatcher. It disintegrated in the light of now.

"Perhaps you should take a seat," Roth said. "Perhaps you're not a hundred percent yet."

"I am." As soon as I said it, I knew it was true. I had never felt better, never felt more bulletproof.

"All right," Roth said softly, consolingly, unlike I had ever seen him before. "Then what are the marks on your skin?"

I shook my head. "Don't worry about that. They won't hurt me, and they won't hurt you either."

Roth swallowed. A long silence spun between us. I seemed to be coming back into consciousness, and he seemed not to know what to do. "Is there something I can get you? Are you hungry?"

"No," I said, "but I could use a drink."

"A drink," he said, and he smiled. "That I can do."

He nodded to Jasper, and Jasper spoke into his walkie-talkie, instructing someone on the other end to bring liquor, glasses, and cigarettes.

Roth motioned toward me warily. "If you don't mind, I'd like to let a doctor look you over."

"I don't think any doctor should see what I am."

"This one is trustworthy."

I laughed. "How do you know?"

"Because I will kill him and his family if he speaks a word about you to anyone."

The heavy, frank words seemed to rock against me. Even if a white monster existed, Roth carried weight somewhere, with someone. It bothered me. My mind begged me to leave.

"I want to take a shower. As long as one of your men doesn't shoot me, I will survive a shower."

Roth took a deep breath, looking at Jasper and then me. "I'll have some decent clothes brought to you."

"A turtleneck," I said.

He nodded. "Yes. A turtleneck." He gestured toward the door behind me.

"The bathrooms and showers are that way."

"Where am I?"

"Deep, deep in the underbelly of Purdom," he said, "where almost no one goes and comes out alive."

I stared at him, thinking that I almost hadn't. I left Roth and went to wash the blood from my body.

CHAPTER 23
NEW

THE WARM WATER HEATED MY cold skin. The blood rinsed off me, as if it had never been there, as if I had never been shot in the chest and bled to death. I shampooed my hair three times, washing all the filth away—including the dirt from McFadden's grave—and conditioned it. I ran the soap over my skin multiple times and scrubbed where the black lines crossed me in branches. Like ash, would it rub away? It wouldn't.

I felt strange. A second engine had started in my core and hummed along. I awakened, more aware; I smelled things more acutely. The soap contained subtle woody herbal notes. A slight mildew permeated the air. The scent of Roth's cologne and odor of my blood lingered.

I felt strong, as though things could not hurt me as they had before. I was peculiarly unafraid. I did not fear others seeing my nakedness or the black lines. I did not worry about someone trying to shoot me again or hurt me in another way. My mind and body rose above everything and retired from anxiety of this particular world.

The kernel of my power, deep inside me, flowed steadily throughout my body, itching to be used. That kernel had always seemed like a muscle ready to be flexed, a circuit that had to be completed. Now it was in constant use, coursing through my mind, body, spirit, not just my center. I noticed a crack in the shower wall and kept an eye on it, in case it filled itself in, in case reality began renewing itself in my presence, just like it had in Lutin's presence. The crack, though, remained.

After I dried off, I walked to the mirror and ran the towel across the damp glass from top to bottom. When it cleared, I studied at myself. Not only had lines appeared across my body but a piercing blackness filled my eyes, and something that appeared to be charcoal dust touched just beneath my cheekbones. I appeared very much like Lutin and his brothers.

Lutin's words rang, as though he stood very near, informing me about the piece of himself he had given me. *It will become more a part of you than any other part of you. Soon enough, they won't be able to take it back anymore.*

My mind flashed to a dead rose I had hidden beneath my bed when I lived at Cyrus's. After Lutin had given me part of himself, I had retrieved the rose and brought it back to life. It was the first time I had resurrected anything. I had come a long way since then.

What could this body do now?

CHAPTER 24
PLAN

ROTH'S DOCTOR EXAMINED ME, KEEPING any comments about the black lines on my skin to himself, probably reserving such commentary for a later one-on-one that excluded me. He checked my heartbeat, pulse, and blood pressure, which registered a healthy 110 over 85, my hearing, eyesight, and reflexes. He did not say anything beyond commands. When he stared into my eyes, he paled. Sweat beaded on his forehead.

He rose from his stool and wiped his face. "You're healthy," he said. "I... I don't know how, but you are." His chin wobbled when he opened his mouth to say more, but he refrained and left the room. Roth followed. I sat alone with Jasper.

After a few awkward seconds, I said, "Did you deliver McFadden alive or dead?"

"Alive." He chuckled, like he expected me to ask. His arms crossed over his chest. Unlike the doctor, he did not seem to fear me. I couldn't tell if it was an act meant to spare my feelings or if he really didn't care. "I wanted there to be no question. Later in the day after you...well..."

I nodded.

"He was unconscious when I dropped him off at a hospital with a note strapped to his body. Then I had someone deliver an anonymous tip to the news stations that James McFadden was actually alive and at the hospital. There had been so many paranoid theories about his death, and it's a hot enough case, that they ate it right up. The police released Roth from all charges."

"Well," I said, pressing my lips together, reaching for the whiskey waiting on a clean table beside me, "good for him." I poured myself a glass and downed it.

"You're angry, and you should be, but I promise you that Roth and I had nothing to do with it. It was a rogue employee."

Even if that was true, it didn't necessarily matter. On a long enough timeline, under the right amount of pressure, everyone goes rogue. My turning on Cyrus proved it; he had treated me like a daughter. "How many others are there?"

Jasper looked to the floor. "Unless you have a way of determining if someone is lying, you know the answer to that."

"Any guess why that particular employee wanted me dead?"

Jasper answered slowly, judiciously. I lit a cigarette. "I don't think everyone can handle what you're capable of. It scares them."

"An eighteen-year-old girl scares *them*?"

"Is that what you are?" he asked. "A human? A girl? Eighteen? You don't talk like it, and you don't act like it."

"I was raised differently than most people."

He smiled as though something both mysterious and funny existed in the corner of the room. "I don't think that's what it is."

My eyes narrowed as I took a drag. No, that's not what it was. I just hoped he wouldn't know that I knew.

Roth returned. He held out his hands and said, "The doctor says you're clear, so you're clear. You can bring that bottle with you to my office." He smirked. "Things have *changed* in the past week. We are very close to catching Alex now."

My back stiffened at the mention of my brother's name. The image of Alex on a metal table, a large white monster towering over him, flashed in my mind. "How?"

He pointed his chin toward the door. "I'll show you."

I stubbed the cigarette out and walked with him. He led me through the doors and down a long gray hallway to an elevator. Jasper followed.

When the elevator doors closed, on the way to the fourteenth floor Roth said, "Jack, I know there's currently no way to reassure you of our allegiance, but I promise you, I will tear Infinitum apart person by person, stone by stone. Exactly as you want. I hope in time you and I will become more settled with one another. This could be the beginning of something...big. If we let it."

I looked at him. His raised eyebrows questioned me. "Hm?"

Slowly, I nodded, although the large, shiny white monster that could crush Roth as quickly as he had nearly crushed me occupied my mind. Yes, this could be the beginning of something big, if something bigger hadn't existed. Roth didn't know my motivation had shifted. It wouldn't have mattered if he did.

The elevator doors opened onto the inner sanctum of Roth's office. Several men lounged inside, and a large television blared as we entered.

On the screen, a woman wearing a red blouse and blazer spoke in a vague accent about an anonymous tip leading reporters to James McFadden at Vickery Hospital. She said that it was beginning to appear that a man named Jonathon Roth, as well as two other individuals who had been arrested for his death, had been victims of shoddy investigative work and potentially the largest framing that had ever taken place. McFadden's death, at least as it seemed so far, had never actually occurred. The anchor summarized the story of McFadden's supposed demise. I stole a glance at Roth.

He smirked.

I momentarily wished I had been present when Jasper had dropped the resurrected man at the hospital entrance, just to observe whether Jasper had worn a satisfied smile as he left a small gift in the world that would allow everyone, if they looked hard enough, to know that the laws of reality were mere illusion.

"Before we begin," Roth said, pulling me from my thought. From his pocket, he retrieved a black rectangle. "Your cell phone." He handed it to me. "Fully charged."

I pressed the button, and the screen illuminated. Three missed calls from Patrick in three little gray boxes. The first was seven days old. The last had been left today. I shut the phone off and slipped it into my pocket. I would listen to the messages later.

Roth spread his hands wide. "Thank you for ensuring they cleared me of all charges. And for blessing us with your presence again. I did not know you were immortal."

He seemed to expect a reply, but I spoke nothing. I wasn't about to tell him that I was also unaware. I had hardly been alive long enough to think of myself that way. Was it true? Could I not be killed? Ever?

He hugged me briefly. We sat around the table to the left of his desk, and he took a deep breath. "I'm not going to forget what you did. It seems I will never be able to repay you, either for Emily or for setting me free," he said matter-of-factly. He waved at the television, and Jasper muted it.

I nodded and gazed down at the table. "I have to admit that I never expected that to happen to you, a man who seemed so invincible."

Roth scratched his chin, and his eyes shifted to the window. "It surprised me too," he said in a low voice. "You understand what it is like to battle someone from your past for dominance. A variety of dirty tricks gets pulled. Your feet get knocked out from under you from time to time. In this way, we are similar."

"How do I know it won't happen again?" I asked. "That you won't disappear into thin air?"

Roth leaned forward. "I could promise you that nothing outside of this room will ever enter into our lives and disturb them, that I won't ever be framed again, and that no one will ever attack you, but you and I both know that that would be a lie…" He took a breath. His eyes locked on mine. "But we will do our best, and our best is very good."

We quieted for a moment, and then I asked him, "What's the news?"

He reached forward, grabbed a remote from the table beside him, and pressed a button. The television shut off, and a soft rumbling entered the room. The sound seemed muted, as though emanating behind a very thick curtain. It sounded like wheels turning, and an image of Cyrus's bookshelf appeared my mind's eye. I attempted to brush the memory away but found it difficult. The wall that anchored Roth's television moved forward and shifted to the left, as though on a set of wheels. Behind a thick pane of glass appeared a very large white room. In the center stood a silver rolling cart. On it sat a small, vibrant gramophone.

My mouth dropped, and I shot to my feet.

"Very interesting contraption," he said. "Killed four of my men before we were able to turn it off. Funny you never warned me about it."

My mouth went dry. It was true. I hadn't warned him about the device inside 405 Brimmer. I hadn't known if I should. "It's an…"

"*Arca*," Roth finished.

I turned and looked at him in astonishment.

"I know. Harlowton told us."

The dryness that parched my mouth tickled my throat and then shifted into my stomach. I ached. "When?"

"When we asked him. Admittedly, we had to ask him many, many times, and we had to work on him a little, but he told us." Roth smiled again. This time, his smile seemed twisted, evil. Something in the core of me wanted to flex, and it poked at me like a ball of nausea in the pit of my stomach.

"So you found him, and you tortured him, and he told you…"

"Everything," Roth answered, without malice this time. "About the ferrics. About what you are. What you can do."

"Oh?"

"Mm hmm."

"What else did he tell you?"

Roth blinked languidly before he spoke. "We recorded the conversation. Would you like to see?"

He had recorded Harlowton's interrogation—why? In case I returned? Or for a different reason? Did I want to see it? No. I didn't. I'd seen enough.

"You don't know everything," I told him. "Even if you know all of that…"

He straightened in his chair and smoothed his blazer, giving me the floor. I sat down, eyeing the gramophone in the center of the room behind the glass.

"For instance, Patrick's father owns Lucient."

"Yes." Roth gazed at me curiously. "I discovered that as soon as you asked me to look into it."

That surprised me, but at the same time, it probably shouldn't have.

"Let me start from the beginning then."

"Please do." All the men in the room drew nearer as though to better hear me.

Taking a deep breath, I told my story. I explained about Cyrus—not that he was the lunatic leader of a cult who had swallowed too many pills, injected too many chemicals—but, rather, that he had been a brilliant and nearly paranormal man, far more capable than anyone I had ever met. I said that Cyrus and others owned boxes with magical powers, and I explained how these boxes worked, that they varied in appearance and had their own specialties. The one thing they seemed to have in common, so far, was that, when open, they bleached the color from everything they touched.

As I spoke, an image of the white monster flashed briefly in my mind, and I shivered, but I did not reveal the vision I'd experienced when dead. It was mine, for me only.

It seemed Mr. Bryan Flannigan owned such a contraption, I explained. His son, Patrick, had shown it to me. I described how Flannigan's men had discovered us in Building 1C and what I had seen: the paint, the machine, the rose. I told him about Bryan Flannigan hitting Patrick.

The entire time I spoke, Roth tuned in completely. He did not take notes, and he did not interrupt me, but I felt his mind working like a lawyer's. It operated quick, invasive, and would detect any inconsistency.

He never questioned the validity of my statements, but I expected that he had assigned a giant red flag to the whole tale. It was, after all, an unbelievable story. If not for the fact that I had resurrected his daughter and McFadden and that I myself had returned from the dead, he would not have believed me. I finished, and he sat motionless, his hands pressed together beneath his chin, his eyes down. When he spoke, he seemed to rise out of a dream. "I knew about Lucient because Harlowton told me."

A jolt of shock hit me, bringing me back to awareness. "Harlowton knew?"

He nodded. "But you confirmed it, and that's just as important. How did the two men discover you in Building 1C?"

If Harlowton knew about Lucient's machine, then Infinitum had to be using it for something. I bet Roth knew the answer to that, too. "They said it was the alarm."

"No surveillance?"

"They did not say, but there were two cameras in the hallway."

"How did Cyrus's box work? What did it do?"

"It identified the traitors in the group."

"How?"

"I don't know. It just named them."

He rocked back in his seat. "Seems like these boxes do a lot of naming."

My eyes searched his face. "What do you mean?" At the same time, an image of a black sheet of paper falling from the left side of Lucient's machine popped up, like my brain were waking after the deep freeze of death. As though I still wore my black coat, I moved to reach into my pocket.

"Are you looking for this?" Roth asked. He walked over to his desk, opened a drawer, and retrieved a black rectangle. He returned and placed it on the table. If it had been folded or crunched, no evidence remained. It was crisp, smooth. Where it sat, the table looked as though a hole had been cut out. A line of gold writing shimmered up and out, as though a hologram.

"Yes," I said. I gazed upon the sheet of paper, beginning to realize there might be nothing Roth didn't know, that I limped far, far behind. I slid it toward me, touching the surface with my fingers tentatively.

"I've never seen anything like it," Roth whispered. "The black is astonishing. It's heavy. Like flexible stone."

Considering what Roth had told me—that many of the machines seemed to produce names—I said, "There's no name though. Only an address. The same address where we were at the time. I don't think it names traitors."

"You're right," he said. "It doesn't name traitors."

He appeared smug, unafraid of me, despite the black lines on my skin, despite the fact that I had returned from the dead. I should've seen it. He already knew. He had a name for a creature like me, a place for me in his understanding of the world. Otherwise, he would have killed me. "What does it name?" I nevertheless asked, as though my prodding him to say it would give me the upper hand.

His eyebrows lifted ever so slightly. "Ferrics."

With a wary twitch of my fingers, I drew my hand away from the sheet of paper and leaned back in my seat.

"If we were to lay out a hundred bodies for you now, how many of those individuals could you resurrect?" Roth asked.

"All of them," I answered, not bothering to hide.

"In the same evening."

"Yes."

"So bringing them back to life doesn't drain you."

I shook my head.

"You are miraculous, Jack," he said, surprising me. "Not in my wildest dreams could I have imagined someone like you exists. Not in all of my nightmares. You and I have much to discuss beyond our current concerns. But that is a conversation for the future." Roth smiled knowingly and lifted his hand toward me. I stared at it and realized that he wanted me to clasp his hand with my own. "I know exactly what you are, and I accept you. I want you to work with me. In return, I will burn Infinitum to the ground. I know what they are doing with Lucient's box, and I will tell you. But first, I want you to shake my hand so we have an agreement. We won't destroy one another but share everything. I do not want any more surprises, like my men walking into 405 Brimmer to be attacked by something like that gramophone. If I am going to help you, I don't want anything withheld. I need to know *exactly* what I am getting into. Do we have an agreement?"

The image of the white monster immediately entered my mind. I would never speak of it, never tell him. I stared at Roth's hand and immediately knew that my shaking it meant nothing. I wouldn't hold to the agreement. Neither would he.

Nevertheless, I slid my hand toward his. "I am sorry. I would have told you before your men went to the house, but things…got in the way. I will be timely with any future information, and I won't withhold anything." We shook three times. Perhaps it was for the benefit of the others who watched us. Perhaps it was for the aspects of us that wished this relationship could work out, that it could be the answer.

Where he touched my hand, the fresh black lines on my arm crackled and fizzed.

"Thank you," he said.

I swallowed and returned my hand to my lap.

Roth answered my unasked question. "The box turns the paint at Lucient white. The paint is then shipped out for painting address labels on curbs for houses and apartments."

"Address labels?"

"That's what your brother chose. It could have been anything, apparently, that belongs to the houses."

The image of Alex on a table, a white, gooey being slipping a piece of itself inside him, came to me. My smile faltered. I pushed the image away, cleared my throat. "Why isn't Alex keeping the box near him?"

"Because. He wants it to be visible."

"Why?" I asked.

"To lure the ferrics in."

"What do you mean, *lure* them?"

"As Harlowton put it, the white isn't white when the ferrics are near it, apparently. It reverts to its original color. Your kind returns color to the world, and this particular box keeps track of which items shift back. The location is passed to the owner of the machine. The paint serves as a web across the world. A ferric is the fly that catches its wing on a thread. The box allows Alex to know immediately where a ferric is because the machine provides the address, or addresses, of all the places where white shifts to color. If he chooses, it immobilizes them until he can arrive. They can't move. He brings another box that weakens or kills them."

I shuddered. Tribal lines now covered my body, like a ferric. Did this mean that I, too, would return the white paint to its original color? That I would be trapped?

Roth gazed at me, waiting for a reaction.

"And he is doing this to catch one," I said, realizing the truth of it as I spoke.

I should have known. Alex intended to follow in Cyrus's footsteps. Cyrus's immense power he owed in large part to Lutin, and it was obvious what Alex was scheming to do—feed pieces of a ferric's soul to a box from the Builder, expand it to an immense size, make it ten times capable, perhaps more.

When the mechanism in Patrick's father's lab spit out the address, it provided the location where *I* was, and it had appeared after I had turned a can of paint red. The thought made me nauseous.

"If the box is at Lucient," I said, "how would Alex know when an address is provided? Does he stay there?"

"I don't know. Harlowton doesn't know."

"Are you sure?"

Roth's glance distanced, as though he were remembering something difficult and significant. "I'm *sure*."

My eyes dropped. I frowned, thinking. "What's in it for Flannigan?"

Roth gestured vaguely. "It's an investment perhaps. He is a funder. If you were offered a chance at capturing a creature who could resurrect the dead, wouldn't you be intrigued?"

The back of my neck flushed with heat, but I refused to react. If I did, I'd be admitting something. Fear. The possibility he'd lock me away, the same way that Flannigan and Alex wanted to. The lines on my body vibrated, itching, like they were trying to release some pent-up, never-before-used energy.

"No, I wouldn't," I said. "Because those who own ferrics are doomed."

Roth cocked his head, as though not entirely doubting that might be true.

"Alex is seeking ferrics. I should have realized. If he finds one, if he hasn't already, then our ability to catch him will be a thousand times more difficult. Ferrics make an *arca* far, far more powerful." Not only that, but if he ever did find one, it would likely be subjected to a reality far worse than death. I shook my head. "Everything you just told me sets us back. Lucient Laboratories has to be dealt with. Before we do anything else. Before we try to find and help any children. Before anything. It's not safe for me to resurrect anyone until this is taken care of. If I do, Alex will find me."

I was not quite a full ferric—though that might have changed since my death—but I nevertheless caused the address to appear in the laboratory where Flannigan's box worked. When I had exercised that bit of power on the can of paint, the machine had spit out the address where I was. Wherever I went, whatever I did, I might be discovered and caught. I would never get the jump on Alex.

Roth gazed at the ceiling. His eyes seemed to pass over invisible writing in the air. "Yes. I have been thinking about this. Alex has a way of tracking you," he said "If you're near that paint it turns red?"

"Yes."

"And that sheet of black paper with the gold writing... It fell from the machine and provided your location because you had turned the paint red?"

"Yes, but it happened after I'd released my power on one of the cans... only then. I think, with the others, they only have to walk past before it happens immediately."

"But you are one of them, are you not? At least that's how Harlowton described ferrics to me." His eyes twinkled, a new kind of light behind them, more like a series of sparks than a steady flame. It seemed to accuse me of failing to inform him about myself. But there had been no reason to, in the same way I knew little about Roth.

"He is both right and wrong about me."

"How is he wrong?"

"I don't...*exactly* look like them."

He gazed at me, unconvinced. "Then what are you?"

I paused. I wasn't like him or Jasper. Neither, though, was I entirely like Lutin. At least, not yet. "I'm halfway between."

"*Half* way?"

He smiled, glanced at Jasper, and then returned his eyes to me. He took a deep breath and opened his mouth. His smile vanished. "When we started out, I admit I wondered if it was some spell that you cast. I wondered if you had learned some kind of black magic from Cyrus. Then one of my men killed you while under my care, which I do apologize for, and it became obvious to me then that it wasn't magic. It's *you*."

I waited for him to arrive at his point. "Is that a problem?"

He shook his head. "No. No. There will never be a problem. Understand that here and now.

"I am only thinking that if Alex wanted you dead, he must not know that you are one of these creatures, these ferrics. Otherwise, he would have had us capture you, not kill you." His eyebrows drew down pensively. He spoke slowly. "And those in 405 Brimmer would not have attempted to kill you. *None* of them know, do they?" He looked at me. "Not a single person knows what you are."

His intelligence shone brilliantly.

"Just you."

If that satisfied him, he didn't show it. "How were you able to keep the secret from them when you were involved in Infinitum?"

"You'd be surprised how strongly men in power want to believe every miracle is their own doing."

He grinned. "Cyrus's fatal flaw? Thank goodness for self-obsession, hm?"

"Yes."

He stared at me for a long while, sending a frisson through me. He rose from his chair and crossed his arms. "This is good." He paced back and forth in front of the table before he turned to me. "We can proceed with our plan. They want a ferric. The paint shows Alex where he can find one, any one, *any* nameless creature like you who can resurrect the dead. As for you, you turn the paint red. Let us trick him then. We will let Alex believe he has found a random being. You could, however you do it, change one of the house addresses to red. That will alert him, and we can be there, waiting. When he arrives, we will kill him."

It was a good idea, except for one problem. I thought of my vision of the white creature standing over Alex, inserting something into him and healing him. It felt real to me, but had it been? Or was it just a fever dream brought on by death?

"Alex has tools. He is powerful."

"Yes." Roth's eyes wandered to the gramophone in the room behind glass. "But obviously not powerful enough. Why would he be searching for these creatures otherwise? He has no ferric to resurrect him. He is not on the side of life, or immortality, not like we are." Roth, a kill-for-hire manager, winked. "If we lose against him, you'll bring all of us back, and we'll fight him again. It all works, as long as we have..."

"What?"

"Your word."

I assured him, "You have it, but..."

Roth nodded and cut me off. He rubbed his thumb against his fingers intently. "It should work. It's the best shot we have, now anyway, to catch and kill the man who murdered Emily, or at least one of the men related to that man. We can destroy the man who plots to enslave those who can resurrect the dead."

He looked at me as though he hoped I would remember this, that it would stick with me that he wanted to help. I nearly rolled my eyes.

"I cannot endorse this idea."

He looked surprised. "Why?"

"Waiting around while Alex brings some weapon that could destroy ferrics, or paralyze them, or wear then down... Whatever it is, no. If a device can do that to a ferric, then neither I nor you stand a chance."

"For all you know, his weapon only targets ferrics. And with the boxes, you have to lock a person in the same room and open it. We just won't allow ourselves to be locked in with one of them."

"It's not that simple."

"A bullet will make it simple. Alex is just a boy, a human, flesh and blood boy. You've had problems with these people, I know, because of their numbers. Well, now you have numbers too, as many numbers as you need. As long as you resurrect us, we will protect you."

"I always had bullets."

"And did you shoot him?"

I paused. The utter atrociousness of the fact I had never turned a gun on Alex during my time with Cyrus made me wince with embarrassment and rage.

"*We* will shoot him," Roth said.

"This is not how I would go about things."

"Well, this is how we are. We will lure him to us and kill him. You said yourself that he must corner us and open the box. We will not allow either to happen." He smiled. "You are in experienced hands. It will be fine. We will make it so."

I tapped a finger on the table and looked at Jasper's resolute face, and Asher's, and the other men. I turned back to Roth, relaxed in my chair, and clasped my hands together. His death would be his own. I would flee, if need be, and be done with them.

I nodded. "All right."

CHAPTER 25
RUN

ROTH LOCATED AN OLD HOUSE for sale in the north of the state and purchased it under another name. For a mile in either direction, there existed no other residences, businesses, or buildings. It was perfect for his plan to lure the blond young spider in.

An extraordinarily brilliant white address gleamed on the concrete curb beside the cement walkway, despite the house's isolation. When Roth showed it to me, I said, despite the fact I disapproved of the plan, "As good a shot as any." It looked like fresh paint, like Lucient's paint, and I did not stand too close. I worried that it would immediately turn red when I neared it. After all, my eyes gleamed black, my face looked like charcoal had been dipped beneath my cheekbones, and black lines traced themselves all over my body. Even more telling than that, the electric current of energy still itched inside me—pressure ready to release. The white paint shined at me, as bleached as ever, implying I was not a full ferric. Nevertheless, I kept my distance.

Twenty men filled the house. An array of weapons, from knives to Glocks to AR-15s, covered on the floors, the kitchen counters, the bathroom sinks, the mantle.

Roth had asked me before if I recommended that he take any precautions. Was there something they could do to throw Alex off when he arrived?

I had glanced up from my seat at the large table in his vast office, and a thought came to mind. The thought had not arrived earlier because I'd assumed they would fail. "Yes, actually. There is."

"What?" he asked.

"You can dress the part."

Inside the house, along their bodies men taped wires, which trailed down their arms and hands and up over their necks. These wires burned reddish orange and crawled, just like my lines, all over their forms. Over the thick, glowing wires, they donned their shirts. When the lights switched off, the orange trails incandesced through their clothes. It was striking.

"This is what a ferric looks like?" Roth asked, assessing himself in the mirror. The room's overhead lights had been dimmed, and the similarity was close to perfect.

"Yes."

"When did you first see one?"

"Down in Cyrus's basement. He kept one there. And then, later, I saw more of them."

"How did you become one of them?"

"I'll have to tell you some other time."

He looked annoyed. I didn't care. I wouldn't answer.

"How many exist?"

"I don't know."

"How do you find them?"

"I guess you find a box that hunts them down."

"And how do you get a box?"

I paused. I looked at Roth, in front of the mirror, resembling an older, tired-er, more human version of Lutin, and for the first time I realized that before I had died, I'd felt a sense of security with him that I never had before. He was a powerful man in a world I had been trying hard to join and survive. No twilight monstrosities concealed themselves in his closet. He boasted no gramophone that crooned sinister staves, no pictures with moving eyes, no followers. I wondered if his employees might be considered followers. Sure, they filled most of their days with coffee and cigarettes and chit-chat, and that was all normal and good. Sure, they didn't believe in anything grandiose, like conquering the world. Still, I couldn't ignore the similarities—a powerful man of the world with employees resembled a powerful paranormal man with followers. Roth even had a ferric, or at least three-quarters of a ferric, helping him.

"For the first time," I said, narrowing my eyes, "I'm wondering why you don't know. Why you don't have one of those boxes."

Roth stared at me in the mirror as he adjusted his headset. A small, thin wire curved down the back of his head to his ear; a tiny microphone aimed toward his mouth from his cheek. Each of the men wore them. They gave me one, as well; it waited on a nearby chair.

"Probably because I have no use for such an item."

"Believe me," I said, "you would find a use." I crossed to the wall and looked out the window at the lawn in the late afternoon light. The sun would begin descending soon. In little time, I would turn the paint red.

"I like you because you brought back Emily, but before we went to St. Matthew's and you resurrected her, there was a moment I seriously considered killing you."

I turned to him, my eyebrows arched low. This revelation did not surprise me. "Why?"

He flipped the light switch on, and the stripe of eye black on his face gleamed under the electric illumination. Any similarities to Lutin evaporated. I could see the eye black for what it was—makeup. I could see the wires taped to the back of his hands.

"Because you frightened me. You were no joke, no toy to mess with. You were, I realized, perhaps an evil that needed to be destroyed. Now," he smiled, "I realize you are a good to be helped.

"And my general view of the paranormal, aside from believing it's bullshit, is that it is less of an asset than a hindrance. It is a deviation from a set path, the right path, and when one follows it, he begins to spiral down into nothing. Nothing becomes knowable. What would it profit a man to gain a ghost and lose all sense of the world?"

I searched his face and remembered he'd had Emily resurrected in a church. "Are you not...religious, Roth?"

"I am, but I am also practical. The enemy of anything mystical. Except..."

"What?"

"You are surprisingly efficient." He laughed as though the idea were impossible. "No shadows or ghost stories, no candles, no reading in tongues from a book, no crystal balls. Excluding the fact that you took your sweet time with resurrecting Emily," he winked, "you get the job done quickly and without question. *That* is worth protecting and working with. But this entire system of boxes and invisibility and brainwashing... I couldn't care less. The fact is, if I put a bullet through Alex's head, he will die." He shrugged. "It might take two. But that requires no boxes, nothing extra. It involves very little cost. Nothing is more streamlined than a bullet. I don't need a spider's web, white paint turning back to red. I don't want an infinite number of things that can go wrong. I just want what works." He held up a forefinger. "One bullet. It solves a thousand problems in the space of a second, and it's good enough for the majority of us. It will be good enough now."

I nodded. "That's respectable." I didn't necessarily believe what he just told me—I did not trust his no-bullshit nature would hold under the temptation of supernatural power—but nevertheless he loathed and hunted Alex, and that meant a great deal to me. "The only thing I can say is that's not me."

"I know." He smiled. "But you are useful. A useful mysticism."

I looked out the window. "Most likely," I said, "Alex and Cyrus didn't care about efficiency or business or, in the end, even money. It is the elaborateness of death that interests people like them. I guess that's why you were never offered a box," I said, picking at a thread on the cuff of my gray sweater.

"What do you mean?" Roth cocked his head.

"As I understand it, the Builder offers boxes to certain individuals who prove themselves worthy."

"And I'm not worthy."

I laughed. "Don't take it badly. I wouldn't work with you if the Builder had." I looked up at him. "In case this all goes horribly wrong..."

"Don't." One word. Nothing more.

I withheld my comment.

His gaze released me, and he glanced at his phone. "Time to go downstairs. Jasper should have returned by now."

He shut off the light and stopped me in the doorway. "Alex will come to the house."

"Yes."

"And he will bring one of these boxes inside."

"Yes."

"And we must kill him before he opens it."

I nodded.

"Jack," he tapped my face kindly, "we *will* kill him before he opens it." With that, he walked out of the room. Tentatively, I followed him downstairs.

Jasper wore a long brown coat, a duffel bag slung over his shoulder, likely filled with his own weapons, headset, and wires. The silver in his salt-and-pepper hair glinted. He nodded to the others as he entered the room.

For the next hour and a half, they reviewed the plan repeatedly. I glanced again at the missed messages from Patrick on my phone. Oddly, he had never complained about his father; he had kept up the pretense as Flannigan preferred. I doubted that the first time Flannigan had hit his son was in 1C, with me standing there. It did not escape me that people like Patrick, born and bred in hard circumstances, seek similar people. I wondered if that was why he was comfortable with me.

Violence observed is violence forcibly adored. Trauma repeats. That's how it works. I wondered what patterns I repeated.

Was I building another cult?

I shivered. If we survived the night, I would leave Roth and his men behind.

If we survived the night.

⌒

AT EXACTLY SIX IN THE evening, Roth, Jasper, and I left the house, proceeded to the end of the concrete walkway, and waited beside the curb. The darkening sky had not entirely lost its blue, and the energy of the land seemed dim and distraught. The grass was yellow, and the leaves had already dropped and darkened. Moisture scented the air, not like dew and not like rain, as though a storm hovered very close and would just graze us.

Roth's dark eyes scanned both directions, and he nodded to me.

I exhaled and approached the side of the curb, keeping an eye on the white to see if it would turn red when I got too close. To my relief, it remained colorless. My hand reached above the tiny pebbles and glistening trails of snails. I let the spring inside me unwind, and as it uncoiled, the delicious energy that was already humming inside my body exploded and eagerly passed from my center to my fingers. It landed on the address label, and the numbers shifted red.

A movement at the front of the house caught my eye.

Not only the numbers on the curb turned red. So had the front door.

"Damn," Jasper said.

Roth looked at him, and they exchanged something unspoken. It seemed they were noting my power and its usefulness in a refreshed way; that they needed to take full advantage of it, of me. But one huge impediment remained: the box in 1C.

"We end this tonight. We have better things to do," Roth said.

Jasper assented. I rose, and Roth placed his hand on my shoulder and squeezed. He kept his hand there until we reentered the house.

When we stepped inside and shut the door, the room quieted with renewed energy. Roth said to me, "You stay away from the windows when they arrive. If you see one of us go down, bring him back, but otherwise, we'll take care of it."

"*You'll* take care of it?" I nearly laughed. They still did not quite understand what they were getting into, despite my warnings. "All right."

He shook his head dismissively before he led the majority of the group out the back door. Four remained in the living room, and they switched their electric wires on. Their fiery false veins glowed, visible from the road in the twilight.

About fifteen minutes passed before Roth said, "There are several cars driving up." We heard his words through our headsets, but because I stood close, I sensed the urgency and focus of his voice. "Five in all. There may be more than we expected."

I crept to the window and peered out. Three cars, two SUVs, and one van appeared on the street.

All five of the vehicles shut off in succession and waited in the road. I stopped breathing as I searched the vehicles, wondering if my brother sat in them.

Roth shifted the gun at his side, and metal clicked. His lights were not illuminated, and I reached to the button at his wrist and pressed. The orange spread across his hands and up his neck.

Another man shifted his toe, and a floorboard creaked.

"When they leave the vehicles," he said, "remember—five yards from the house. No farther. No closer."

Every person in the room, and every man outside, held his breath. I could feel it. It was like a deep freeze.

A man in the third vehicle opened his door and stepped to the back. He opened the passenger door, and a man wearing a pin-striped suit exited. His dark hair, flat face, and pointed chin immediately invoked his name.

"Flannigan," I whispered. "What is he doing here?" I assumed he simply funded Alex, not actively pursued what the box might yield. Which party in the agreement had given in? Had Flannigan been forced to take part by Alex, or had he wormed his way into a situation he couldn't possibly understand?

Roth spoke flatly into his mouthpiece. "Wait."

Patrick's father buttoned his jacket and smoothed his hair back. He looked toward the house, seeming to notice the red door and the tiny stripes of orange glowing through the windows.

"He sees us," Roth said, as though reassuring the others.

Flannigan retrieved a cell phone from his pocket and made a call. He paced back and forth beside the car, nodding and toeing the rocks and dirt.

When he slipped the phone back into his pocket, Flannigan gestured with his hand, and men began opening vehicle doors. This group reminded me of the Outfit. They were uniformly dressed and obviously disciplined.

"Wait," Roth repeated.

After the SUV trunks opened, two men proceeded to hand weapons to the others. They appeared to be as well-armed as Roth's group. They turned toward the house and crossed the yard to the walkway. Roth aimed his M4 more precisely.

"On the count of three," he said. "One."

Flannigan remained at the cars. He folded his arms and leaned back against the hood. The other fifteen or so fanned out, in no hurry at all, and surrounded the house. It would only be a few moments before they reached the backyard. There, they would find six individuals waiting for them.

"Two."

Seven men stood in the yard in a small semi-circle. They gazed into the windows. I stole one more look before I pulled back and covered my ears.

"Three."

The four men in the living room fired their rifles twice in the space of a second, shooting out the glass of the windows and killing those on the lawn.

From the backyard came the rapid reports as several automatic weapons fired.

No long and tiresome shootout commenced. The process ended in the span of a few seconds.

Roth opened the front door. He and Jasper left the house and shot three more people on their way out. Flannigan dashed into one of the cars and started the engine.

Asher grabbed a shotgun from the mantle and ran out of the door. He called to Roth and threw him the weapon. Halfway across the lawn, Roth turned and caught the twelve-gauge expertly. Just as Flannigan pulled out,

Roth shot the car engine twice. The engine died, and the car rolled back into the SUV behind it with a crunch. Roth walked up to the car window and pumped two more rounds. Blood and glass exploded.

Patrick's father died. Staring at the car, unable to see inside, I felt strange, conflicted even, not knowing if this had destroyed Patrick or released him from an oppressor.

"All clear," Roth said.

Three more *all clears* arrived in my earpiece. Shaking away my thoughts about Flannigan, I walked out to the front lawn, my boots crunching through the dead grass, and stared at the blood splashed across the yard. The Outfit's men at the back of the house walked to the front.

"How many bodies?" Jasper asked.

"Sixteen total," Asher answered.

"Are any of them Alex?" Roth asked.

Three more voices called, "No."

I waited beside Roth as his men dragged the corpses to the center of the yard. "Jack, do you see him? Look closely."

I didn't need to look at their faces. I had already seen them. None of them were Alex. Nevertheless, I searched each body, checking for anyone from my past.

"Seemed to me they were waiting for someone else to arrive," I said as they dragged over more bodies for me to observe. None of them were familiar.

"Yes," Roth said. "We'll prepare for a second round."

After they laid out all fifteen bodies, I confirmed I knew none of them. The men carried them into the house.

Roth approached the third vehicle and pulled Flannigan's body out. His face was unrecognizable. Nausea filled me.

Jasper followed and climbed into the car; five other men surrounded it and began pushing it to the back of the house. Roth carried Flannigan's body inside.

A sick feeling flooded my stomach, a sensation of uncertainty, and I thought of Patrick as Roth and his cargo passed by.

Roth's men inside twinkled through the windows with the fluorescing orange delineations. I retrieved the gold cigarette case from my inside jacket pocket and plucked one out. A large C carved itself into the front of the case, and I slipped my thumb across it, frowned, and returned it to my pocket. I placed the cigarette in my mouth and lit it, inhaling deeply.

I looked up the hill. It rose high above the house. Tall trees speckled the land. Except for an occasional brush of wind, the area remained quiet. The air turned cold, the sky almost completely dark, and I didn't expect the sounds of birds or dogs or people, but the silence struck me nevertheless—heart-stopping almost, like the moisture in the air.

Up in the trees, the figure of a man appeared.

I cocked my head, the cigarette planted firmly between my lips, and I bit down reflexively, cutting the filter in two.

Moonlight began to cover the land, and it illuminated a tiny section of yellow-blond hair among the trees. My heart leaped, and I almost cried out, "*You!*" But I kept quiet. He did not seem to notice me.

Thirty feet from the house, I glanced through its windows, realizing that the man on the hill witnessed what I saw—a house apparently full of ferrics. There was no knowing how long Alex had been standing there, what he had heard or witnessed.

I moved past the perimeter of the yard and gazed up the hill.

The figure also moved. He bent low, hunkered down. I whispered into my mouthpiece, "There's someone on the hill behind the house."

Every glowing movement in front of the windows stopped.

"Get inside," Roth instructed. Trying to avoid attention, I began to creep ahead. Then I stopped. Something strange happened on the hill.

A tiny waterfall dropped from the figure, painting a line through the landscape. The flow became violent, no longer clear, but churning white and gray. The waterfall expanded, widened, stretched, finally colliding with the ground about fifty feet down before it bounded up again. Sections appeared more like powder than water. The flow tossed whirring grains into the air, coating everything. Powder, though, is light and loose. This was solid and eerily silent.

In just a few seconds, the substance splashed against the house and exploded twenty feet skyward. The blue trim went white, as did the grass and nearby trees.

"Impossible," I muttered. The cigarette dropped from my mouth. This box worked *outside*.

"Run!" I screamed.

CHAPTER 26
PROOF

As I turned, Roth and several others leaped from the porch.

I raced at a diagonal angle, hoping to veer from the white liquid trail. Behind me, it expanded its path, quickly approaching. The house and Roth's men were no longer visible. Everything suffocated in the soft, thick false snow.

I launched myself over a short wooden fence along the road and raced across the land beyond it. My heartbeat thrummed hard and loud. If anyone called to me, I would not be able to hear him.

As I entered the tree line, I scanned the trunks, looking for one I could climb. I rushed among them, glancing back only once to confirm that the white froth still followed. Indeed, it chased only a few yards behind.

On my left, I spotted a tree that should work and bolted toward it. My calves burned as I launched myself at the tree. I jumped high, caught a branch, and swung my feet up and over. As the white fog rolled under me like silent thunder, the tree creaked and swayed. Holding myself onto the limb, my waist against the branch, I lifted my right foot up, and then my left, and stood, carefully balancing. I reached higher, caught another limb, and lifted myself the same way, pulling my legs over, swiveling around the limb, then upright with the branch at my waist. I wanted to climb higher, but no sturdy limbs remained. I bent low, gripped the trunk tightly, and steadied myself, my muscles on fire, my heart pounding. The white rolled under me.

White trees now populated the entirety of the woods, as though a disease had spread underground and soaked the sap from them.

In all my life I had never witnessed anything like this. Cyrus's boxes had worked on a small scale, indoors, hidden from the rest of the world. This, however, affected nature, where I had always believed it was safest to be. Four walls weren't closing me in, yet the rolling, bleaching tide trapped me.

From high up and far away, the current weakened. The height of the silent, mysterious fluid diminished. I released a slow, steadying breath, trying to calm my panic.

When I tried to speak into the mouthpiece to ask who was all right and who was not, my tongue froze on the tip of my teeth. It was possible that if even one of Roth's men died—and likely several had—the figure on the hill could have walked inside and taken one of the headsets. I didn't want to announce that I was alive, let alone the only survivor. I chose to keep my mouth shut, and I knew that if any of the men had survived, they would do the same.

They couldn't have survived, though, could they? Roth had been at least thirty feet from me. He could not have made it when I almost hadn't.

Below me, the fog began to clear. The fleece-like mass rolled back like a tide lowering and dissipating into nothing. A few wisps of smoke curled around the tree roots. They evaporated, and all stilled. I wondered if all the poisonous stuff was gone.

Bark had scraped my hands, and a smear of my blood stood out against the white trunk. I looked down at myself and realized that my clothes stuck out as the only dark features in the landscape. I would be noticed immediately and might already have been. I needed to get out of sight.

Trusting that the floor of the woods was now safe, I clasped the branch I crouched on and swung down until I dangled by my arms. The bark ground into my skin and beneath my nails. Suppressing a grunt, I tentatively dropped to the next branch and landed perfectly on it, balancing with one hand against the trunk of the tree. Instantly, I squatted and steadied myself. I grasped the last branch carefully and lowered myself again. I hit the ground.

The grass and dirt felt particularly dry beneath my boots. I dug at the ground with the toe of my right foot; beneath the white grains that fluoresced under the moon arrived fresh, black earth, as dark as coffee, and that comforted me.

I questioned if I should continue the way I was going or return to the house.

Either way, the land was clear, particularly so, the forest colorless, tinged a faint lemon hue from the moon.

A twig snapped behind me, and I turned.

Alex stood there, smiling. At the sight, my heart seemed to explode, and both terror and delight flooded me. Seeing him, a reminder of the old world, someone sharing my origin, made me experience something akin to nostalgia.

He stood between two white trees, his head slightly cocked. "It's been a while," he said. He pointed behind him, toward the house. "The costumes. Smart." He shook his head and sneered. "So smart. You had me fooled, I confess."

I took a deep breath and steadied myself. At least four months had passed since I'd last seen him. He and I had both changed.

"You're taller now," I said. "You must have grown a foot."

He nodded. "Your hair is longer."

That's not all, Alex, but I guess it's hard to notice in the night.

He stepped toward me. It sounded like he broke bones as he walked across the white twigs and leaves, through the white trees, his path lit brilliantly with moonglow. It was surreal to see him after so long, and in such a place. I slipped my hand into my pocket and clasped my knife. I thought once again of my vision of him on the table, the white monster looming over him, working inside him. In that vision, Alex's face and hair had whitened, and he had moved robotically. The Alex that stood before me appeared human, and he moved like I remembered. It made me wonder: If he had changed like I had changed, would I be able to see it? In the light of the moon from a distance, he did not see my transformation.

"Yes, the costumes were smart." He lifted his chin inquiringly. "But how did you turn the address red, and the door to the house? Plus that can of paint, hm? Oh yes, I see the realization in your eyes, and you are absolutely right. I know you were at Lucient. Flannigan showed me a tape of you there."

I said nothing. He began to walk around me, crunching through the grass as though it were ice. "No, no, that can't be the most important question. I haven't gone back far enough, have I? Let's start at the beginning. Why aren't you dead? How did you convince the Outfit not to kill you? To kill Julian instead? Answer me that first."

As he spoke, I tried to plan my next move. "If you don't know, you haven't looked hard enough."

"Oh?"

I opened the knife in my pocket carefully, making sure it didn't click as it locked into place. In the distance, behind Alex, white lights speckled the land—the unmoving lights attached to the bodies of Roth's men no longer burned orange.

"Wait. That's not the question I want answered either, is it?" Alex asked, smiling, seeming absolutely pleased with his own thought process, as though I might as well not even be there, he enjoyed it so much. He looked too much like Cyrus as he approached. The baby fat had disappeared from his cheeks. His hair glinted short, trim. He towered tall and thin. "No, no. The *real* question is, how did you help Lutin escape? How did you kill our father?"

I swallowed and tried to appear as calm as possible. I answered him honestly. "He made a mistake."

"What mistake?"

"Of underestimating me."

When Alex came closer, a box appeared in his right hand, and I stopped breathing. He lifted it, swung the object through the air and released it. It did not fall. It hovered three feet off the ground, as though resting on an invisible shelf. I marveled, until he reached into his pocket and retrieved a revolver. Alex pulled back the hammer.

"Have I underestimated you?" he asked. "I probably have, haven't I?" He looked me up and down. "What is it, then? What did my father not see? What have I not seen?" His eyes narrowed. "What could *you* possibly have to prevent a group of experienced men from killing you?" His eyes searched me, angry, probing.

As he walked around me, I readied myself. I planned to thrust my power out as far as it would reach, toward the glowing bodies in the field. Maybe I could resurrect them. If so, I didn't want Alex to see them rise before they had a chance to come to me.

"Yes... What is it about you, Jack, that would stop men hired to kill from killing? What did they see?" His eyes locked on me. Just as his view of Roth's men in the field was about to be obscured, he shifted direction. Silently I cursed.

"How were you able to turn that can of paint back to red? Did you collect Lutin's blood? Bury it somewhere? Keep it for future use?" he speculated quietly, more to himself than to me. "No. You would have needed *a lot* of blood for all that you've been up to."

He stopped circling, his blue eyes focused on the grass where I stood. I glanced down. Had my power slipped? Had the white shifted to color? He seemed fascinated. I saw nothing. All remained pale.

When I met Alex's eyes again, he tilted his head inquisitively, as though wondering why I had just checked the ground beneath my feet.

"Unless," he said, "there is a ferric there?" He waved the pistol outward.

"What is the Builder giving you," I asked, "in exchange for your loyalty? What is it you think are you getting out of it? Immortality? Transcendence?"

Alex continued as though I hadn't spoken. "One can of paint turned red when you were down in that lab. But when I questioned Patrick, he said he had never seen one of the creatures I described. Neither had Flannigan. So—how did you? Tell me now, before I shoot you. How were you able to—"

Alex stopped and stood perfectly still, silent, his pistol still pointed toward me. He gazed back across the field. "The image is half of it," he said pensively. "And the other half..."

How he reached the conclusion so suddenly, I couldn't comprehend, but he did. He gazed upon me with wide eyes, his realization clear to me. The pistol barrel drooped.

"Oh Jack, Jack, Jack... You..." He scanned me up and down, and then his eyes settled on my face, tracing the contours of my cheeks, searching the black of my pupils. "There is something about you that... You must trigger it. The can of paint. The door of the house. That would be the only way to explain... Ah!" He gasped. "There is something about *you*."

His eyes grew alight; he released the pistol to his side.

I nodded. The horridness of everything nearly made me chuckle. "Perhaps you are smarter than Cyrus."

I lifted the knife from my pocket and threw it. It penetrated his shoulder, and he dropped the gun.

He reached toward the box to his left, but I launched myself at him, landing my right foot just past him to trip him as I pushed. He fell backward and landed hard on the ground. I dropped to a knee, slid my hand around the knife handle, and wrenched it from his shoulder. His scream filled the night.

I raised the knife and stabbed down, but he covered himself with his arms. Instead of slicing into his chest, the knife cut through his jacket and entered his arm. I ripped it free and brought it down again, but Alex freed his foot and planted it firmly in my stomach, kicking me backward.

I landed on my back and felt the wind burst from my lungs, but the fall did not hurt me as much as it might have. When I gained my feet, Alex rose at the same time. I rammed my shoulder against him as he reached toward the hovering object.

We both collapsed. On the white floor of the woods lay the pistol. I reached for it. Alex slammed his hand on mine as I touched the pistol grip. He caught me around my neck with his other arm, cutting off my air. He rose to his knees and began to stand, lifting me. My left hand slipped inside my boot for the other knife.

When Alex heaved me up, my hand slipped. Using all the strength I had, I brought my knees to my chest, pressing his elbow more deeply into my neck. Black dots flooded my vision, but I ignored them. My hand fumbled at my ankle, until finally I found it.

Circling my hand around the handle, I pulled it free from my boot.

I prepared to stab him, and he shoved me forward. I landed on my knees and swung toward my left, but I missed.

When I rose from the ground again, his bloody arms were outstretched. "Wait," he gasped. "Wait!"

I staggered unsteadily between him and the box.

"You and I both know they'll enslave you!" he shouted. "It's only a matter of time. But I swear, if you come with me voluntarily, I won't."

"Bullshit," I said, my voice raspy and high. I gasped for air, unable to pull it into my lungs fast enough.

"I swear," he grunted as he stumbled. "Come with me. Resurrect our father, and all can be forgiven. It will be like it was." His chest rose and fell rapidly. He put his hands on his knees and attempted a smile. "Truly. I mean, do you not miss it? You must. This world...it is magicless. Meaningless. Boring." His hands dropped from their defensive position.

To bring back Cyrus—that was what he wanted? Or was it simply the appeal of joining him? Either way, I didn't want to repeat my childhood. I didn't want a father again. I wouldn't have it. "Fuck that."

He stared at me as we both struggled to regulate our breathing. "Jack, these are no friends of yours. They might let you believe they are for a short period of time, but we both know how this will end. There will be a chain around your neck, just like Cyrus put a chain around Lutin's. Don't pretend you don't know where you'll end up. He probably already has a basement prepared for you." An image of the white tiled room with silver gurneys flashed in my mind. My blood covered one of them. I shut the thought away.

"You're suddenly so worried about my neck?" I said. "Let *me* worry about my neck. You worry about yours."

I bolted toward him. He drew back a few steps and darted to the right, around me. I raised the knife, my fingertips on the blade. I tilted it just right and leaped at him.

As he jumped toward the box, I managed to slip the knife into his back, just above his kidney. I pushed it inside his body to the hilt.

There was no question. The wound was fatal.

He gasped and pushed toward the floating object, his hands reaching out. Before I could stop him, he fell on top of it. When he connected, the box and his body both vanished. Only white dirt and grass remained, small splashes of blood in the leaves. The person it had come from was gone. I stood in the woods alone.

What?

I circled, ready to defend myself, ready to attack. There was nothing. Silence. I stood there, stunned.

I dropped to my knees and scrabbled at the dirt in rage. His body should have been right there! His corpse should have been at my feet! I should have been watching the light leave his eyes.

Alex's blood covered my hands. It glittered black in the moonlight and darkened the white ground. Blood and blood and blood, and yet no body. It made no sense.

He had to be dead, no matter where his body fell. He had to be. Yes, he did. But was he? God damn it! *Was he*?

I cried in rage and leaned forward on my hands, clutching the blood-soaked leaves into two fistfuls. For the next several minutes I sat there, heaving, trying to steady my breath and my fury. But both seemed to rise and rise.

I gazed toward the white lights in the field, all the dead men, Roth's men, and I blamed them for not listening to me. If Alex was alive, he now knew what I was. He would want to collect me.

But he had to be dead, didn't he?

The vision of the monster opening him up returned, and my breath caught in my throat. I watched it again. Something inside me knew it was happening somewhere, not so far away but not in this world. As I sat there in the dirt, my vision came true. That creature was the Builder, and the Builder placed a bit of itself into Alex. I had no doubt. As soon as the knowledge came to me that it happened, it ended. Somewhere, Alex transformed into something new, and the curtain closed again.

I wiped my hands on my pants and walked to the road, toward the corpses, and soon stood among them, staring, not moving, not resurrecting them. It would be better to leave them as they were. It would be best to leave New York.

A pair of headlights on the road crested the hill. Then another and another. Four pairs of lights approached, blinding me with their light, and my body surged with adrenaline.

Reflexively, I channeled my anger down into my core and loosed the inner spring. The sensation of fizzing carbonated blood filtered through me. The trees and grass shifted back to their original hues. Color returned along the hill and through the woods, reversing the damage of the box. In my earpiece, gasps from ten breaths resounded in unison. The glowing orange stripes on the flat earth began to move, rise, and straighten.

"Jack, is that you?" a voice said into my headset.

"There are cars on the road. Someone's coming," I replied.

I began to run toward the house, out of view of the SUVs, before Roth replied, "I know. I know. I called for backup. They're coming to help."

I stopped, and my heart sank. "Oh," I said, my voice flat.

"Are you hurt?" Roth asked. Among the vast darkness and the now-moving men, one of them emerged, walking toward me. It was Roth.

"No."

"Good." A confused expression swept over his face. He looked me up and down, and then his hand ran over the blood-stained places on my clothes.

"Shit."

"It's Alex's." Ten men exited the vehicles and convened with those I had just reanimated. "I stabbed him."

He sighed in relief and looked toward the trees. "Where is he?"

"Gone."

"Dead?"

I winced. Fuck. "I don't know. His...body disappeared after I stabbed him."

Roth gazed at me. He patted my arms. "Show me."

"We should get her checked out first," Jasper said, suddenly standing next to me.

"I'm fine."

"She's fine," Roth said emphatically. "Now, show me."

I walked him to the area and described everything that had taken place. When I finished, he peered warily around, seeing nothing and no one but nevertheless on edge, as though someone else might be there, someone bigger, more monstrous, ready to kill him. "Come on. It's time to leave this place."

He called his men in, and they walked to the vehicles. Reluctantly, I followed. Roth's breath streamed into the air slower and slower. His stride shortened, but his grip on my arm never slackened. It never would. I wouldn't have resurrected him if the SUVs hadn't arrived. I thought they had belonged to Alex or Flannigan. Roth's backup had saved him in a way he didn't realize.

"You shouldn't have gone about it this way," I said, half to myself. "These new boxes have evolved."

"We will regroup," Roth replied. "Plan again." His voice rang flat, like a bell landing on concrete.

He escorted me to the car.

I did not blame him for sounding uncertain or for escorting me. We had both just realized he was not enough.

CHAPTER 27
UNITY IN BLOOD

ROTH DIDN'T HAVE A PLAN for Alex, but he did have a plan for Lucient, and he exercised it quickly. In the comforts of his office, Roth and I sat at the large conference table. The windows were cracked open, and the mint curtains swayed in the light wind. We sat in two comfortable leather chairs and observed on multiple television screens his men driving onto Bryan Flannigan's property. They breezed through the gate after one of Roth's men killed the security guard.

I had already pointed out to them Building 1C on a map, and Roth and I watched through the men's bodycams as the Outfit swarmed it. Several cars veered left and right to other areas in the complex, while one particular vehicle stopped outside the door Patrick had taken me to. Four men bolted out of the car.

One of them shot the lock and yanked the door open. Men filed into the dimly lit hall and turned right. Arriving at the glass door, they shot through it and walked inside. They fired through the next lock. At last, they marched across the grated balcony and trotted down the stairs.

I feared the mechanism would not be there, that someone would have moved it, but when they reached the ground floor, there it stood—open, quiet, waiting for another can of paint to bleach. I breathed a sigh of relief.

All around them towered white paint cans.

"That's it," I said. Roth looked over the table at me.

The man with the bodycam rounded the structure once, placing his hand on it, exploring its tiny grooves. In the distance, beyond the walls of the building, burst the *pop, pop, pop* of gunfire.

"Doesn't look so intimidating to me," the man observed. Someone handed him two blocks of orange-red putty, and he pressed the substance along both sides of the machine.

"You have no interest in seeing how it works?" I asked Roth, testing him.

He smirked and sipped his bourbon. "That is not the sort of power I am interested in. This," he said, waving to the camera, where we could see the man attaching red putty along the machine, "is my power. And it has always worked."

After the man applied the explosives to the base of the machine, another man checked it and nodded.

Clean. Efficient. There was no mystical destruction, no white thing crawling around taking lives. There was just the red brick putty, minus the detection taggant, that would blast the brick, stone, and concrete away.

It was normal power to a paranormal level.

They left the building the way they came and retreated to the car. Car doors slammed, and the driver transported everyone beyond the gate. There, three other cars waited.

"Take one last look," Roth said to me.

I gazed at the massive Lucient buildings visible on multiple screens.

From within one of the vehicles, a man pressed a button, and an explosion followed. Another. Another. Five in total. Though miles away and safe at Purdom, I felt the pulse of power and wave of heat. In the live video, the blast rocked the vehicle. The man who pressed the first button waited a few seconds and then pressed another. Three more explosions rocked the air.

I smiled as the night sky illuminated on the video. I couldn't help myself.

"And we're out," Roth said. The car began moving. All four vehicles went on their way. Roth pressed a button on the large remote, and the screens went black. Silence.

In the aftermath of a battle that, this time, we didn't fight, I sat back and breathed. Asher poured us some coffee, and the same no-name doctor-on-call who had checked me after I had died inspected the bruises on my neck, the remnants of the scrapes on my hands. They were nearly healed already, and when he realized that, he pursed his lips and began to sweat. He whispered something to Roth about me being fine before he hurried out of the room. Roth eyed me.

"There is a better way to go about this job. Something safer for us and more efficient," he said.

It took a while to summon the energy to respond. "Oh?"

He pressed his hands together into a steeple, the tips of his middle fingers beneath his chin. "We have the maps from 405 Brimmer. They identify the locations of many followers' houses, hundreds of them, all across the country.

"If you were to resurrect some men for me, say a hundred and sixty men I have known over the years—trustworthy men—we could enter all of those houses in one, maybe two, nights and execute them. It would be quick."

We locked eyes as he spoke.

"If we execute Cyrus's group in two nights, there will be no time for them to prepare or plan. We can rescue the children more quickly. And, if Alex is alive—hopefully the bastard is not—but if he is and the others are dead, he won't have any place to run. There will be no Infinitum. And in this plan, there is no waiting for *him* to come to *us*."

I pictured again the shiny white monster bending over Alex and bit the inside of my lip. "Ensuring Alex's death by proxy," I said halfheartedly. "That's a good idea. What is an injured, perhaps dead, king without his rooks, bishops, knights, and queen?"

Roth nodded.

I betrayed no reaction, but inside, I winced. That plan required a lot of trust, and I did not trust Roth anymore. More importantly, I wouldn't trust one hundred and sixty newly resurrected individuals.

"I know what you're thinking. This requires a lot of confidence on your part," he finished for me. "But I guarantee that if you grant me the lives of these one hundred and sixty people, I can have this problem taken care of in one or two nights."

Two nights.

The words echoed in my head, and the greedy part of my heart that so desperately wanted Infinitum dead lunged toward the idea. I imagined my past problems completely obliterated in the span of only two evenings. But then I thought of Alex's words. *You know they are going to lock you up.*

The way that Roth spoke, he didn't expect a fight from me. It was as though he anticipated I was already thinking yes.

But I wasn't. If I did what he asked, he would become unstoppable.

I sipped the bourbon Roth had shared.

"I will accompany your *living* employees to each of the houses," I said. "If they die, I will resurrect them, but I'm not going to resurrect others. I'm not going to build you an army." I shook my head. "I just won't."

Any warmth in Roth's gaze disappeared. What sat before me was Cyrus, but without the charisma.

"That's unfortunate," he whispered, almost robotically, "because the bodies are being extracted as we speak, and they're coming here tonight."

I cocked my head, my heart beginning to thrum hard.

"Then I guess you'll have to rebury them."

"I'm not reburying them." His tone rumbled even, level, assured.

I swallowed. The room grew quiet. Jasper stood very near me, and I suspected he might grab me if I attempted to stand. Fear, fear that had already visited me when Roth's backup arrived, resurfaced.

"You promised me," I said, "that you could do this job because you were the best. You never mentioned needing one hundred and sixty more men to do it."

"You never told us what Alex's box could do," he said. His eyes narrowed. "We died for you, went out of our way for you to the fullest extent. You now owe us a favor to the fullest extent. Besides…something in my own life, has come up."

"What?"

He sighed and pursed his lips. "Someone I know very well, someone who tried to do me in with that unveiling of new DNA evidence in McFadden's death, has declared a war on me. I can't fight your war and my own at the same time. Not right now."

Whether or not this was true didn't change anything for me. With my power, I could grow a group of formerly dead individuals out of proportion with the natural laws of the world. But that road could only lead to dangerous, chaotic, and irreversible consequences.

"It sounds like that's your problem," I said. "I'm not going to resurrect those bodies."

Without warning, Roth jumped at me. His eyes narrowed, and his mouth opened wide, like an animal's. He stopped just inches from my face and banged his fist on the table. He swept my bourbon and coffee off the surface, and the glasses shattered against the wall beneath the television. He roared at the top of his lungs, "*You will!*" His eyes widened, his face flushed red. Spit splattered the table and my clothes. "*I have done enough for you!*"

I punched the base of his throat. He choked, gagging. I pushed my chair back and took off, but Jasper caught my arm and jerked me back, hard. I fell against him. "Sorry, kid," he said, and something sharp slid into my neck just as I elbowed him in the side. He grunted. His grip slackened, but he didn't release me.

A warm burning entered the left side of my neck, and then the sharp sensation relinquished. I drifted, as though suddenly in a room made of dough or clouds. He'd injected me with something hard and unyielding that demanded I go down. I did, hitting the floor, boneless and feeling nothing. Roth's black shoes appeared in front of me. He knelt, rubbing his throat. His face blurred, as did the whole room. He said one last thing before I passed out: "Alex is moot until things are in order." A hand grabbed my chin and lifted my head. Roth's breath covered my face. "So it's in your best interest to help me. Hm?"

I woke on gray concrete. An endless line of blue tarps stretched out before me with pale, decomposing bodies on them. A pair of boots entered my vision. The person who owned them squatted down.

Roth's face appeared, the deep-cut lines in his cheeks particularly dark beneath the fluorescents. He opened his arms wide. "This is your first lesson. You are here, with us, permanently. We are your new family, and you will help *us*."

My mouth felt dry, and when I spoke, my throat squeaked. "*Your* first lesson," I said, "is that I'm not the sort of person to allow you to tell me what to do."

Roth's black eyes narrowed. "I guess we're about to find out whose lesson is law, aren't we?"

Jasper and Asher arrived on either side and lifted me. They set me upright in a chair and held me, steadying me amidst my drowsiness. The garage brightened, darkened, and then brightened again. The hum of the fluorescent lights drowned everything. Before me, lines of dead bodies seemed to stretch for miles. Their stench hit me in waves.

"You're going to resurrect them," he said.

I took a deep breath and shook my head to rouse myself as best I could. "No."

He hit me, hard, straight in the mouth. My head snapped back, my neck cracked. My lips split against my teeth. The medicinal taste of iron dripped into my mouth as I lowered my head. The blood that slipped down my chin tickled. I waited for the shock from the punch to relent, and it did. Far more quickly than it should have. Was it the drugs? I didn't think so.

I opened my eyes and looked around the room, realizing that I could see everything clearly, as though Roth hadn't just hit me.

My gaze flicked to him. "You're going to have to punch me a lot harder than that, Roth. I don't feel things like I used to."

"Jack," said a voice behind me. The deep, gravelly sound belonged to Jasper. "Don't bring it to a boiling point. You won't win."

"He's right. You won't," Roth said. "You'll save yourself a lot of pain if you just do what I ask now."

Staring at him, considering my options, knowing where this headed, I began to feel true fear, as true as being in the grip of the shining white monster from my vision. It bloomed in every crevice of every capillary and vein. I tried my best to hide it.

"I wouldn't hurt me, if I were you," I said, latching onto the first argument that came to mind. "The others—the ones who made me—are going to come, and it only takes them seconds to burn through thousands."

Roth stepped back. "See, I've been thinking about that." He clasped his hands together, as if in prayer. "I don't think they will come. Why would they leave you here alone if they wanted you? Why didn't they take you in? Even when you died, they didn't come. Even while I had my men working on your cell, they didn't come."

Cell? Roth had been building a cell?

I tried to swallow, but my mouth dried.

"My guess is that you aren't their type." He tilted his head. "You're not quite like us...but you're not quite like them either, are you?"

My mind went blank. How had he known? Had the truth been so obvious?

"Maybe," I admitted. "But I don't think they're going to enjoy the idea of hundreds of *your* type coming back to life."

He smiled. "Perhaps." His smile disappeared. "It's a risk I'm willing to take. Now, I'm giving you one more chance, Jack."

"Do it," Jasper urged behind me.

I shook my head, feeling my hair hit the sides of my face. Some of it clung to the blood on my chin. Already, my lips no longer hurt, as though the skin had sealed itself. It was as though no one had ever hit me.

Roth shrugged. "So be it."

Jasper and Asher cuffed my arms to the chair. I shivered. I had no gun, no knife, no options. Five people, all of them killers, surrounded me in the depths of a secluded garage. I didn't stand a chance.

I winced and waited for the punches to commence, wondering how long I could hold out. Maybe five minutes? Ten? The truth was, Roth was right. I might save myself a lot of pain if I just did as he asked, and it was possible that resurrecting those bodies was inevitable.

The elevator door dinged behind me, and its doors opened. The squeaking of a cart's wheels resounded as something rolled out. The sound traveled across the floor of the garage, closer and closer to me, until it arrived in front. On top of the cart sat a small gramophone with a shining brass bell.

I straightened in the chair and gritted my teeth.

Roth reached across the gramophone and lifted the arm, moved it above the record, which began to spin, and deliberately began to drop it.

"Roth," I said, my heart lurching, my voice warning him like one would a small child swinging a pair of scissors, "you don't know what you're doing. Put it down."

Roth's head swiveled toward me. His eyebrows arched high. His hand perched, dangling the arm and needle perfectly above the vinyl.

If he let go, the lively white goo would ooze from the widening bell and consume me. Trapped in the chair, I would have no chance. And there was no knowing how it would grow with a soul half or more ferric.

"Are you ready to help us?" Roth asked.

I licked my lips, wondering if the gramophone would even work outside the confines of the Victorian house, away from the man who had originally owned it. My bet was that it would—just as the paint worked away from Lucient, just as Alex's box worked in the forest. Not only that, but for all I knew, this gramophone might alert Infinitum, as well as the Builder, to exactly where I was.

Roth dropped the arm further toward the record, which spun faster, excitedly, as though it knew who and what it sat in front of. The bell expanded slightly in size, like a stomach preparing for a meal. The men around me moved back.

It felt like I was already falling into the center of the bell, into the black pit, unable to help myself. The needle hovered, bare centimeters from touching down.

"Stop," I said, unable to stand both my surrender and what Roth threatened. "Turn it off. I'll resurrect them."

Roth did not stop the spinning record, and he left his hand where it was. Tormented by the idea of him dropping the needle, I assured him once again that I would resurrect the men, and, slowly, he lifted the gramophone arm. I collapsed against the chair and broke into a cold sweat.

"You don't know what you're doing," I said.

"No," he replied. "I have a very good idea of what I am doing. You are just now figuring it out. Now, as you were told." He swung his arm toward the bodies on the tarps. They stretched on and on. How anyone could dig up so many in such a short time I didn't know. How long had I been knocked out? Days?

"I need to get up to do it," I said.

Pursing his lips, looking like he doubted my sincerity, Roth nevertheless motioned for Jasper and Asher to undo my restraints.

When free, I got up. I walked between the bodies, Roth right behind me the entire time, until I stopped halfway down the line. I glanced back at Roth just once to check his resolute expression. Faster than they likely expected, I let the power trickle out of me. I woke the corpses four at a time, walking down the space between them. Sixty individuals woke in rags spoiled by human gases and liquids. The acrid smell that filled the garage decreased remarkably. When I finished, the men exclaimed, most of them wondering, some of them demanding to know, what had happened and where they were. Jasper grabbed my arm and tugged me toward the elevator. I resisted, jerking away. But then someone grabbed me by the neck and propelled me forward, and I fell into Jasper's hands again.

"Brothers!" Roth called out to the living men. "I have woken you!"

Cyrus might as well have been the one speaking. My heart leaped. Tears welled as I crossed the threshold of the double doors. The terror inside me bloomed. At the last second, I dashed out of the elevator and began to call one of the men I had just reanimated for help, but Jasper slapped a hand over my mouth. He and Asher hauled me back in before the doors could register that my body stuck halfway out.

I screamed against Jasper's hand, and a needle pricked my neck. The elevator became swimmy, and I expected to drop. Rather than blacking out, though, I felt groggy, so groggy that fear abandoned me, so groggy I couldn't stand. The elevator dinged, going down, deeper into the core of Purdom. Asher supported me, or perhaps both of them did, and then the doors opened onto a terribly bright white room with a white tile floor. I recognized it. I had died there.

They took me to the gurney.

"Relax, now, Jack," Jasper said. "I don't want to hurt you."

Something stung my arm. He'd inserted an IV at the bend in my elbow. A line of red blood flowed into a bag hanging from a metal hook. I should have been scared, but fear had disappeared along with every other sensation.

"Ever since you resurrected Emily," Jasper said, his hands in his pockets, his eyes narrowing, "we have been wondering what else your blood can do—if it can heal, if it can prevent men from dying… at least for a period of time. We wondered even more after you died and came back."

He stood at the head of the table, and I looked up at him, upside down, through a fog of chemicals. "And what can it do?" I said.

"We are going to find out."

Somehow, through the haze, rage blossomed in my chest. As Jasper walked to a nearby table, I managed to grab the IV with my left hand and jerk it out of my arm. I slid off the table, fell, and crawled forward, toward the doors. Blood streamed from my arm. Arms arrived to surround me, lift me, and Jasper muttered, "What a mess." Another needle pierced my neck. "Sorry I have to do this."

The bright white sterile room darkened, and a peaceful nonexistence washed over me.

It was like I was dead again.

CHAPTER 28
HIVE LIVES

I WOKE ON A METAL gurney. An IV bag full of my blood hung beside me. To my left, ten—no, fifteen…no, twenty—more bags of blood rested on a shelf.

Twenty. How long had I been out? How was I not dead?

"Your body replenishes itself quickly," someone beside me said. It was Roth. He leaned against a counter, arms crossed over his chest. "And that's good, because it turns out that your blood can heal people. Not only that, but it can prevent people from getting hurt for about twenty-four hours. After twenty-four hours, they just have to dose again."

I went to move, but blue ropes strapped down my ankles and wrists. My first memory of Roland came to mind, and I felt nauseous. I fell back against the surface, letting my head drop with a bang.

"We still need you to resurrect about a hundred more bodies that we are bringing in, but after that, it seems we can just use your blood to prevent damage."

He walked around the table to my right, and two individuals joined him—Jasper and someone I had never seen before. The man held a pen and a journal, making notes. He stood beside a tall table that had once held the instruments for removing the bullet from my body. It now held three objects that appeared to be asthma inhalers.

Roth said, "We experimented to see how much of your blood we needed to keep men alive, how much was necessary to heal their wounds. About three drops will do it, or about 150 microliters. It has to enter the bloodstream, however. You can't just rub blood on the skin.

"So John here," Roth slapped a man on his back, "one of the wonderful people you resurrected, had a brilliant idea." The man named John chuckled. "He started experimenting with a reliable delivery system, so we don't have to inject it. In the heat of a fight, that takes too much time. He came up with this." Roth picked up an inhaler.

"Metered dose inhalers," Roth said. He turned the small device over in his hands.

"It delivers the exact amount the men need. It's inconspicuous, so if anyone were to find one, it wouldn't be like discovering a syringe on a body. They'll carry brown prescription labels, as though for steroids from a pharmacy. You know, in case they're discovered for some reason by someone outside Purdom."

He set the inhaler down on the table. "I guess even if someone had asthma, this would clear it up," he remarked wistfully.

"Minimal waste is involved. The blood won't dry up or solidify. It's transported straight to the lungs where it's absorbed into the bloodstream. I've already tested it. Each metered dose provides four drops of blood, not three—that seems to prevent gunshot wounds or knife wounds for up to twenty-four hours, but only *once* every twenty-four hours. If we are shot, we have to take another metered dose."

He sighed, as though relieved. "This whole process has been... miraculous. The only really unfortunate thing was how we had to figure all of this out. We had to shoot ourselves to ensure it would work. Trial and error, again and again. No pain, no gain, though." He smiled.

"How many doses per inhaler?" Jasper asked calmly, looking at John.

"I'm limiting it to ten," John said. "And we should require the men to log each dose. At the end of each day, the inhalers are returned to the vaults. At the beginning of each day, they're picked up."

"Excellent," Roth said. He glanced at me, seemingly pleased. Why shouldn't he be? He possessed an unstoppable army, armored with my blood.

"Don't look so unhappy, Jack. Many of these doses will go toward stopping your brother. I told you I would destroy him, and I will. There's no knowing what he has planned next, but your blood will help us. And, as I told you before, we have our own problems. Our line of work is the most hazardous…or it used to be."

Roth's expression shifted. "Now that I'm confident you're not going anywhere, I'll be frank with you. I owe you that, I suppose. Purdom is having territory problems with our competition. During wars like this, there are, of course, casualties. You would not believe some of the familial costs we have suffered."

Jasper studied me, as if to check my reaction.

"But we can correct that, too."

The hive of Purdom buzzed around me, the men planning, creating their own technology to benefit from my blood in more places than I could possibly be at one time. It had expanded much more quickly than I could have foreseen. Worse still, I couldn't react. Whether from the drugs or the loss of blood, I could barely move.

"And that isn't all," Roth said, smiling.

He walked to a table and retrieved an object I had never seen before.

"Insulin pump. Wounded men can't always reach for an inhaler, especially if they're unconscious or dead. So we're trying out these. They should work, especially if your blood continues to become more potent. Someday, when you become fully ferric, as I suspect you will, your blood may be able to resurrect."

How long had I been out? Months. It had to be months for all this to have happened.

He stared, waiting for me to say something. There was nothing, though, for me to say. I could do nothing. I couldn't even move or think.

"All we need you to do now is produce your life-saving blood. Luckily, it seems that since your death, you produce blood as quickly as it is taken from you."

Roth set the insulin pump on the table and came to stand beside me.

"After we collect the blood we need, I will let you rest in a room nearby. We don't want the men to see you. We don't want them to know about you. Right now, they think this power is coming from me. It's safer for you that way."

He kept waiting for me to say something. Instead, I turned away from him, closing my eyes.

Roth pressed his hand to my arm and shook me. "I know you probably want to sleep, but there's one more thing I need you to do, Jack. And you must be awake for it."

I looked at him.

"Patrick has been leaving texts and voice messages on your cell. I need you to tell him you've left the state, that you are all right, but you are not coming back. He seems to be worried about you, and as his father's disappearance will more clearly mean his father's death, all of Flannigan's assets are going to go to him. He will be able to start searching for you with that increased level of money and resources, and we don't want that.

"If he figures out where you are, I will kill him. For the boy's sake, you need to call him and say good-bye."

I breathed deep and let the breath out slowly.

Roth retrieved my phone from his inner pocket and held it out to me.

Though I loathed him, he was right. I didn't want Patrick snooping around Purdom, and I didn't want Roth to destroy him as he had destroyed Bryan Flannigan. I looked into Roth's dark eyes and nodded. "Give me the phone." My voice cracked.

Roth released my restraints, and I sat up, woozy and drained. I wondered again how long I had been down here.

I grabbed the phone. Roth held on to it until I looked at him.

"If you tell him anything, I will kill him."

"I know you will."

He relinquished the phone.

CHAPTER 29
EXTIMATE

PATRICK PICKED UP ON THE third ring. The relief in his voice resonated, palpable. "Jack, I've been calling you for a month."

There. That was my answer. They had kept me out for a month. I winced.

"I know," I said. Noticing my weak voice, I sat straighter and breathed deeper, urging my tone to become strong and certain. "I haven't been picking up because I've already left the city, Patrick."

"Why?"

"I, uh, I had some family issues down south, in Louisiana. I had to come here for a little while."

"Well, when are you coming back?"

"I don't know." Tears stung my eyes. My chest filled with grief. "I don't know if I'm coming back."

Roth watched me from the other side of the room.

"I see. Listen, Jack. I called to apologize for what happened at the Lucient banquet and to let you know I'm all right. You might not have heard, but my father went missing, and a group of individuals bombed

Lucient. I am really, *really* freaked out. I'm not sure… I think he's… I'm not sure he's ever coming back."

I stifled the sob rising in my throat. "I'm so sorry. I didn't know. Why would someone bomb Lucient?"

"No one can even guess…I've just got this feeling…Things have gone horribly wrong. I don't feel safe."

"You should trust your feelings," I said. "I'm sorry, whatever comes of it."

During the long pause that followed, I had no idea what Patrick was thinking. I had already said my part, and I had come across as distant and insincere. But it had been enough to get the job done.

"Look. It seems like you're busy or something, so I'm going to let you go. Before I do, though, I want to thank you."

I frowned and wiped a tear from my eye. "Thank me? For what?"

"For what you said to me, at Lucient. You are right. I am a child, or I have been, far longer than necessary. And, well… I've decided I'm going to start taking control. It looks like I may have to take over Lucient. I enrolled in a rehab program, and I just want to thank you for helping me take responsibility for my actions. I'm planning on going back to school and making something of myself."

"That's so good to hear, Patrick," I said. The praise in my voice sounded genuine. "I had no idea I had that effect on you."

"Me neither," he said, "No one has ever called me out on my bullshit. I've never had to take control. And it's tough. Hell, it feels like I'm trying to grow a supernatural power. It's all alien and scary, and it feels completely unwieldy, but I'm getting better. I'm getting more powerful, now that I'm working it." He laughed.

I smiled. "It makes me so happy to hear that. It was the last thing I expected you to tell me."

Patrick chuckled. "They expect a flicker from me, and I give them stars."

I closed my eyes and hung onto those words.

"I'll let you go. Let me know if you're ever back in Manhattan."

"I will," I said. "Best of luck to you, Patrick."

"Keep it," he said. "The Irish have whiskey, and that's good enough."

"Good-bye."

"Bye, Jack."

We hung up, and I lingered on the edge of an emotional abyss until Roth held out his hand. I surrendered my phone. He slipped it into his pocket. "Very good, Jack. Now we'll go up a few floors so you can resurrect the rest of the men I need, and then I'll show you to your new quarters."

"I don't think I have it in me."

Roth grabbed my shoulder and squeezed hard. "You do."

CHAPTER 30
CAGE

AFTER I RESURRECTED THE HUNDRED men in the garage, Roth and Jasper escorted me to the elevator, which began dropping through the basement levels.

As we descended, Roth said, "As soon as we bombed Lucient, the entire state became full of red doors, mailboxes, and address numbers. Articles online described it as a mass prank. Unfortunately, this did not happen before Infinitum burned the cathedral where you resurrected Emily. I checked on it after we bombed Lucient, realizing it might have already been given a white address label, and you might have turned it red. Sure enough. And they utterly destroyed it."

I wasn't sure why Roth thought I would care.

"A gorgeous building gone. I am paying to have it rebuilt. The place is worth rebuilding. Protecting. My daughter's second birthplace."

When the doors opened, we walked down a single hallway toward what appeared to be a round vault. At the sight of it, my heart pounded, and I screamed inside. I would go insane if they made me step past the threshold. I struggled to turn back.

Roth and Jasper grabbed my arms and held me in place. They forced me, step by step, toward my cage.

Past the rounded threshold, they held me firmly. "It's not much, but… it's yours." He waved openly.

A cream room met me, half behind a set of bars, half not. Behind bars sat a bed, a desk, and a chair. To the left stood a bathroom. On the other side of the bars a desk, a computer, and a chair faced my barred living area. Four video cameras, one in each corner of the room, pointed toward my side of the cell. The shiny, metallic walls mimicked a vault.

"Various men will take shifts to keep an eye on you, so you will never actually be alone. In addition, I'll observe you from my office. We would have put certain measures in place if we thought you might try to kill yourself, but I'm fairly certain you can't die, even by your own hand.

"We'll take blood from you daily here.

"If you show no resistance, after a period of time I'll consider allowing you in the higher levels now and again, but I haven't decided.

"Anyone we need you to resurrect, you will resurrect here. You will not be allowed to leave. Anything you might need, we will bring you. We'll place a treadmill over there." He nodded toward the left wall.

I looked around at the sparse surroundings. "My clothes?"

"They'll be brought down tomorrow. In the meantime, I suggest you get some rest." Jasper escorted me into the cell, and the bars clanged behind me.

"Thank you for not resisting so much this time," Roth said before he left.

His footsteps faded. The other men and Jasper turned and walked away. Only one person remained, sitting at the desk.

The lights extinguished, and the glow from a computer screen lit his face.

"Go to sleep," he said.

Without bothering to change clothes, I walked to the bed and lay down. I pulled the covers over me. With the comforter piled on top of me, I did something I'd promised I wouldn't do.

I prayed to Lutin. I whispered in the dark as I cried.

"Don't leave me down here. Not after all we've been through. Not after what you've given me. I'm sorry I fucked up. Don't leave me. Please, don't leave me here."

This prayer circled my mind on repeat.

But my intuition was right.

Lutin never came.

CHAPTER 31
A FEW LESS THAN INFINITY

Jasper took my blood daily, and he brought me my meals, as well as things from my apartment.

While I gave blood, I stared at the ominous golden thing they had put on the other side of the cell, pressed against the wall—the miniature gramophone. Its eye, like Roth's, never veered from me.

I gave three pints of blood daily. Otherwise, I paced around my small room and prayed. I didn't ask Roth what he did or planned. I didn't care. I just wanted Lutin to come and save me. I had never asked to be saved before, but now I begged for it. I wondered if I were the same person. Was I breaking down into something unlike myself with each and every prayer?

Sometimes I watched whichever man sat behind the computer. I'd scratch my nose, and he would scratch his nose. I'd cough and lean back on the bed. He would cough and lean back in his chair. I would think. And so would he.

And then I'd stare at the gramophone.

I became bored, so bored that eventually I decided to test the boundaries by refusing to give blood one day.

"Don't play with me," Roth said.

"I'm not playing. I want to see the sunlight. I want to go outside."

"There will be no conversation. You'll do as you're told. Sit down."

"No."

The man behind the desk winced and looked down at his hands.

Roth loomed before me. He pulled his fist back and punched me in the face, hard enough to let me know he wasn't joking. The hit blinded me momentarily, but I recovered. The pain passed, and I balanced again. In less than half a minute, I felt fine.

Roth pulled back and hit me again, even harder. I toppled. On the floor, I checked my nose for blood. None appeared, and all discomfort vanished. I looked up at him, my eyes open, my mind clear. No nausea filled my stomach, no sting from tears.

"You heal quickly now, hm?" He shook his hand. He was the one in pain.

I couldn't help but smile.

"Laugh all you want, but I'll figure something out. Next time, maybe it won't be you I hit. Next time, it will be Patrick. Or maybe I'll play that gramophone."

I bit the inside of my cheek, thinking perhaps I shouldn't test the boundaries. I didn't want Patrick hurt, and I didn't want Roth to use the gramophone on me. I sat down on the edge of the bed, relenting and rolling up my sweater sleeve. I offered my arm. "When are you going to let me out of here?"

"When I can trust you," Roth said.

For another week, I spoke to no one. I weakened. My eyes dried and glazed from the recirculated air and synthetic lights. With nothing to put my mind on, my thoughts lost delineation, and I transformed in a way I had never expected—receding.

I studied the gramophone and considered allowing them to use the device on me, let them drop the needle and play the record. It would be better than staying in this cell forever. Lutin might have been able to bear it for ten years. I couldn't last that long. Whatever they chipped away in me would not grow back, not in the way it had popped back, full bloom, in him. Not a full-fledged ferric, I didn't have the mental wherewithal to last a decade in a cell. Nor did I have the strength to snap everyone's neck and flee.

I felt stupid—stupid for trusting Roth in the first place, stupid for making an agreement with him, stupid for having been so hell bent on destroying Infinitum and Alex. I had failed at everything. And if I had succeeded, it would have been nothing compared to the shiny white monster in my vision. The Builder had saved my brother after I stabbed him. My victories were pointless wastes of time and energy.

Lutin's brother, Osric, was right. Evil was a metonymy. A shot, a stab, a murder, a theft, a disease, and on, and on, and on. Getting rid of a few of infinity never altered infinity. There was the cult, and there was Roth, and after Roth there would be something else, and after the something else would come another something, if I lived that long.

If I wanted to stop the metonymy, I couldn't deal with the few. I had to go to the source itself. I had to stop the monster, the Builder. So I considered again the gramophone. If it linked to the Builder, perhaps I could speak to him through it. Perhaps he would hear me.

The outer room door opened, and Jasper stepped inside. I frowned and readied myself. My eyes drifted from the gramophone to my arm, and I rolled up my sleeve. The man behind the desk stood to meet Jasper. Jasper held a black pistol and shot him three times. The guard fell backward, over the desk, toppling the computer to the floor. His body jerked as blood poured from his wounds across the desk and onto the concrete floor. He slammed against the ground.

My jaw dropped.

At my cell door, Jasper swiped his card. With a *click*, the door opened.

"Come on," he said, waving me through. "We don't have much time."

I jumped from my bed and sprinted toward the open cell. "What did you do?"

His mutt-like face curled with a brief grin. "The video cameras are on loop for the next five minutes. A car is in the garage. I'm getting you out of here."

Something in my chest swelled, the shadow of hope, and I wasted no time. I rushed to the body on the floor and grabbed the gun from the guard's holster. Jasper nodded, a grim look on his face, and we left the cell. I shivered with delight over both the terror and excitement. My pulse pounded in my throat, and my mind scattered in a million directions.

We cleared the hall and jogged toward the elevator.

"Why are you helping me?"

"You are too important for Purdom."

Jasper had propped a brick against one side of the open elevator door. He kicked it out and pressed the button for the garage level. When the doors closed, he readied his weapon. His forehead glimmered with sweat, his breath ragged. He checked his watch. "Three minutes."

I held the gun in both hands, ready for when the doors opened. My eyes met Jasper's, and a trickle of sweat rolled down his weathered face. He looked like he needed a vacation.

"I'm sorry about the blood," he said. "I had to, though."

I almost laughed. "I get it."

The numbers ticked up and up. We arrived at the garage level. "The car is on the left," Jasper said. "Run."

I readied myself to bolt. The doors opened.

Roth and ten men appeared. In horror, I lifted my gun and shot Roth in the head several times and again in the chest. With every shot, he winced, but nothing more. Where the bullets pierced his forehead, the wounds closed. He looked down at himself as if his clothes were just a little disheveled.

Jasper fired, ripping into the men's bodies before us. The fabric of their suits exploded, and their bodies jerked. They stood unmoving, as if it were nothing.

The elevator doors started to close, but Roth put his hand on one side, stopping them. "I don't think so."

Two of the men jumped on Jasper. I hit one of them in the back of the head with my gun, but hands grabbed me from behind, and I sank under their weight, unable to reach the surface.

They dragged Jasper out of the elevator. He screamed, his voice echoing in the garage. Someone jabbed a familiar needle into my neck.

The elevator doors closed, cutting Jasper's scream off. Roth turned me around and grabbed my jaw. "You will never see the light of day. Never."

I grew groggy, and my vision threatened to evaporate. I fought it, fought to stay awake, and, to my surprise, I did. I clutched hard to the edge of a precipice, a black void beneath me. Still, I clung.

Roth eyed the syringe in his hand, confused as to why I remained conscious. The elevator dropped. "Interesting," he said. He smiled. "Seems like the old stuff isn't quite doing the trick anymore, is it? That's all right. I brought two, just in case."

To my horror, he retrieved another syringe. I cried, "No!" and attempted to grab it, but he moved quickly. The needle plunged into my neck like a knife, and the blackness that followed hit me, heavy and unstoppable.

"Don't hurt him," I whispered.

"Who?" Roth asked. "Jasper? Come on, Jack. Be realistic."

I began to cry.

"You know who we are," he repeated. "Jasper will be in his own hell for this mistake, and so will you."

Hell and hell and hell. I couldn't bear it.

CHAPTER 32
ECHO CHAMBER

WHEN I WOKE, ROTH STOOD on the other side of the bars, and I was back in my cell. He ordered me to resurrect the guard Jasper had killed. I peered through the bars and noticed they had cleaned the desk and floor of blood, had replaced the computer. Everything was as it had been before, except for the body, which they had cleaned up and prepared for resurrection.

I thought of Jasper and sought his vibration psychically. Nothing. His particular hue no longer existed in the Purdom spectrum. His disappearance sapped the remaining energy from me; my body felt like an inert weight. I turned away and placed a pillow over my head before I waved my hand and resurrected the man on the floor. I pulled the covers over myself and did not look at either of them. I fell asleep.

I stood outside Cyrus's burning house. The crisp air wafted over my skin. The smell of smoke filled my nostrils. Lutin loomed at my left, staring at me and smiling. The darkness around his eyes, his pale face, and the fire in his body sharpened, beautifully wild and untamed. Unjailed. It was as though he had never been kept prisoner in Cyrus's mansion. The beauty of his face seemed magnified, as though I viewed him with preternatural new eyes.

"I'm not going to learn to stop biting, am I?" I asked. "We're never going to see each other again."

Lutin walked toward me, one step on the soft grass at a time, and slipped his arms around me. He pressed me against him, and I softened against his warm and comforting body. The fire rolled over the house, but we were our own little island, protecting ourselves from the heat and the memories being burned by it.

"Why won't you help me?" I asked. "I helped you. Why are you leaving me here? Is there something in me that deserves this?"

Lutin's hand slipped into my hair, and his fingers trailed along my head and against my neck.

"Why won't you answer me? Why won't you do something?"

He continued to stroke my hair. I pushed him back and looked into his eyes. It was no longer Lutin I was looking at, and I was no longer beside Cyrus's burning house.

Jonathon Roth stood in front of me, eye black on his cheeks, false wires attached to his arms. "You are an efficient mysticism, Jack. I didn't know whether to kill you or kiss you the first time I saw you resurrect someone." He smiled. "Did you know there are superstitions that talk about spirits and how to lock them in? I read up on them as soon as I learned about you. *Lead* supposedly blocks the soul from leaving or entering, as if it were a speck of radiation. There are tales of people using it to try and capture spirits. Just in case, I had your whole cell lined with it. Just in case the ferrics wanted to come for you, or you decided to call them here, I wanted to do my best to make sure they couldn't hear you. I didn't know if it would work, but I took the precaution. And see? You remain mine."

I looked around me, at the cell where Roth and I stood. I saw the lead in the walls, not only around my cell but through the floor above me and through the floor above that, creating a perfectly air-tight container. He caged me in pod upon pod of lead.

"You are the mystical, and I am the real. The real wins, every time." Roth smirked.

I gasped and woke.

Anger cleared my mind instantly, despite the fact I had been unconscious. My body felt cold, reptilian, and I planted my hands on the bed and pushed myself up. The man behind the computer turned to me.

"Did Roth line this cell with lead?" I asked, my dark eyes burrowing into him.

He frowned, and his mouth opened, his expression confused. His eyes wandered, and where they landed answered my question.

I grimaced and gritted my teeth. My eyes traveled over the walls. I wanted to see the lead throughout them as I had in my dream. Was it possible that this was why Lutin had not heard my prayers? Had Roth figured out something that I never had? I recalled an image of the metal door in Cyrus's mansion that swung shut on Lutin's cell, as well as the metallic bookcase that guarded the bodies of Lutin's brothers. It had been quite an elaborate mechanism. For the first time, I realized that no ferrics had come for Lutin or for his brothers during that time. I always thought it was the red box, but had Cyrus lined the walls with lead?

Roth had accounted for far more than I had. If he had truly blocked me from the outside world, and any hope of reaching Lutin, that meant the only possible way to escape was through... My eyes flicked to the gramophone.

I rose and walked to the bars of the cell. The guard glanced between me and the contraption.

The man had reddish brown hair and a strong chin. His eyes sparkled dark blue, but that blue might as well have been dark brown or black. Not impressively tall, he was nevertheless muscular.

"Did I resurrect you?"

The man nodded.

"Then why is your loyalty to Roth and not to me? I gave you life, after all. I brought you back from the dead."

The man didn't blink. "Ms. Harper, I'm going to have to ask you to stop talking."

"Why? Is it *blasphemous* to speak against him?" I sneered. I had nothing anymore. No hope. And I was going to get to that gramophone, one way or another. I didn't care what I had to do.

"I'm not supposed to talk to you," he mumbled.

"Why?"

"Those are my orders."

"Fuck your orders."

The man rolled his eyes and sighed. "Ms. Harper, you really need to stop speaking now."

"No!" I shouted. My voice boomed against the walls. It growled preternatural. The new-voice in my voice ricocheted across the walls, and the man winced. "Fuck that! *You know what should happen?* You should get over here and let me out of this fucking cage. As the person who gave you life, *I demand you let me out of here!*" My voice towered to an impossible height, as though I were fifteen feet tall.

"Let me out of here!"

He stood so swiftly it scared me. He marched toward my side of the room.

He stopped inches from the bars. If he'd wanted to, he could have reached through and grabbed me. Rage transformed his face, but as I stared into his eyes, that rage shifted to confusion. He walked to the cell door and retrieved his key card. He swiped it over the electronic sensor, and the metal clanked.

"What are you doing?" I asked, my voice soft again. Human.

He stared at me, eyes wide. "I don't know."

Fear radiated from him. His head jerked, and he looked down along his body, as though it were no longer part of him, as though he had just been split. His eyes shifted to me, circling in panic. He had opened the cell because I told him to.

I gasped, breathless. "Come into the cell."

Robotically, he swung the door open and stepped inside, his expression pure horror. He took a deep breath, as if to scream.

"Be quiet," I ordered.

The scream coiled in his throat. He swallowed it down, and it disappeared into nothing. He stared at me, still fearful but quiet and unmoving.

Patrick's words came to me. *I think I just...never learned to take control before. Hell, it feels like I'm trying to grow a supernatural power. ... completely unwieldy, but I'm getting better.*

My back muscles tingled; the black lines on my limbs pulsed as though carbonation was trapped just beneath the skin.

I quickly stepped through, as though he might close the door on me at any second.

"Why are you doing this?" I asked. "Answer me."

"I don't know," he said. His eyes widened, wild. He looked down at himself, as though his body were a puppet and the strings no longer belonged to him.

"Step outside the cell."

He did as I asked.

Relief flooded me. "Oh my God."

The realization arrived in an image, not in words. I saw two hundred men in a building more than twenty stories tall—men with my blood in their veins, men I had resurrected.

"Bring your gun," I said, "I'm getting the fuck out of here. Protect me." The man moved in front of me, cleared the hall, and waved for me to come out. The strange expression on his face shifted toward something akin to acceptance, as though the difference between me telling him to do something and his deciding it himself faded.

The elevator at the end of the hall dinged, and we both stopped. The doors opened, and Roth and Asher emerged.

"Wilton! What are you doing?" Roth demanded.

"Don't come any closer!" Wilton called, "or I'll shoot."

Roth and Asher raised their pistols.

"Stop!" I yelled. "Roth and Asher, stop walking and drop your weapons!"

They immediately stopped, looking astonished. They stared at their feet, spellbound by their unmoving legs. Two pistols clattered to the floor.

I walked toward them, as mesmerized as they. When I reached them, I said, "Don't touch me." Roth's eyes betrayed that he wanted to do exactly that, but he nevertheless remained still. I stepped around them, studying them. They seemed to be dipped in wax that gradually solidified. I stopped, closed my eyes, and took a deep breath.

Though still deep underground, still close to my cage, I realized the blessed truth. I feared that if I mentally acknowledged it, it would disappear. Despite the drugs they had dosed me with, despite contributing gallons of my blood, despite the cell and the lead in the walls, despite my prayers not being answered, a solution had always been there. I just hadn't realized it until now.

Searching deep within myself, I urged my power to control outward, upward, toward all the men in the building, instructing them as their resurrecter to stop whatever they were doing. Even though I couldn't see them, I sensed they obeyed my command. Everyone in Purdom froze.

Pleasure erupted throughout my body. Beneath my clothes, the black lines etched across my limbs like tree branches burst, filled with fire and surged with power, a power that had only needed a spark to ignite. I stared at the fire that stoked within me, shocked, relieved, fulfilled.

I bloomed powerful, purposeful, no longer a cracked being. I was whole, and that wholeness brought me fully to myself. All thought and fear evaporated, replaced with being and certainty.

I returned to my surroundings, taking in the minimalistic hallway of the lowest level of Purdom, and it was as though I had never been imprisoned there. I walked forward and, without saying anything, willed the men behind me to follow. They did, their clacking footsteps trailing. We entered the elevator.

Pressing the button for the lobby, I stood silently among the three of them, until we emerged from the depths. The doors opened onto a sunlit room.

Several men stood unmoving, as if frozen in time. I walked between them. Roth, Asher, and Wilton followed. We strolled through the doors at the rear of the lobby, and then into the sunlight on a small patch of grass. Cars honked on busy Manhattan streets.

Life buzzed around me, humming. The day shined brilliant. The air warmed, summer near. I squinted, adjusting to the brightness, as the cars zigzagged on the roads, and people passed by in business suits. I trembled at the immensity of the world. Compared to my cell, it swelled vast and overwhelming.

I turned back to Roth, Asher, and Wilton. My eyes traveled up the length of Purdom, taking in its floors upon floors upon floors. Millions of inhabitants in Manhattan, and no one knew what existed here—a dead army of two hundred men led by a dead woman whose body now gleamed with firelight.

Beneath the lapel of Roth's suit, in his pocket, a dead red rose poked out. Asher's and Wilton's suit jackets contained the same.

It dawned on me that these resembled funeral boutonnieres. That they perhaps served as a reminder of their revivals. I made the one in Roth's pocket bloom.

I looked into his eyes. "We have work to do."

Slowly, against his will, I made him nod.

CHAPTER 33
RESCUE

I HAD ROTH'S MEN ENTER the houses in the west of the state. Though I wasn't participating, I smelled the dirt in the air. A trickle of sweat rolled down the back of my neck, and I bit my lip. One of the balcony doors in Roth's office was open, and the mint green curtain twisted in the light breeze. Cool air crawled across my body.

My army and I closed in. Jack was no longer one but many. I watched the television screens.

Multiple groups of men, all with bodycams, hit fifteen different houses at once. They wore black technical gear and bulletproof vests. They could have been SWAT teams. The men had all dosed themselves with my blood, injecting themselves with a small amount right before exiting the vehicles. I made them do this.

I gripped the edges of my seat and took a deep breath.

A man spoke cautiously on the center screen, one of many live feeds.

"Approaching the gate now," he whispered into the mic. The camera recorded everything in night vision, so the image filled with green shadows, moving awkwardly. The feeds fluoresced.

My chest expanded like a balloon. *This is the moment,* I said to myself, *that the cult will finally fall. When Cyrus's old kingdom will be ground down and turned to dust.*

I gripped the left side of my coat, and my list of names crinkled. It represented all the children who had sent me letters over the past years. I would discover if any of them were real, and I would save them.

On the center screen, the garden gate opened soundlessly as the operation leader pushed it. Several of the videos displayed sudden, inaudible movement as men rushed to the front of the house. They paused, low to the ground, weapons drawn.

My breath quickened as they cut the gate's lock. When they finished, the door to the home opened; the men paused. Tinkling sounds from a jewelry box softly played, barely audible in the video. The men waited.

The song finished, followed by a crack in the air. A barely perceptible wave incandesced across the night, like a ripple in water. An *arca*. But the videos did not go black, and the men did not fall. Nothing, in fact, happened to them. The inhalers protected them beautifully.

I held my breath.

"Go," the man on the feed said. Wilton went first, and the others followed. They walked straight into the house and met an astonished man in the hallway who tried to run. They shot him.

The brightly lit home nevertheless registered as eerie, run down. My recruits marched through the house, each clearing a room on his own. Gunfire and screams pierced the mic. The video feed that belonged to Wilton showed him clearing the kitchen before he went upstairs. He entered a hallway lined with three closed bedroom doors. He cleared the first two, shooting the individuals inside. He reached the third one. It was locked.

He kicked it several times before the door swung hard on its hinges into the room. Two more men joined him. As soon as the door opened, they swept inside. It appeared empty of people. One of the men lifted the mattress from a bed and pushed it off, revealing a person.

Wilton swept the weapon away, and when the gun discharged, the bullet hit the floor to the left of the bed.

"It's a child!" Wilton said. He held his hand out. "We've got a child! Nobody shoot!"

My eyes widened.

Wilton bent down and assisted what appeared to be a young girl with red hair. He held her arm and walked her out of the room and down the stairs. The others followed, escorting her to the car. "What's your name?" Wilton asked.

"Elizabeth," she said. Her voice quavered.

"Elizabeth what?"

"Elizabeth Smith."

Retrieving my list of names from my pocket, the names of all the children who had written to me, I sifted through them, looking for Elizabeth Smith. Near the bottom of the page, I found her. I looked up at the screen and silently told Wilton to say the words.

"Jack came for you."

To my surprise, the little girl smiled. "I knew she would."

For the next ten minutes, the men thoroughly searched the house. They discovered no one else, and they found no bodily remains. In the back, behind the house, they searched an old shed, but it revealed nothing of value.

One vehicle went to a fire station with Elizabeth. The others continued to the next house on the map. All in all, it only took twenty-five minutes.

After they destroyed the first five houses, I had them continue, and the subsequent houses fell the same way. As multiple operations occurred simultaneously, I usually watched only one-fifth of what occurred, but I felt it all, down in my core, in my marrow. I moved every chess piece.

Infinitum's followers were unprepared for the sudden invasion. Shock exploded across their faces, unmistakable even in the grainy videos. Not every house harbored kids, but Roth's men managed to retrieve those they found unscathed. When the children said their names, I checked them off, one at a time, until only one remained. Annette.

Each time the men went to another home, they dosed again with my blood. By the time the sixtieth house fell, and the sense of victory impassioned me, Roth/I released a second wave of men, all stocked with my blood, as well, though these only had several vials' worth.

Sixty men boarded three private planes that would fly them two states over. There, they would continue the operation. The two groups would work in waves, never stopping until Roth eradicated every house on Harlowton's map.

As the hours wore on, the first morning light crept into Roth's office. The first group of men found hotels for a few hours' rest. The second group continued to work.

One of the men discovered a small body wrapped in cloth in the basement of a house in the western portion of the country. They unwrapped the corpse, revealing the body of a young woman. Her lips were drawn back, but her features were discernable. The body's excellent condition surprised me. An image of the girl in the video Infinitum had sent me flooded my memory. I was fairly certain it was her. If not, I would still resurrect her. "Bring her to me," I said.

The man rewrapped the corpse, and two of the Outfit carried the body out of the basement to a car. The driver informed me when he began making his way to New York.

House by house, Infinitum collapsed. The foundation of my horrific childhood and young adulthood disintegrated. The followers died, easily eliminated. In another day or two, the remaining houses spanning the entire country would be wiped out.

The world would be rid of a virus, a virus that honed evil and destroyed innocence, stole children from their homes, and supped at the marrow of ethereal beings. The people responsible for Lutin's imprisonment, whether or not they knew of him, whether or not they had ever ingested his blood, would die. The being who had given me to myself would be avenged, even if he never knew it. The children would be avenged.

The elevator dinged, and several men dragged something across the floor toward me. I gave it a quick glance and realized who lay there—Jasper. His corpse won my attention away from the live feed. I analyzed his mutt-like face, which was covered in dark bruises. His head was swollen to twice its normal size. The rotting smell of him intensified. I shot my power toward him, urging him to live again. In just a blink, Jasper lived, completely healed, staring into the track lighting overhead. I broke into his view.

He smiled. "Mm hm. That's what I thought," he said, color returning to his lips.

"You were always the smarter one, weren't you?" I smirked.

"I have keen senses."

"For that, I am grateful. Want to watch the rest of Infinitum fall?"

Jasper looked around at the men in the room, as he sat up. His eyes landed on Roth in the distance and remained locked. Roth analyzed the television feeds, directing men in the field. "How..."

"As it turns out, I can control them."

His eyes flicked to me, and his eyebrows drew down. "Because of the blood?"

I shook my head. "Because I resurrected them."

His expression revealed his shock. Jasper stood and stepped out of the body bag, gazing warily around him.

"Don't worry. They won't hurt you. They can't. And they can't hurt me either. No one can."

I held out my hand. Jasper looked at it, then at me, eyes wide. Slowly, he took my hand. We shook. "Welcome to freedom," I said. I led him to the table and pulled out a chair. I picked up another glass from the middle of the table, poured him a drink, and sat. Together, we became absorbed in the screens.

After he spent a few minutes adjusting to everything going on around us, he asked, "How many houses have been taken down?"

"One hundred and thirty."

"How many more to go?"

"About that number again."

"Halfway," he said. "Find any children?"

"Many."

He sighed, sipped the bourbon, and nodded. "Good. How long was I dead?"

"A few days."

He bit his lip. "Efficient."

"Take away politics and the bureaucratic machine, and it's always efficient."

"And where did the children go?"

"To the authorities," I said. My mind filled with images of them. Most of the children had looked unbelievably thin, with dark circles under their eyes. I hadn't seen any that might have been brought up more along the lines of Alex and me. "One," I added, "is coming here." I met his eyes, and he understood she needed resurrecting.

"They'll never know," he said, "that all this led to their new lives."

That was true. "I guess not."

Jasper raised his glass, the liquid glowing in the screen light. We toasted wordlessly.

At six the next morning, the last house fell.

I gasped when the man said, "All clear," and leaned forward, pressing my forehead to the table. A physical weight that had been lying deep in my gut like a stone, a stone placed there when I was seven years old, evaporated. I savored the promise of a peaceful, quiet world. The fever had finally broken.

A pair of hands pressed on my back. Jasper hugged me, briefly, wordlessly. Then, he went off to sleep. Sleep, at least in the usual sense, did not seem to matter to me as much as it used to. I could stay awake much longer and still feel energetic. I stared at a fiery stripe in the flesh on the back of my hand.

Roth's radio buzzed, and he answered. Annette's body had made it to Purdom. It awaited me in the garage. I nodded to him, despite the fact there was no need to—it was like nodding to myself—and I slipped inside the elevator. When the doors at last opened to reveal the garage, a black car with dark windows greeted me, still running, the trunk open.

Inside heaped a bundle of rags, holes rotted through the cloth, and I reached my hand to it. The holes closed in until the blankets became seamless, soft, and plump. It reminded me of the first time I had been in the presence of Lutin and his brothers, when the scar on my right hand disappeared. The cracked wine bottle beside me had repaired itself.

I tugged the blanket free. There lay a green and black body with yellowed eyes and drawn lips that revealed teeth. Seeing her features closely, I knew for certain they belonged to the girl in the video. The shape of the head was right, the color of the hair. "Put her in the back seat," I said.

Wilton picked up the body and settled it along the backseat. I stepped behind the car. "Drive off as soon as she wakes," I said. He nodded and got in, shut the door, and placed his hands on the wheel.

I let the power rise out of me, toward the vehicle, until it bumped against the girl.

The power brushed against the body, reanimating it, righting it, as well as her clothes, and the soil disappeared. The scar disappeared from her throat. Her curtain of hair lengthened and thickened. She sat up, the top of her head barely visible over the seat. Wilton shifted the car into drive and went on his way.

I was finished.

CHAPTER 34
LEAVE

I WASN'T REALLY IN THE world anymore, and the world was no longer the same. Cyrus's following had been eradicated. I had expunged thousands of individuals from Earth over the course of three days via Roth and his men, a massive undertaking unlike any other.

I slept for a long time in one of the rooms in Purdom, deep and dreamless. When I woke, I rose and walked to the window to observe the lowering sun. I collected a new set of clothes and then showered. After gently patting myself dry, I grabbed a brush and gently separated the tangled strands of my hair. I squirted lotion into my hand and rubbed it into the skin of my face and the tops of my fingers. I dressed, experiencing the denim jeans in a new way, feeling the cotton of the shirt as though I had never felt cotton before. The beautiful dark teal color brought out the blue tones in my black hair.

Looking in the mirror, I blinked several times.

Dark shadows coated the bends of my body, and fiery light crawled over me like a vine beneath my clothes. I thought of the children rescued by the men I had forced out into the world. A saying came to mind. I wasn't sure where I had heard it before.

Beckoned or not, the god will come.

Staring at my reflection, I knew it wasn't that I was the god.

But I could see the god. Just for a moment. Like a tiger stripe through the tall grass. In how things had come to be.

It was time for me to leave.

CHAPTER 35
BASILLE

NO AMOUNT OF DISTANCE FROM Roth or the others diminished my control. The very first thing I commanded them to do remotely they completed with great success.

"You will reconvene at Purdom. You will destroy all evidence of yourselves. You will sell the building and vacate. When you have finished, you will come to me in Basille, Louisiana, with all the *arcas*. I will be waiting. Do not tell anyone about what has happened, or about me, and do not fail to complete this assignment. You may not do anything but what I tell you. I will see you in Basille."

They nodded, in all their parts of the world, and then they turned, leaving me, abandoning their robotic motions, doing what I commanded as though they had thought of it themselves. As I selected a car from Purdom's parking garage, they were already on their way.

In one full day, I drove halfway to Louisiana, and they destroyed half of everything they needed to. In two full days, I arrived in Basille, and Roth, under Jasper's watch, prepared to sell the building.

I had one thing left to do, and I would finish before they arrived.

I reached the crumbled, burned-out lot on a familiar road I had left behind only six months before. I stood in the daylight, taking in fresh air, enjoying it in the same way that Lutin had when I had helped free him. I stared at the empty lot, where the grass refused to grow, and I imagined the burning building. Its scent lingered in the air.

I knelt and extended my hand. I beckoned the pieces of him to gather, from wherever they were, however small they might be—the pieces of Cyrus.

From the charred stone beneath my hand, the deeply buried molecules emerged from the dirt and land. Very few collected, but with my now-potent power, they were enough.

I willed the power within me to bring my maniacal mentor back. I needed to know what he knew.

When I opened my eyes, Cyrus lay on grass and stone, completely naked, his gray hair and gray eyes remarkably bright. He looked around in confusion, and then he saw me. He took me in, new form and all. He snarled and lunged at me.

I fell to the ground, only somewhat surprised by his sudden attack, but not really feeling it, not really feeling anything. He was much smaller than I remembered, weaker.

He pulled back his arm to punch me in the face, but I simply said, "Stop."

He stopped.

Surprise replaced the rage in his eyes. He stared at his fist as though it were foreign, and his face contorted, as though mid-torture. I crawled out from beneath him. Falling hadn't hurt me at all.

Cyrus rushed me again.

"Stop moving," I said quietly. He did.

His lips contracted, baring his teeth. "You bitch."

"Be quiet."

Cyrus's lips pressed together. At six foot two, he towered over me, but he did not in any way seem powerful. Worlds of experience existed between us, and fear was needless. He could not speak if I commanded him not to. He could not move if I required he be still.

"I am here now, and I am in control," I said.

I walked toward him, letting my intuition take over my voice, letting my gut be in charge. "I want you to do something for me. I want you to think back to the first dark moment we shared together—the one that formed me for the longest time. You took me to your basement. You strapped Roland to the gurney, and you taught me how to kill him. I want you to switch positions with me in your mind. You are a child with a needle in his hand, and I am the adult, there with you. Look into my eyes and see me as I saw you—as bigger than life. Listen to me as I listened to you."

I hugged him. I closed my eyes, and I pretended we stood down in the basement, a cave that surrounded us. And there lay Roland—a man whose life apparently hung in the balance. "There are so many people, so many creatures," I said, "that cannot help themselves, that are at the beck and call of those with more power, and it is important to notice their plight. If we do not, they will be alone, and they will die. We do not want them to be alone or die. We are not murderers. We respect all life. Say it with me."

Cyrus spoke against his will, repeating my words.

I commanded him again. "Say, 'We are not murderers. We respect all life.'"

"We are not murderers," he said. "We respect all life." He choked back a scream, as though it hurt him.

"Now, in your mind, I want you to take a good look at the needle and put it down." I envisioned it, just as he envisioned it, because I commanded him to. "Unstrap the man on the table." In my mind, the young child with blond hair and blue eyes—young Cyrus—stepped down from the stool and cut each of the blue ropes free, one by one.

"Now wake him." The child Cyrus walked back to the stool and climbed on it. He grabbed Roland's arm and shook it.

As Cyrus also imagined this, I let my hand hover above the burned lot, seeking particles of Roland, anything that hadn't been scattered by wind or time. In the search, I strained; the land stretched on and on, and any speck of carbon that had once belonged to him was almost indistinguishable to the other molecules.

"Try to wake him," I whispered again in Cyrus's ear.

The child Cyrus nudged Roland's torso, trying to make him animate himself in the basement that resembled a cave. Simultaneously, I searched through the rubble, the grass, the dirt, the trees, for any speck.

Finally, I found some. He had been reduced to ash and dispersed by the wind across the land after the house had burned.

I called all the remaining particles of Roland to gather. And collect they did. They flowed to me from every direction, tumbling across leaves and filtering free of the dirt, until a speck the size of a strawberry seed rested in my hand.

I enclosed it in my fist, shut my eyes, and then opened my hand.

"Wake him up," I whispered again, and I thrust my power forward to unite with the molecules. Just as Cyrus had instantly appeared on the grass before me, so did Roland.

I caught my breath as I stared at him.

I turned Cyrus toward Roland, who rose from the dirt.

Before either of them could react, I waved my hand, urging the wreckage to coalesce. The blocks of brick had started to arrange themselves as soon as I'd arrived, but at my command, the entire mansion formed, pulling all of the parts it needed from the world. That the process required so little power from me and happened so quickly astounded me.

Soon, we stared into the home that had terrorized me for years. Although it appeared to be the same house, it wasn't. *I* owned it, and I would determine what would and would not happen within.

"Come," I said. I walked up the path to the large front door, opened it, and stepped inside. Cyrus followed. He peered around quietly, hesitantly. He refused to look at me. Roland also entered. I hugged him.

"Where am I? What is all this?"

"I will explain everything, but it will take a while."

After I separated from him, Cyrus, though held in place by my will, managed to snarl, "I'm going to rip you limb from limb. I'm going to eat your heart."

"No, you're not," I said. My voice resonated as matter-of-fact. He seemed quaint and feeble, fragile even, to me, not dreadful. Part of that was because I now understood he had no sense of self. That was why he needed followers—to fill in the sense of self that he did not have.

"You are not going to harm me because why?" I asked.

Speaking against his will, he muttered, "We are not murderers. We respect all life."

I nodded. "That's right. Now go. Find some clothes."

Cyrus made his way upstairs. Roland watched this exchange with awe. Once we were alone, he collected a blanket from the living room and pulled it over his shoulders.

"I'm so sorry," I said immediately. "I need your help."

He peered at the house, as though he hadn't seen it for a very long time. He listened to the birds outside like he knew he had been dead for the past six months.

When he looked at me again, he said, "You're…different. You're…like Lutin now, aren't you?"

I nodded.

He smiled, wincing, still somewhat waking. "That's all right. You made it out then, didn't you?"

"And much more."

He cocked his head. His expression shifted among confusion, elation, and fear.

"What has happened?" he asked.

I closed my eyes and thought of the shining white creature, the Builder. I sighed. "I'll let you know, but not just now."

CHAPTER 36
THE SHINING WHITE THING

ROLAND AND I ARRIVED IN the dank room with bits of fire floating all around. Cyrus and Roland both dressed exactly the way I had last seen them and always pictured them. Cyrus waited in a black trench coat, gray shirt, and black pants. Roland wore a gray three-piece suit without the jacket.

Cyrus tilted his head when we arrived. He stepped back, wary of me. His fear and uncertainty were new, and they refreshed me. Perhaps his mind now opened to the idea of someone who didn't need his approval, something that existed outside of his control and desire.

"You are going to tell me *all* about the Builder, and I mean everything. Immediately," I said. "Both of you."

Cyrus's throat hummed, but his lips didn't move. He grimaced and struggled to speak, fought against his own body, which obeyed me. His battle lasted the longest of any of the resurrected so far.

Eventually, though, his mouth opened. "He is like the devil," Cyrus said. "There is only one of him, and he builds boxes to distribute himself, in the same way that ferrics travel to distribute good. It is the only way he can keep up with them. He does not have the same amount of power that ferrics have, but he is indestructible."

"Indestructible?" I asked. "So he can't be killed?"

"He can," Cyrus said, "but it doesn't matter if he is. He simply regenerates. Ferrics resurrect *others*. The Builder is *self*-resurrecting. It doesn't matter how many times they kill him, he simply comes back. But he can kill ferrics, and he does so quite easily."

"What else do you know?" I asked.

"Nothing."

I waited for a while, to ensure he hadn't withheld information. But he remained quiet. I found his limited knowledge outrageous. With as much power as Cyrus had pretended to have, he should have known far, far more. He had made it seem like he and the Builder were best friends. It appeared, now, that that, too, was façade. Nevertheless, he had given me something important, and I fumbled with this new information like a child with a Rubik's cube.

Roland turned to me and said, "I met the Builder only once."

That surprised me. "You?"

He nodded. "He was the man on the water, the one who came to me playing the violin, and made that cross..." he said pointing to me, "turn in on itself. He was the one who told me to work for Cyrus, said we would make a good team."

I frowned. "I thought the Builder was shining and white?"

Roland tilted his head inquisitively. "He takes many forms. With me, he was a musician."

"With me," Cyrus said, "he was my best friend."

"But no one has ever seen his true form," Roland added.

I recalled the image of the plastic white being leaning over dead Alex, whom I had successfully killed. "I don't think that's true."

CHAPTER 37

EMERGE

WHEN NIGHT FELL, ROLAND MENTIONED his hunger. I gave him the keys to Roth's car and some of Roth's money so he could buy food for himself and the house.

I sat in the living room of the old mansion, listening to the quiet and thinking. Cyrus sat across from me, still and silent, just as I commanded.

Some of Roth's men would be arriving in Basille soon enough. I wasn't sure how we would proceed once they did. I had an idea, but it was so radical and dangerous that I might be insane for even thinking it.

The doorbell rang.

Both Cyrus and I turned. Nobody knew this house existed. My heart fluttered. "Does the Builder knock when he wants in?"

Cyrus's eyes flicked to me. "Sometimes."

A shiver ran down my spine. I stood, my imagination bouncing between picturing a monster and picturing Alex transformed by that monster. I had my hand on the .38 in my pocket when I crept to the door, eyeing its shiny gold surface. It seemed possible to me that the paneling could buckle and morph into some monstrous being. The light shone on the wood too brightly.

I reached for the handle cautiously. I twisted it and pulled the door open just a crack.

An arm appeared. A cream shirt covered it, and through the fabric shivered orange light. The luminescence vibrated, increasing in intensity and fading back. I closed my eyes, and my breath shook.

"Lutin?"

"Yes, Jack," replied the familiar voice, a voice I had memorized. I wanted to welcome him. At the same time, anger stormed inside me. He had abandoned me six months before. And when I had prayed for him to rescue me from Roth, he hadn't.

I turned so that I wouldn't see him through the crack.

"I don't know what you want," I said, "but I'm thinking we should remain apart and continue on our own paths. You have your life, and I have mine."

A long silence stretched. Lutin didn't leave or push his way in. "Jack, I am here because I felt Cyrus reanimate. I need to ask you what you are doing and why. I'm not leaving until you explain." His voice rumbled both gentle and firm. It balanced between love and destruction.

I bit my lip. "So *that's* what it was." The reappearance of Cyrus had brought him here. Not me.

I swallowed back tears. "I guess I won't keep you in suspense." I opened the door wide and returned to the living room. I sat on the couch and waited for him to follow.

His bare feet padded softly against the floor as he entered the house and made his way to us. He stopped at the threshold, and the odor of something between cinnamon and a chimney entered the room.

"Jack," he said, surprise in his voice. "You're a ferric."

I tilted my head. "Yes."

"I didn't know. I didn't feel it when you shifted. I should have felt it."

That slightly eased my conflicted feelings. Was it possible that Lutin hadn't known? That he hadn't heard my prayers? Because Roth had lined the walls of my cell with lead? Had it shielded everything that had occurred inside?

"Why won't you look at me?"

"I don't know why you're here. And I don't know when you will leave again."

He sighed. "Please, after everything, we should be able to talk."

Tears filled my eyes, and I wiped them away. "I prayed for you to come. You didn't come."

At last, I looked into his eyes. He frowned. "I didn't hear you call for me."

I searched him, a hand pressed against my mouth because I didn't want to react. He radiated just as beautiful, as gritty, as real, as wild, as unnatural as I remembered. Black eyes that never blinked, like holograms on his white face. A cream boatneck shirt and gray sweatpants. Lines of tribal hellfire all over his body. He did not look as weathered as he once had. He seemed to have recovered fully from the years of imprisonment, and it added to his exquisiteness.

"I didn't hear you call me," he repeated sadly. He came and sat on the couch and leaned toward me. He wrapped his arms around me, pulling me close. My ear pressed against his warm neck, and his heartbeat thudded exactly in time with my own, as if the piece of himself he had given me had synchronized our bodies. As he held me, the fiery lines on my skin brightened. It felt like my power expanded. I took a deep breath and relaxed against him. Lutin ran his fingers through my hair.

"If I had heard you call, I would have come to you, even if I was invisible to you. I would have come to you if I had sensed you shift. The most spectacular light shines when it happens. I would have come to you, but I didn't see it."

I nodded. "I believe you."

"Before we discuss anything further, I must know—why is Cyrus alive?"

I answered him by turning to my old mentor. "Cyrus," I said, "why don't you come here and kneel before Lutin?"

Cyrus rose from the couch and walked straight to us. Lutin pulled back, his body tense, as if preparing for an attack.

Cyrus dropped to his knees in front of Lutin and bowed.

"I want you to tell Lutin that you are sorry for all that you did to him."

"I am sorry for all that I did to you," Cyrus repeated.

"I want you to tell him what you think of us and of life now."

"We are not murderers," he said. "We have respect for all life."

"I want you to tell him that all you feel for him now is love."

"All I feel now for you is love."

Cyrus trembled and appeared ready to wail.

Lutin's jaw dropped. He sat bewildered, as still as a statue, his ethereal black eyes locked on the man curled on the floor. "Jack, what did you do?"

I told him. "I can control those I resurrect."

He searched me. It seemed he didn't want to accept that this could be true. "How?"

"I don't know, but I can."

Lutin's eyes flicked between me and Cyrus. "There haven't been many humans who became ferrics. Perhaps the combination…"

I nodded. "I considered that."

"…created something new."

As though willing to concede the possibility for just a moment, he asked, "Why, though, did you bring back Cyrus?"

"I needed to learn about the Builder. I saw him, Lutin. Something happened to me. I was attacked, and I was killed. When I died, I saw the Builder, and he terrified me. He must be destroyed. So I sought the only people I knew to ask about him. I thought Cyrus would know everything, but he doesn't. What he has told me, though, has given me an idea."

Lutin's eyes wandered over me like an angel thinking a million thoughts in the span of time it takes a human to think just one. He closed his eyes and sighed. "We have so much to discuss. This was pointless, Jack. The truth is, no one can stop the Builder. All we can ever do is trim the weeds. That's what ferrics do. We trim back the evil in the world, destroy the *arcas*, rein it all in."

I nodded. "I know. That's all *you* can do."

Lutin tilted his head and regarded me.

"I can control those I resurrect. Like Cyrus here, or the two hundred men now on their way. And I've been thinking—what if I kill the Builder? *And then*, before he can resurrect himself, what if I resurrect him *first*?"

The realization of what I proposed dawned on Lutin—if I could resurrect the Builder, then I could control him, and if I could control him, I could stop him from creating *arcas*.

Lutin stood restlessly and rubbed his hands together, as though to warm them, as if my imagining this possibility had chilled him, affected the flames in his veins. He stepped over Cyrus and stood in the middle of the living room.

"That might work," he said. He did not sound satisfied, but rather scared. Like we held in our hands the single vial of a life-saving drug that might be crushed at any moment and spill onto the carpet.

"I don't know," he said, his voice low, "if my brothers will be okay with this, though. They might kill you for what you are."

A chuckle rose in my throat, but laughing would have been a drastic mistake. Instead, I smiled. "You've forgotten."

"Forgotten?"

"Who brought them back to life."

Lutin's posture stiffened as the realization hit him. I had resurrected them, months and months ago, and persuaded them to tear through the house, killing all the men who worked for Cyrus. It seemed likely that I could compel his brothers to stand with me, whether or not they wanted to. Lutin realized the extent of how dangerous I could be—potentially more powerful than any ferric.

"I know what you're thinking. The question isn't whether or not I'm the best person in the world to wield this much power," I told him. "The question is whether you would rather deal with the Builder or deal with me."

I had already thought this through.

"I was supposed to stop biting. I know," I said. "That's what you told me when you left—that you would return when I learned to stop seeking violence. I'm not sure, though, that that's the sort of person who could stop the Builder. I think this particular task requires a lot of bite. Don't you?"

He nodded, rubbing his hands together. "Perhaps you're right. Perhaps we need someone between, on the border between good and evil. Someone human...but more." Lutin loosened his shoulders with a shake and took a few steps until he loomed over Cyrus, gazing down at him contemplatively.

When he looked at me again, his fear had dissolved.

"I like you, Jack. I always have. Are you sure you want to do this? Do you want to be connected to this being?"

I frowned, disturbed at how he used the word "connected." Connection had nothing to do with it. "I want to squelch the source of evil in this world," I said. "Whatever it takes, that's what I want. I am tired of seeing all this...*trauma* repeat."

Lutin's dark lips curled up wonderfully. He nodded. "Perhaps you have learned to stop biting...in your own way."

He stepped over Cyrus to reach me. I stood, and he held me to him.

"The threshold will be dark," he whispered, his cinnamon-coal breath against my ear, "and the inner realm even darker. He will never give up."

"Neither will I," I said. "I'm ready. Even if we lose."

"Even if we lose," Lutin repeated softly. He pulled back and beamed. His eyebrows lifted. He said, with certainty. "Beckoned or not, the god will come."

I gazed at him in wonder. The same exact thought had arrived just a few days before, as I stared at myself in the mirror, at the changes in my body, wrestling with abstractions and how reality had come to be.

"Beckoned or not the god will come," I whispered, my heart as one, connected, with Lutin's.

"The tiger between the tall grass."

"The tiger...between the tall grass."

"Our life, our death, but its law."

Acknowledgments

WHEN I FIRST CREATED *PIVOT*—THE first of the Jack Harper Trilogy—it and *Perish* were interwoven. The strange amalgamation that was the first instantiation slipped back and forth between past and present. Neither timeline, though, had been developed enough to exist as its own book. When my wonderful agent, Jonathan Lyons, took a look at the creation, one of his first recommendations was to split the book into two and build up each portion. This wasn't the first time that someone had recommended I divide up the novel. Wayne Alexander and Ryan Lewis, two individuals who had seen something of worth in the trilogy, before the book had ever been sent to an agent, had asked if this was something I would consider doing. I declined.

I also declined when Jonathan suggested it.

I did so because I'd spent half a year refining what *Pivot* was, building it up—even as the timelines were interwoven—and I had been so particular about it that, by that point, I could not see the forest for the trees.

Jonathan sent the book out, and the response from publishers was an echo of his, Wayne's, and Ryan's advice—they all said that the book needed to be split into two. By that point, I'd had some months apart from the novel, and when I went back and looked through everything, I agreed. It did need to be split, and I wasn't sure why I hadn't seen it before.

So, I took a deep breath and divided what was the original *Pivot* into *Pivot* and *Perish*. Frankly, I'm thankful that Jonathan had even been willing to send out the original version with such a glaring issue. I built *Pivot* up so that it could exist on its own and, to my surprise, liked the book better with a linear timeline. *Perish*, too, improved, though its revisions required a little bit more than I ever could have expected, and I talk about this more below. I have, since this experience, heard of at least one other author who'd been advised to split her book into two (due to a non-linear timeline) and refused to do so, only later stating that she realized she had erred, once she and her agent had gone separate ways. I'm thankful that I was willing to revise. In essence, I understood that the version I'd already created was already done—it was in the bank, so to speak—and so there would be no harm in creating other/new/ experimental versions. It just turned out that I liked the new versions better than the prior one.

Thus, I give many thanks to Jonathan, as well as Wayne and Ryan, for being patient with me and guiding me gently towards yet another huge (and quite daunting) restructuring of the book/s.

Many writers say that writing one's second book is more difficult than writing one's first, and for me this was true. I had, somehow, been able to make the first book work, and I wasn't sure how to repeat that process with an entirely different plot. Fortunately, I had anticipated this problem and entered into an MFA program (Stonecoast, to be exact), which had—among many other extraordinary individuals—Nancy Holder and Liz Hand at its helm. Nancy, who was my mentor for two semesters and workshop leader/ professor for two residencies in the program, was a godsend. Her two craft book recommendations, as well as her brilliant insights into the first third of *Perish*, helped me move forward in a way that wasn't purely trial-and-error, and I thank her a thousand times over.

By the time Robert J. Peterson of California Coldblood Books took a look at the revised *Pivot* manuscript in 2018, I'd completed *Perish* and was able to submit that book to him, as well. Bob offered me a three-book deal for the trilogy, with the understanding that *Peak*—the third novel—would be on its way shortly. I am fairly certain, had Nancy not been there to guide me, and had I not finished *Perish* in time, my contract would likely have been very different.

As it is, I'm incredibly grateful to Bob for taking a chance on a new author with not one book, not two books, but three whole books. Thank you so much, Bob, for putting such trust in me.

In addition to thanking Bob, Nancy, Jonathan, Wayne, and Ryan, a sixth individual deserves gratitude, and his name is Weston Ochse. Back in 2014, at my first World Horror Convention, he was one of the many wonderful authors I met in Portland, Oregon. During the whirlwind, three-day adventure, Weston advised me on pursuing what my heart desired—writing creatively—and he highly recommended that I check out MFA programs, as he himself had attained his. I appreciated his push towards an MFA program greatly, and it ended up being the right call for me, especially in terms of finishing PERISH in time. Many thanks to him not just for the nudge towards writing and the MFA, but for the wonderful blurb on the front of this book.

The fantastic Sue Ducharme I must thank for her wonderful copyediting work on the novel. Not only has copyediting been a magical process with Sue, but it has helped me improve as a writer.

Kate Kastelein I would like to thank for the one question she asked about my manuscript during our workshop with Nancy, which spurred a whole new scene in the book.

I want to also recognize my best friend Adam Setliff for always being willing to read my work and lend his ear. He is an amazing human being, and I don't know what I would do without him.

Finally, I would also like to thank my Mom for always being so supportive and encouraging when it comes to my writing. Life is nonstop and unrelenting, but she tirelessly cheers me on.

About the Author

L.C. BARLOW is a writer and professor. Her work has been published in a variety of magazines and journals and garnered praise, winning multiple awards. Barlow lives in Dallas, Texas, with her cats Smaug and Dusty.